KILTY SECRETS
Clash of the Tartans
Book One

by

Anna Markland

Copyright © 2017 by Anna Markland
Print Edition

Published by Dragonblade Publishing, an imprint of Kathryn Le Veque Novels, Inc

All rights reserved. No part of this book may be used or reproduced in any manner whatsoever without written permission, except in the case of brief quotations embodied in critical articles or reviews.

*Dedicated to my grandfather, Richard Gaskell,
aka Richard Wilson, aka Dick Lowe
~a man with secrets of his own.*

"Life is under no obligation to give us what we expect."
~Margaret Mitchell

Books from Dragonblade Publishing

Knights of Honor Series by Alexa Aston
Word of Honor
Marked By Honor
Code of Honor
Journey to Honor
Heart of Honor

Legends of Love Series by Avril Borthiry
The Wishing Well
Isolated Hearts
Sentinel

The Lost Lords Series by Chasity Bowlin
The Lost Lord of Castle Black

Heart of the Corsairs Series by Elizabeth Ellen Carter
Captive of the Corsairs

Also From Elizabeth Ellen Carter
Dark Heart

Knight Everlasting Series by Cassidy Cayman
Endearing

Midnight Meetings Series by Gina Conkle
Meet a Rogue at Midnight, book 4

Second Chance Series by Jessica Jefferson
Second Chance Marquess

Imperial Season Series by Mary Lancaster
Vienna Waltz
Vienna Woods
Vienna Dawn

Blackhaven Brides Series by Mary Lancaster
The Wicked Baron
The Wicked Lady

Clash of the Tartans Series by Anna Markland
Kilty Secrets

Queen of Thieves Series by Andy Peloquin
Child of the Night Guild
Thief of the Night Guild

Dark Gardens Series by Meara Platt
Garden of Shadows
Garden of Light
Garden of Dragons
Garden of Destiny

Rulers of the Sky Series by Paula Quinn
Scorched
Ember

Viking's Fury Series by Violetta Rand
Love's Fury
Desire's Fury
Passion's Fury

Also from Violetta Rand
Viking Hearts

The Sons of Scotland Series by Victoria Vane
Virtue

Dry Bayou Brides Series by Lynn Winchester
The Shepherd's Daughter
The Seamstress
The Widow

Table of Contents

Sacrificial Lamb 1
No Choice 4
Andrew 7
Searching for Solutions 9
Disheartening 11
Accident 14
Kiliwhimin 17
First Meeting 22
He Thinks I'm Ye 29
New Plans 33
We've Been Tricked 37
Caught in the Act 45
Secrets and Lies 51
Complications 57
Mischief Afoot 62
Makings of a Good Laird 67
Wild Deer Chase 72
The Hairpin 75
Simpleton 79
Stricken Warrior 86
Playing the Buffoon 91
Plot Thwarted 96
Bitter Truths 101
Secret Feelings 107
Pledging Vengeance 110
Search 113
Clues 118

Something Rotten 122
Trial 127
The Tunnel... 133
Superfluous.. 138
Important Matters 142
Responsibilities 147
Marking Time... 155
Ups and Downs 160
Off His Head... 168
Are Ye Deaf?... 174
The Corpse 179
The Pack 182
Two Weddings... 186
Ninth Inch 192
Rapture 198
Cocoon 206
Under Attack 210
Kith and Kin... 214
Who is This Man?.. 218
Historical Footnotes 222
About Anna 223
More Anna Markland 224

SACRIFICIAL LAMB

Roigh Hall, Inverness, Scotland, 1666 AD

GLAD HE'D RECEIVED no invitation to sit, Ewan Mackinloch folded his arms and scowled at his cantankerous father presiding regally at the head of the Council. "After all the blood spilled o'er the last three hundred years between our clan and the MacCarrons, ye expect me to marry a wench from that cursed tribe?"

The elders gathered around the narrow table in the Chart Room flinched when Laird Duncan Mackinloch leaned forward and brought a gnarled fist down heavily on the scarred wood. "Such an alliance will seal the bargain struck last year at Clunes," he growled. "How else are we to hold the MacCarrons to the deal and make sure they pay the rest of the seventy-two thousand *merks* they promised for Loch Alkayg? For hundreds of years we've proven time and again that land came to Angus Mackinloch in the year of our lord thirteen hundred and twenty-one, when he married Eva, daughter of…"

Ewan had lived and breathed the history of the feud's origins his entire life and could recite the story in his sleep. He studied the rafters while his father droned on about Angus Mackinloch fleeing the wrath of the Lord of the Isles, the occupation of the lands by the MacCarrons, the Battle of Drumlui, the confirmation of Mackinloch rights by no less a personage than King David himself.

He clenched his jaw, reluctant to breathe the fetid air that reeked of too many nervous men, and did the unthinkable. He interrupted his father's monologue. "If 'tis such a good idea, why are ye nay scheming to betroth my brother to the lass?"

"Come now, laddie," his spluttering father replied, "ye ken only too weel we canna allow a MacCarron to be the wife o' the laird o' Clan Mackinloch."

It was the inevitable answer he'd expected, yet it left a bitter taste. "I'm to be the sacrificial lamb, then?"

His Uncle Jamie spoke up. "It might not be so bad. They say the MacCarron women are bonnie."

Despite his affection for his soft-spoken uncle, Ewan snorted. "Whereas the several friendly clans of our own Chattan federation boast few comely lasses."

"No need for sarcasm," his red-faced father retorted. "The MacCarrons are in agreement."

Ewan narrowed his eyes. "And how did ye convince them?"

A chill settled on his nape when Duncan averted his eyes and mumbled—something he never did.

Frustrated, Ewan threw his hands in the air and looked to his uncle for an explanation.

"We agreed ye'll bide a wee in Creag Castle after the handfasting," Jamie told him, "until yer bride is comfortable wi' traveling to Roigh."

Ewan rolled his eyes. "Bide a wee? What the *fyke* does that mean? Ye're talking hand-fasting now?"

"A twelvemonth," his father spat. "As is usual."

A glimmer of hope flickered. After a year and a day he'd be free to abandon his unwanted bride and return home. In the meantime, however, he'd be a hostage in enemy territory. The MacCarrons might not let him leave—alive. He'd have to take a fair-sized contingent of clan warriors. "And I'm to go alone?"

"Nay," Jamie replied. "The MacCarrons will allow some o' yer men." He peeled muck out of his fingernails. "Two to be precise."

Two!

Ewan bit back a blasphemous retort. "And when does my banishment begin?"

His father looked him in the eye. "Ye'll leave on the morrow. We must show the MacCarrons we expect them to keep their promise to pay the compensation within two years. Three installments. I myself shared a wee dram and exchanged swords with their chief—dead shortly after, God rest his soul. We must hold his successor to the agreement."

Evidently, the coin was more important to Duncan Mackinloch than his son's life. Too angry to speak, Ewan turned on his heel and strode out, resentful he'd gone to the bother of donning his best plaid for the meeting. Arguing further would be a waste of time. He'd less than a day to find bodyguards willing to accompany him into the lion's den—and one night to bid a fond farewell to his sweet Kathleen.

No Choice

Creag Castle, Highlands, Scotland

SHONA STALKED TO the door of her uncle's solar, then turned, fisted her hands on her waist, filled her lungs and shouted, "I willna marry a Mackinloch and ye canna make me. Ye're nay my father."

Seated in his favorite chair by the hearth, Kendric MacCarron sighed wearily. "I told ye, lass, I had to agree to a hand-fasting. And I am yer laird."

Blood pulsed in her ears. She knew Kendric grieved the recent death of his older brother, but it was a bitter reminder that he had inherited the lairdship. She lost the last vestige of control and gave her anger full rein. "My father must be turning in his newly-dug grave. What worthy *mon* will want me after I've warmed the bed of a cursed Mackinloch for a twelvemonth?"

She hurried out before he had a chance to reply, slamming the heavy door hard. Panting with the effort, she kept the tears at bay until she reached the privacy of her own apartments a few paces along the narrow hallway.

She shoved open the door and from somewhere found the strength to slam it behind her. Out of the corner of her eye, she noticed her auntie's wide-eyed surprise. Jeannie struggled to extricate herself from the deep upholstered chair by the window as Shona flung herself onto the bed and wept into the bolster.

Her aunt hurried over to perch on the edge of the mattress. "Whatever ails ye, lass?" she asked, stroking her hair. "What has my foolish brother said to upset ye so?"

Shona found comfort in the familiar scent of rosemary. She rolled over and accepted the offer of a kerchief. Sitting up, she blew her nose, which helped clear her ears but seemed to make the hiccups worse. "He's betrothed me," she said hoarsely.

"Weel, ye're of marrying age. Yer dear father would have done the same."

Shona slid off the rumpled bed and readjusted her disheveled clothing. "Da would ne'er have betrothed me to a Mackinloch."

Jeannie gasped. "A Mackinloch?"

Shona paced, the kerchief clutched tight in her fist. "Aye, and not even the laird's eldest son. Some second or mayhap third in line. I didna catch his name. A nobody."

Jeannie shook her head. "Kendric cares for ye. He must have a good reason for doing this. Yer father took part in the talks at Clunes. Perhaps…"

Shona appreciated the difficulty of her aunt's position. She owed loyalty to her brothers—one dead and one now laird. But Jeannie was the babe of that family, a bairn born to a woman thought past her childbearing years. She was closer in age to Shona, more a sister than an auntie, especially since both their mothers had died bringing them into the world.

She chose to ignore the possibility her father had gone along with the plan to wed her to a Mackinloch. "Kendric claims he had nay choice. The agreement with the Chattan federation has to be sealed. But he agreed only to a hand-fasting."

Jeannie brightened. "Weel—"

"'Tis worse than marriage," Shona wailed. "I'll be soiled goods when yon Mackinloch abandons me after a year and a day."

"Aye," Jeannie whispered.

Shona was instantly contrite. Her aunt's husband had supposedly abandoned her after a hand-fasting, citing fears his bairns might inherit the lazy eye that marred Jeannie's otherwise beautiful face. It was a false excuse put forth by a coward. The bitter truth was he'd been banished from MacCarron lands by Shona's father as punishment for his brutality.

"Forgive me," she murmured as she sat down next to her auntie and took her hand. "I'm thoughtless. My mouth runs away with me."

Jeannie forced a smile, the afflicted eye wandering more than usual. "Dinna fash. I'm nay sorry Ailig is gone. He was a cruel *mon*."

It was the closest Jeannie had ever come to speaking of what she'd endured at Ailig's hands, and Shona feared it might be an omen. Her heart sank. "Surely my uncle wouldna betroth me to a brute," she whispered.

ANDREW

Striding through Roigh's dusty bailey, Ewan espied wee Andrew coming in the opposite direction. They fought an ongoing mock battle whenever their paths crossed. He loved the canny lad and it was of some consolation that at least his sister's son would be sad to see him go.

His grinning seven-year-old nephew drew a wooden sword and challenged him. "Halt, scurvy knave."

Ewan slowed his pace, but didn't stop. "Sorry," he replied, "no time to play this day."

The smile had disappeared from the boy's face by the time he caught up. "What's amiss, Uncle?"

How to explain to a bairn that his life had fallen apart? He paused and hunkered down. "I'm to undertake a long and difficult journey, and I must gather companions to accompany me."

"I'll go with ye," Andrew replied without hesitation.

"I wish it could be so," Ewan said with a wry smile, "but I'm bound for MacCarron lands."

Andrew braced his legs and brandished his toy sword. "I'll help ye fight that evil clan."

Ewan touched a finger to the wooden point. "I'd be proud to have ye fight at my side, but I'm going there to be wed, not to make war."

Andrew frowned. "Wed? To a MacCarron?"

"Aye."

The boy slashed the air with his weapon. "Who sends ye to such a fate? I'll slay him."

"The Mackinloch. Yer laird."

The boy studied his feet as he put up his blade. "Oh."

Ewan tussled the mop of red curls. "Dinna fash. 'Tis only for a year and a day, then I'll return."

"With yer bride?"

Ewan bristled as he stood. "I hae ma doots about that."

Andrew hurried to keep pace with him as he set off again. "Who will ye choose as yer escort? I'll warrant my da will go with ye."

Ewan shook his head. "I'll nay expect men with wives and bairns to bide a year with our enemies."

Out of breath now, Andrew panted, "And I suppose men with sweethearts willna wish to go either."

For the first time, the complexity of the task he faced struck Ewan—a problem a bairn had foreseen. Most young Mackinloch warriors boasted of a lady-love.

"I always thought ye'd marry Kathleen," Andrew remarked.

Ewan looked askance at his red-faced nephew. He was fond of the sweet Kathleen, but marriage had never entered his head. Mayhap if they were to wed quickly, there'd be no question of hand-fasting a MacCarron.

It was a way out of his dilemma, and would surely infuriate his father. However, truth be told, he knew in his heart he didn't fancy being married to a biddable woman. He wanted passion.

He stopped at the door to the barracks. "I think I prefer a feisty lass with a sense of humor," he said.

Andrew eyed him as if he'd lost his wits.

SEARCHING FOR SOLUTIONS

"We'll be late to the hall for supper," Jeannie cajoled, smoothing her skirts as she exited the *boudoir*. "Hurry and get ready."

Shona paced the chamber, shaking her head. "I'll nay sup with my uncle until we've thought of a solution."

"The solution is that there's no escape," her auntie replied, tucking a wayward curl behind her ear. "I'm hungry and, besides, yon Mackinloch will be smitten as soon as he sets eyes on yer golden hair."

Shona stopped abruptly, hands fisted on her hips. "We could stay locked in this chamber until the fellow gives up and returns home."

Jeannie rolled her eyes—well, at least the one she could control. "Aye. If we dinna starve to death, we can then wait until the Mackinlochs descend on us with an army to avenge the insult."

Shona chewed her bottom lip, reluctant to admit Jeannie was right. "I could pretend to be ill…afflicted with some noxious disease…the pox. Who'd want to wed a poxy woman?"

Her aunt headed for the door. "Ye're daft."

Shona couldn't bear the thought of being left alone with her dilemma. "We'll run away."

"To where? And forget the *we*. This is my home."

Panic tightened Shona's throat. "We must have allies who will grant me sanctuary."

Jeannie snorted. "We're MacCarrons, or have ye forgotten? Any allies we may have willna risk the wrath of the mighty Mackinlochs. Besides, 'tis foolhardy to travel alone."

"I would take Ruadh."

Her auntie laughed heartily. "That hound is afraid of his shadow. He'd lead ye round in circles chasing his own tail."

Jeannie's broad smile reminded Shona of what many people said of the two of them, that they looked like sisters. It sparked an idea and she decided to try a different, more subtle plan of attack. "Ye ken, Auntie," she wheedled, "'twould be prudent, would it not, to size up this Mackinloch afore I say yeah or nay to his suit?"

The smile turned to a frown. "And how do ye propose to do that?"

"If someone else were to take my place…"

Jeannie grimaced. "What are ye plotting in that wee head?"

"If I could watch him, but he doesna ken I'm…"

Her aunt yanked open the door. "Nay, lassie, running away was a better idea."

DISHEARTENING

In the late afternoon, Ewan left Liath munching oats in the stables. The gelding would have to carry him far on the morrow and he'd already ridden from village to village, across miles of Mackinloch lands. Weary and disheartened, he walked to Kathleen's cottage outside the castle wall.

She rushed at him the moment he came through the door. He put his arms around her as she sobbed on his chest. Obviously, she'd heard the news, but her wailing set him on edge.

He stroked her hair, summoning the will to ask her to be his bride. The words lodged in his throat.

Once the weeping stopped, she turned her tear-streaked face to look up at him. "I'll miss ye," she said hoarsely.

He detected a note of insincerity and suspected she'd already cast about for a new patron. "A year will pass quickly," he replied.

"Aye," she sighed in a way that made him feel he'd already left.

It was her habit to take him by the hand and lead him to bed when he arrived. This evening, she pulled away and went to sit on the stool by the kitchen hearth. Strangely, it didn't bother him. Any thoughts of coupling with her had fled. He supposed the uncertainty of what he faced at Creag Castle had dimmed his enthusiasm.

He wandered around the cottage for a while, picking up this and that—a plate, a comb, a brooch he recognized as a trinket he'd given her.

"Can I keep it?" she asked.

"As a memento?" he replied.

"Aye. Summat o' the sort."

He was tempted to remark that she'd likely have no trouble selling it, but held his tongue. Better to part as friends.

"How long will it teck to reach MacCarron lands?" she asked.

"Two days, three if the weather turns bad."

"Will ye go alone?"

He bristled, recalling the frustrating day he'd spent trying to recruit men to accompany him. "Fynn Macintyre of Badenoch and David Shaw have agreed to come with me."

"Not Mackinloch kin then?"

He clenched his jaw. "Men whose families are loyal to the Chattan federation nonetheless."

"I wish ye safe journey."

He went to the hearth, took her hand and kissed it. "Fare thee well, sweet Kathleen."

"Goodbye, Ewan," she replied.

She made no effort to rise, so he left her there, feeling an odd sense of relief as he walked up the hill to the castle.

Arriving back at Roigh Hall earlier than planned, he decided to check on Fynn and David. Mayhap they'd been successful in convincing other warriors to join them. Just because the MacCarrons had stipulated two men at the most didn't mean he had to abide by their wishes. A man with one hand and a lad with a stutter were hardly an impressive escort for the son of a Mackinloch laird.

After a bit of searching he found them in the stables. Fynn was checking reins and bridles. He was dexterous for a man with a handicap, and fortunately it wasn't his sword hand lost in a skirmish. However, his opponent had been a MacCarron, a warrior he'd cleaved in two with his last ounce of strength. It didn't bode well.

David came close to tripping over his own feet in his haste to greet Ewan. "My…my…my…lord," he managed. "I…I…I was…"

Ewan reined in his impatience. He had to survive a year of the stammer and already itched to shake the words out of the youth. "Did we recruit anyone else?" he asked.

David studied his boots. "N...n...nay."

"Cowards, the lot o' them," Fynn growled. "Afeared o' MacCarrons."

Ewan worried about the man's reasons for volunteering. "We're going to meet my betrothed," he pointed out. "Not to start another war."

Fynn spat into the dirt. "Aye. Yer betrothed. I ken."

The journey loomed like an ominous cloud in the darkening sky. Ewan might end up talking to himself on the way. "Get some sleep," he said gruffly. "Be ready at dawn."

David grinned. "A...A...Aye, my...my...my lord. Soon...soon...soonest..."

Ewan strode away lest he throttle the lad.

ACCIDENT

Shona pestered Jeannie about trading places as they made their way to the hall, but her aunt was having none of it. "Yer uncle will flay us alive if ye even suggest it," she said indignantly.

"Not if I can convince him o' the merits…"

The words died abruptly when a group of agitated clansmen appeared in the hallway, four of them bearing a stretcher on which lay her uncle, his leg in a makeshift splint, his scratched and muck-smeared face contorted in agony.

Memories of her father's fatal accident constricted Shona's throat as Jeannie hurried to her brother's side. "What happened, Kendric?"

He gritted his teeth and shook his head.

"We were hunting to fill the larder for our visitors," one of the ruddy-faced bearers hissed without breaking his stride. "His horse threw him. The physician's on the way, but we must get him to bed. His leg is badly broken."

"And he may have injured his back," another frowning clansman confided once the stretcher bearers had disappeared in the direction of Kendric's solar with their burden, Jeannie hurrying alongside.

Guilt swept over Shona. She'd been trying to fathom a way to keep her uncle ignorant of her plans, but hadn't wished him ill. His injuries were obviously serious and, what was worse, the proud fool had sustained them while out hunting deer to serve to his Mackinloch guest. The visit was already bringing hardship.

She spent the next few hours dealing with distraught clan members and elders who descended on them like a swarm of buzzing bees.

How news of the accident spread so fast was beyond her ken. She supposed they'd only recently become accustomed to a new laird, and now another terrible mishap had occurred. There were whispers of a curse. She shoved aside her own fears and repeated a litany of reassurances.

As she might have expected, the most persistent among the *concerned* relatives was Mungo Morley, a distant cousin who'd offered for her hand in marriage many times. Her father had deemed him unsuitable to be a leader, and Uncle Kendric concurred. The deciding factor in their refusal was that Shona thought him odd. He put her in mind of an overgrown weasel and such a high-pitched voice should never come out of the mouth of a giant of a man.

The physician's arrival provided the opportunity to free herself from Mungo's insistent probing as to Kendric's condition.

"The vultures are gathering, I see," Cummings said.

"Aye," she agreed with a shudder, ushering him into the chamber. "Brings back too many raw memories."

He patted her hand. "I ken, child. We must hope for the best."

Reluctant to witness what she expected would be a painful ordeal for her uncle, she didn't enter the laird's chamber, deciding instead to seek the quiet of her own apartment.

She covered her ears to shut out the shouts of agony that echoed down the stone hallway, adding to her anxiety. When all was suddenly quiet, she plucked up courage and tiptoed into Kendric's chamber, full of dread. Bees buzzed in her head when she espied him lying in the big laird's bed that had once been her parents'—the bed she'd been born in, and where her mother's life had ended. Her uncle seemed to have shriveled beneath a mound of blankets and furs. Mouth agape, he looked like he'd breathed his last. His normally ruddy face was as pale as death.

Her feet felt like they were nailed to the planked flooring. "He's nay dead, is he?" she whispered to Jeannie seated in a chair pulled up to the side of the bed.

Her auntie glanced up sharply, though the lazy eye remained

closed. "I didna hear ye come in, lass," she murmured. "He's sleeping."

Her pallor worried Shona. "Ye need rest. Ye've been here too long. I'll sit with him and send a servant if he wakes."

Jeannie shook her head. "Cummings gave him laudanum when he set his leg, though he protested against the new potion. Wanted old-fashioned *dwale*, not opium. As ye see, the laudanum has done the job."

"'Tis a blessing really," Shona offered, not knowing what else to say. "At least he canna feel the pain."

"Aye," Jeannie said hoarsely. "I doot he'll be in a fit state to welcome yer betrothed."

The terrible accident had shoved Shona's dilemma to the back of her mind, but she hadn't forgotten it entirely. Perhaps her uncle's drugged state was a good omen and Jeannie might be more easily persuaded now that she was exhausted.

She opened her mouth, but the stern set of her aunt's jaw dissuaded her. She took Jeannie's arm and coaxed her out of the chair. "Go to bed. I'll keep vigil."

KILIWHIMIN

At dawn the day after the Council meeting, Duncan bade Ewan farewell with a gruff reminder of his duty. There was no handshake and no attempt at an embrace. Andrew's mother wept and babbled reassurances she was certain all would be well. Her son managed to grit his teeth and swallow his tears until Ewan picked him up and hugged him.

His older brother offered a limp handshake. Colin tended to think he was already the Mackinloch laird. The five years' age difference had stood in the way of them ever becoming friends.

Tight-lipped, Ewan was the first to ride out through the gates of Roigh Hall. There was no sign of Kathleen as he passed her cottage.

He wondered if he'd ever see the castle again. It was the place of his birth and he admitted inwardly he'd taken for granted the comfort and security of the only home he'd known. Few enemy clans had ever contemplated attacking the powerful Mackinlochs.

"Least of all the cowardly MacCarrons," he grumbled, after taking a last look over his shoulder.

Reluctant to indulge in hours of idle chatter with his men, he stayed slightly ahead. For the first hour of the journey to Creag Castle, David tried without success to instigate conversation with Fynn, until the older man cut him off. "Ye mistake me for someone who has the patience to listen to yer stammering prattle," he said.

After that, the trio rode in silence, which suited Ewan just fine.

When the weak noonday sun indicated it was time to eat, he reached into his satchel and found the heel of bread a tearful Alys

Cook had packed for him. He bit into it, though his appetite had fled.

Chunnering over the likelihood Colin may have had a hand in the MacCarron agreement since he'd participated in the meetings at Clunes, Ewan didn't bother to tell his men they'd have to eat in the saddle. Let them figure it out for themselves.

He finished the bread and a lump of hard cheese from which he suspected Alys had pared the mold. As he tipped the flagon of ale to his mouth, a loud shout from David caused him to spill some of the brew. "Loo…loo…look. An ee…ee…eagle."

Wiping droplets from his plaid, Ewan peered at the bird of prey and its mate gliding effortlessly high in the sky. He inhaled deeply as his irritation fled. The rugged grandeur of the Highlands always filled him with a sense of peace. Resentment had turned his mind inward and he hadn't paid attention to the magnificent beauty of the shoreline they followed as they traveled southwest. There was no more breathtaking vista in the whole of Scotland than Loch Ness.

Even Fynn stared open-mouthed at the birds, his good hand shading his eyes, the reins wound around his stump.

As they resumed their journey, it struck Ewan he had a choice. He could wallow in self-pity or make the best of his fate. Mayhap Jamie was right about MacCarron lasses being bonnie, though how his uncle would ken such a thing…

He mused on the color of his betrothed's hair—he liked redheads, or, better yet, golden-haired beauties. He cursed when it dawned on him he hadn't paid attention to the name of his intended. "She'll probably have a warty nose," he muttered, "and be bald as a coot."

"Yer par…par…pardon, I did…didna hear what ye said, my…my…"

"Nothing," Ewan hissed.

Annoyed he'd again lost his temper, he looked to the sky. The eagles were faint dots in the distant clouds. The raptors didn't worry about enemies, and neither should he. The MacCarrons wouldn't dare murder him, lest they bring the wrath of the Mackinlochs down on their misbegotten heads.

Perhaps his conniving father hadn't offered him up as a sacrificial lamb. Forcing the MacCarrons to hold to the bargain was important and he'd make sure they did. In the meanwhile, he'd get to rut to his heart's content, and he could always keep his eyes shut if his bride wasn't comely.

The sky suddenly darkened as it occurred to him he'd have to be careful not to sire a bairn in the process. A child would be an unwanted complication if he was to return to Roigh after a year and a day.

He looked over his shoulder. "We need to pick up our pace if we want to reach the lodge at Kiliwhimin afore the downpour," he shouted, feeling the first drops on his face.

They went as fast as they dared in the uncertain terrain of the moor, but their plaids were soaked by the time they reached the small hunting lodge. Ewan had camped in the rustic cabin many times before and knew the friendly clan that owned it would have no objection to their seeking shelter there.

They took care of their horses in the wee stable, and fed them the oats they'd brought. Fynn soon had a peat fire glowing in the hearth. David fetched water from the loch and set it to heat on the hob.

When the lad disappeared without a word, Ewan assumed he was seeing to his needs. His spirits lifted when the youth returned a short time later, his long red hair plastered to his head, water running in rivulets down his face, and a plump rabbit in each meaty fist.

Fynn drew out his dagger and pointed to a small wooden table. "There," he said gruffly.

David obeyed.

Fynn had the rabbits skinned and skewered on the spit in less time than it would have taken most men with two good hands.

Ewan spread his wet plaid out near the hearth, then sat cross-legged close to the fire to dry his wet hair, inhaling the tempting aroma already rising from the roasted game. A spark of hope glimmered in his heart that the two misfits might prove their worth after all.

Reluctant as he was to strike up a conversation, it seemed churlish to remain silent. He pointed to a roughly hewn wooden chest built into the wall. "They usually keep that well supplied wi' blankets," he said, hoping the caretakers hadn't let things slide since the last time he'd been by this way. The unpleasant alternative was to sleep wrapped in damp plaids.

David eagerly thrust open the lid, pulled out a blanket, and grinned, holding it aloft. When he didn't utter a word, Ewan worried he and Fynn had been too harsh on the lad.

"They might need a good shaking," he advised, wishing he'd been more explicit when the air in the confined space filled with dust motes and several moths startled from the bedding.

"S...s...sorry," David said sheepishly, carrying the bundle to the door and giving the whole lot another shake.

Fynn rolled his eyes when the wind blew more dust back into the cabin.

"Set them here close to the hearth," Ewan told the lad.

David obeyed, then took over turning the spit.

With the heat of the fire on his face, Ewan closed his eyes, listening. Rain danced on the roof, flames hissed when grease spattered, the spit squeaked in protest.

It came to him as the chill receded and he relaxed that a melodious masculine voice was singing.

Nae doot ye've heard o' Jenny Shaw,
  Who lives doon by the burn;
That winsome lass few can surpass,
  Who daily works the churn.
An' tho' she's but a dairymaid,
  She's a' the world to me;
She is my jewel, my Jenny fair,
  Wi' modest grace to see.

He hummed along through several verses of the well-loved tune, feeling the tension drain from his body. Sorry when the song came to an end, he opened his eyes, astonished to discover David was the singer.

He couldn't help himself. "Ye can sing without stammering."

David shrugged. "Aye," he replied, apparently as unsure of the reason as anybody.

"Meat's ready," Fynn announced, deftly carving the food directly on the scarred table. Ewan pulled up a stool, took out his dagger and skewered a choice piece, his right as the laird's son. Fynn and David waited until he'd savored the first bite and indicated his approval before taking their share.

"Well done, lads," he said with his mouth full.

"Aye," Fynn replied, licking the grease off his stump.

David nodded.

"I expect we'll reach Creag Castle by the afternoon on the morrow," he told them between bites. "From what I hear o' the place, this might be our last good meal for a while."

Fynn stabbed his dagger into the wood of the table.

David's eyes widened and Ewan regretted alarming the youth. "Dinna fash, I meant it as a jest," he explained.

A short time later, he lay on the dirt floor in front of the hearth wrapped in a musty-smelling blanket. Staring up at the rafters, he resolved to accept he'd be living in less than ideal conditions for a while. However, they were hardy men fulfilling an important mission for their clan. He'd tried to reassure David, but his expectations of Creag Castle were low. The MacCarrons weren't wealthy.

Sleep proved elusive as worry tormented him. Once the MacCarron wench got her claws into the son of a Mackinloch laird she might not let go. He was, after all, considered an eligible bachelor by the lasses of Inverness.

His bride's interest would wane quickly if he was missing a limb, like Fynn. He chuckled at the notion that if he stammered like David it would likely drive her mad.

FIRST MEETING

WHILE EWAN WAS still abed scheming, Fynn poached the three lake trout David had caught before dawn.

Drawn to the table by the tempting aroma, Ewan grasped the fish's tail and pulled. The skeleton peeled away from the tender flesh.

"Right," he told them, licking the sweet taste of the first bite from his fingers, "this is the plan when we reach Creag Castle."

Fynn raised an eyebrow.

Lines of concentration furrowed David's forehead.

"We're all Mackinloch, nay Shaw, nor Macintyre. I dinna want the MacCarrons to harbor any doots about our unity."

He preferred not to dwell on the fact no Mackinloch kin had been willing to accompany him, and both men nodded their understanding of his instructions without apparent malice.

"Day…Day…David Mm…Mmm…Mac…"

"Mackinloch," Fynn shouted, banging his fist on the table. "'Tis simple enough."

"Aye," David replied. "Simple for ye." His face reddened as he turned his attention to extracting bones from his half-eaten fish. Apparently, his retort had surprised him as much as Ewan and Fynn.

However, there were more important matters to tend to. "I want to size up yon MacCarron lass afore finding myself in a trap I canna escape, so when we first arrive, Fynn will play the role of the intended groom."

Fynn's face turned the same color as the grey stubble on his head. "Nay, laddie. Ye're asking for trouble."

"On the contrary, I seek to avoid a lifetime of it."

"They'll ken something's awry. I'm too old to be ye."

Ewan winked. "Let's hope my bride thinks her intended groom is a greybeard."

"She might fa…fa…fall in lo…lo…lo…love with Fy…Fy…"

Fynn's sullen scowl turned to a snigger of amusement at such a nonsensical idea. "I see yer plan," he said. "Ye're hoping the lass will reject ye. Er, I mean me. Then the blame will rest on the MacCarrons and nay us. I mean ye."

David scratched his head.

Ewan rose from the table and laid a hand on his man's shoulder. "Exactly. Now let's away."

He'd more or less convinced himself his plan was sound when they reined to a halt a few hours later in sight of their destination. "'Tis strange to be in the place where the feud began hundreds o' years ago," he remarked, pointing to the massive tower. "The MacCarrons added on yon show of strength after they seized the castle from us, the rightful owners."

"They cl…cl…claim it was deser…desert…deserted."

"Bollocks," Ewan exclaimed.

"Weel, they've agreed to pay now," Fynn replied, "and we're here to make sure they do."

Heart pounding in his ears, Ewan stared at the castle wherein dwelt the woman he'd been shackled to, unless their ruse worked. "We're clear on the plan?" he asked.

"Aye," David said softly.

"'Tis lunacy if ye ask me," Fynn added.

They rode unchallenged through the open gates and into the bailey.

"Lax," Ewan remarked with disgust. "Just as I expected."

Fynn stood in the stirrups and scanned the wide but almost deserted courtyard. "Odd, I'd say, that no one has come to greet us."

As he spoke, a youth sauntered out from the keep, picking up his pace when he saw them. "My lords," he panted, his eyes darting from

Ewan to Fynn and then to David. "Forgive me. Our laird has been injured and I went inside for only a moment to see how he fares."

Evidently taking his best guess as to the identity of the nobleman, he addressed Ewan. "Ye be the Mackinloch we've been expecting?"

Irritated when his confederate didn't correct the *error*, Ewan was forced to do so. "Nay," he explained, gesturing to Fynn. "This gentleman is the Mackinloch."

The lad recoiled at the sight of Fynn's stump. "I'll see to yer mount, er…" He hesitated, clearly uncertain how to take reins from a man with one hand.

Fynn dismounted and let the leather dangle. "Yer laird is in bad fettle?"

Ewan cringed as he slid from Liath's back. He hadn't factored Fynn's brogue into the plan.

"Aye," the lad replied, taking the reins of the three horses. "'Oss threw him. Shattered 'is leg and they think there's summat wrong wi' 'is back an all."

"Hee…hee…he must…bee…bee…in bed then," David said.

The youth's puzzled stare was predictable.

Fynn shifted his weight, plainly unsure what to say or do next. Ewan inhaled deeply. So far the only thing to go right was the horror on the boy's face when he realized the MacCarron lass had been betrothed to a man with one hand. "Mayhap ye'll inform someone my laird has arrived," he said to the gaping boy.

"Reet away, soon as I've seen to yer 'osses."

He left them standing in the bailey.

"Wha…wha…what…"

"Apparently, we wait," Ewan muttered, gripping the hilt of his claymore, ready to scythe down any MacCarron who dared cross their paths.

"Here comes someone now," Fynn growled, nodding to the door of the keep.

Ewan's fury fled when he espied a tall lass approaching from the castle. The stiff breeze that lent a healthy glow to her cheeks also threatened to lift her skirts, but it was powerless to dislodge even a hair of the long, long golden glory that crowned her head.

He braced his legs, momentarily dizzied by a vision of wrapping himself in those incredible tresses, her shapely breasts filling his hands. If this was the lass he was to wed, all was well with the world.

But she was too fair of face to be a MacCarron.

She frowned. "Ye're the Mackinloch?" she asked Ewan.

"We're all...all...Mac...Mackinlochs," David said with a grin, looking too pleased with himself for Ewan's liking.

Evidently as smitten with the golden-haired beauty as he was, Fynn chose that moment to extend his good hand and play his role. "Nay, I'm the son o' the Mackinloch laird."

Did the idiot nay ken a mon doesna shake a lady's hand?

The color drained from the lass's face as her eyes traveled from the stump to the grey hair and wrinkled features. Holding her breath, she touched her fingertips to Fynn's then snatched her hand away as if she'd been bitten by a snake.

Ewan was about to come clean about the ridiculous ruse, but she spoke to Fynn. "Welcome," she said hoarsely. "I'm Lady Jeannie, sister to The Camron, our chief. 'Tis my niece ye've come to wed. Follow me and I'll show ye to yer chamber. The castle is full of kin who've gathered to keep vigil with my brother. Yer men will have to sleep in the stable."

"Near to deeth is he?" Fynn asked.

Ewan rolled his eyes.

The laird's sister gasped. "We pray he'll recover, but his injuries are serious right enough."

He watched her lead Fynn into the keep, his eyes fixed on the tempting bottom that would never be his to touch. 'Twas incredible that the MacCarron laird had such a bonnie sister—and feisty. There'd been no apology for expecting the Mackinloch escorts to sleep in the stable. The notion of getting to know such a proud and comely lass was appealing. However, pursuing her would complicate matters further.

More disconcerting was the news the MacCarron laird lay gravely injured. From what little Ewan knew of the clan, the man had only recently inherited the lairdship from his older brother. Apparently not expecting to be laird, he'd never married and had no sons. It was possible there'd be a dispute over the succession.

Ewan hadn't slept in a stable since he was a lad when he'd hidden from the licking Da intended to give him for some youthful prank.

"Mac…Mac…MacCarron lasses are bonn…bonn…"

"Aye, bonnie," he muttered, clinging to a faint hope his intended was perhaps even more lovely than the lass with blonde hair. But she was about to meet a man with one hand who was probably old enough to be her father.

Shona clenched her fists in the fabric of her skirts, wrinkling her nose at the odor of horse and leather emanating from the Mackinloch following her. What was her uncle thinking, wedding her to a man with one hand who was old enough to be her father? If Kendric wasn't dead by the time she next visited his chamber, she'd be mightily tempted to throttle him.

To make matters worse, she'd almost thrown herself at his kinsman whose commanding presence and rich attire had persuaded her he was the intended groom.

Now there was a bonnie man. Tall, broad-shouldered, well muscled, and hair of a color she couldn't quite describe—shiny and brown like the shell of a chestnut.

She had no time for any of the MacCarron clansmen who pursued her, but one look at the newcomer filled her head with carnal images involving the removal of all clothing. In a few brief moments he'd roused wanton emotions and needs she was unaware she harbored. Foolish to be gobsmacked by a man whose name she hadn't yet learned and whose station was far beneath hers.

She conjured a vision of dimples if he smiled, though she'd only seen him scowl.

"Mayhap we should come another time," the one-handed man suggested, jolting her back to reality.

A hundred years from now.

Outside the door to the guest chamber, she hesitated, torn between grasping the lifeline he offered and possibly plunging the clan into more conflict with the Mackinlochs. If Kendric died, there'd be trouble. She sensed intrigue already brewing among the kin who'd gathered like buzzards to pick apart the corpse.

She had to convince her aunt to go along with the ruse.

"I must tend my brother," she said coldly. "Ye're welcome to eat in the hall later, but my niece and I willna be there. Ye understand."

"Aye," he replied, shifting his weight from one foot to the other. "Dinna fash. I'll sup wi' ma men."

Fuming, she shoved open the door and withdrew without extending the customary hospitality of asking if the chamber was to his satisfaction. She'd always thought the Mackinlochs a wealthy clan, yet their laird's son spoke like an uneducated peasant.

She'd be damned if she'd allow herself to be shackled to such a man.

Anger gave her feet wings as she hastened down the hallway to her uncle's chamber.

Her aunt startled when she burst through the door. "Hush, child," she admonished. "He needs sleep."

Shona approached the bed, hands fisted at her sides, and stared at the wretch who'd ruined her life. "I'm going to kill him anyway."

Jeannie sighed. "I take it ye've met yer intended husband?"

Shona inhaled deeply and pulled her aunt away from the sickbed. "Aye," she hissed. "He's old enough to be my father."

"Nay," Jeannie replied. "How can that be? Laird Mackinloch isna in his dotage."

"I dinna ken, but that isna the worst of it."

She swallowed hard, not certain she could explain the rest without weeping.

Jeannie put an arm around her shoulders and drew her close. "Tell me," she whispered sympathetically.

"I shouldna fault a warrior for it, but he's missing a hand," she murmured into her aunt's breast.

HE THINKS I'M YE

SHONA WIPED AWAY tears as Jeannie gently stroked her back.

"I ne'er heard anything o' the sort about the Mackinloch laird's sons," her aunt said. "I thought he had just two boys. This must be an older brother, but if that were true he'd be the next laird."

Shona hiccupped. "His name is Fynn. Mayhap he's a bastard."

"Saints preserve us," Jeannie exclaimed. "Kendric will have a fit if that's the case."

They glanced at the stricken man in the bed. Jeannie's face paled. "When he's better, that is."

Shona prayed her uncle would indeed recover, but she'd never been one to shy away from confronting a problem. "What if he doesna get better? There's already speculation among the visitors about who will take over as laird."

Jeannie clenched her jaw. "All the more reason for ye to wed the Mackinloch quickly. I hate to admit it but a laird with ties to that clan would be the best for the MacCarrons. This Fynn would have a strong claim married to ye, blood kin to the former and current laird."

"But if he's a bastard…"

"Ye must ask him, directly," Jeannie replied. "There's too much at stake."

Shona hesitated only a moment before charging ahead. "I canna. He thinks I'm ye."

Fynn perched on a bale of hay in the stables. "'Twouldna be proper," he muttered.

Ewan clenched his jaw, trying to hold on to his patience. "If my betrothed refuses to leave her uncle's bedside then the only way to meet her is to visit the laird. His chamber canna be far from yers."

"Aye," David agreed, earning a scowl from Fynn.

"They'll think it mighty peculiar if ye dinna ask to pay yer respects. 'Twill be considered an insult."

Fynn folded his arms.

Ewan sensed he was wavering. "I'll announce yer intention."

"Seems forward," Fynn remarked.

Ewan rolled his eyes. "We're Mackinlochs, *mon*. They expect us to be pushy."

"I'm a Macintyre," Fynn grumbled as he followed Ewan out of the stable and into the keep.

It was an irritating reminder.

Entering the main hall, they encountered two groups of scowling men huddled around separate trestle tables. The murmur of conversation ceased abruptly. Ewan sensed tension between the factions who soon resumed exchanging hostile glances over the rims of tankards raised to their lips.

One swarthy giant with a scraggly red beard and unruly hair got to his feet and came to confront Fynn. "What the *fyke* are the Mackinlochs playing at? Yer laird sends an owd cripple to wed our Shona?"

Ewan fought the urge to laugh at the man's wheedling voice. He wondered if the fellow was deliberately trying to sound like a fool.

However, it seemed news traveled fast.

To his credit, Fynn didn't back away. He stuck out his chin and looked the man in the eye—no mean feat since the bully was a foot taller. "I'll wager I can gi' a lassie more pleasure wi' one hand than ye can wi' them two beefy mitts ye've got."

A strange silence reigned as the giant faltered and looked at his hands.

David studied the banners wafting in the rafters.

Ewan gawked as the man's face turned as red as his unkempt beard.

Another man from the second table stood. "Seems yon Mackinloch has heard o' Mungo's clumsy reputation wi' the lasses," he shouted.

Guffaws accompanied the racket of tankards banging on wood.

Ewan might have known. For all they were the age-old enemy, the MacCarrons were like any other clan—teeming with rival factions. He had little doubt they'd happened upon a gathering of power-seekers plotting their next moves should Kendric die.

He pitied the clan if this Mungo became their laird. The brute probably wanted Shona for himself. At least now Ewan knew her name. He hadn't even met the woman but felt sorry for any lass married to such a bully. Like most of his ilk, he'd backed down, seemingly too dimwitted to come up with a retort to Fynn's insult.

A peculiar pang of something too much like righteous anger twisted Ewan's innards. He had the makings of a chief; his father had sensibly groomed both his sons for the role—much to Colin's chagrin—and better he become The Camron than the weaselly redhead. If he was to marry this Shona…

He shrugged off the notion and touched Fynn's arm. "The Mac-Carron laird awaits, my lord," he said.

The rumble of plotting resumed as they strode out of the hall. Once they were in the passageway leading to the private chambers, Ewan elbowed Fynn. "That was risky. I'm proud o' ye."

"Me…me…me…too," David said.

Fynn shrugged. "When a *mon* has just the one hand, he learns o'er the years how to deal wi' bullies."

Two MacCarron clansmen leaning against the frame of a heavy planked door suddenly stood up straight, folded corded arms across broad chests, and eyed them suspiciously.

"The Mackinloch, come to pay his respects to The Camron," Ewan announced, stepping back to allow Fynn to enter first.

The guards exchanged a brief glance before one rapped and requested entry.

Ewan was taken aback when the golden-haired beauty he'd met in the bailey opened the door. His unruly cock saluted.

She gritted her teeth and barely glanced at Fynn. "Ye can only stay a few moments. My brother is very ill."

"We'll be quiet as mice," Fynn replied.

"Mm…m…mice," David confirmed.

Ewan clenched his fists.

A second woman appeared at the door.

"May I present my niece, Shona, yer intended," the beauty explained to Fynn.

The newcomer glanced at the stump, hesitated only a moment, then smiled. "Come in. We canna keep the door open overlong," she said.

It registered in Ewan's befuddled brain that the two women looked more like sisters than niece and aunt, but his arousal fled when his body had no trouble realizing he'd been promised to the one with a lazy eye.

New Plans

When Fynn dithered on the threshold, Ewan came up right behind him and gave him a nudge, leaving his kinsman no choice but to enter the chamber. David followed.

Both lasses took a step backward.

Fynn reached for Lady Lazy-Eye's hand and, to Ewan's astonishment, bestowed a courtly kiss upon it.

She blushed prettily and smiled. She'd have been a beauty but for the eye defect.

"My…my…lady," Fynn gushed, still holding her hand.

David scowled, then bowed. "My…my…la..la…la…ladies," he offered.

The MacCarron women stared open-mouthed, probably thinking the mighty Mackinlochs had turned out to be a clan of stammerers.

Ewan affected a perfunctory bow. "Forgive my lord Fynn. He is overcome by…"

He was about to say *yer beauty*, but sensed both women would recognize it for the empty compliment it was.

"…news of yer uncle's accident," he amended quickly.

"Aye," the golden-haired auntie agreed, ignoring Fynn and addressing her comment to Ewan. "He is very ill."

His inclination was to invite the lass to join him outside the chamber where they might continue a more intimate conversation. He struggled to remind himself he was supposed to be a lowly member of Fynn's escort. A dalliance with the aunt of his intended bride was likely to cause more problems.

He glanced across the dimly lit chamber to the mound of furs and blankets on the bed, anxious to get a glimpse of a laird who had a beautiful young sister and an older niece. "I dinna suppose we can speak with The Camron today, about…"

He lost his train of thought as he stared into green eyes welling with tears. "My apologies, ye're upset about yer brother. I shouldna have mentioned it."

The lasses exchanged a strange glance which hinted at a shared secret. Ewan couldn't imagine what it might be, unless the accident was a ruse, and the laird wasn't injured at all. That seemed unlikely given the factions plotting in the hall.

The five hovered near the doorway in silence, avoiding looking at each other for what seemed like long awkward minutes, until Lazy-Eye extracted her hand from Fynn's grip and walked over to the bed.

Ewan again had to prod Fynn to follow. "Go on, *mon*," he whispered. "Pay yer respects."

"He seems shy," the beauty said when only she, Ewan and David remained by the door.

"Aye," he agreed, wishing he'd put more forethought into trying to turn a farmer into the son of a nobleman in the blink of an eye.

"I'm Ewan Mackinloch, by the way," he explained, hoping she would repeat his name. But she merely nodded and walked to her brother's bedside. The aroma of lavender tickled his nostrils. "Not only beautiful, but sweet-smelling," he sighed.

David's echoing sigh of agreement jolted him back to reality. Lowly escorts had no reason to remain in the chamber, but he was hesitant to leave Fynn to his own devices. He couldn't hear the conversation, but his man seemed to be taking more of an interest in Lady Lazy-Eye than was warranted. She was Ewan's intended for pity's sake.

He mocked his own stupidity. Now he was jealous of a one-armed man paying attention to a woman he didn't want to marry anyway.

And if the laird's sister would cease staring at him, he might get his thoughts off bedding her at the earliest opportunity.

He sauntered over to the end of the huge bed, hoping his actions wouldn't be deemed rude. He swallowed hard when he set eyes on the injured man. There was no doubt Kendric MacCarron had met with a catastrophic accident. One leg was encased in a parchment and wax cast from ankle to hip. Though he slept the sleep of a man heavily drugged, agony was etched on his pale features.

Shame prickled Ewan's nape. He shouldn't be relieved the man was indeed very ill, but at least the MacCarrons weren't trying to pull the wool over their eyes. Another emotion plagued him. He'd been raised to hate the lairds of this enemy clan, yet he felt nothing but pity for the stricken chief.

"Ye see the state he's in," Lazy-Eye whispered to Fynn, as if she sensed they had doubts.

Did she also harbor suspicions about the deception the Mackinlochs were perpetrating?

He risked a glance across at the beauty who still stared at him with unmistakable longing. She perhaps thought him free to pursue her, and he surely would if only he could. He half-wished he'd never left Roigh, but then he wouldn't have met the woman who'd bewitched him.

He was tempted to blurt out that he was the Mackinloch laird's son. That while he realized he was meant to wed Lady Lazy-Eye, would the MacCarrons object if he married her aunt instead?

"I think we should leave," Fynn said, shaking him out of his lunacy.

He dragged his gaze away and stalked to the hallway.

"To the stables," he hissed to his men when the door closed behind them. "We need a new plan."

<hr />

"He doesna seem so bad," Jeannie whispered.

"What?" Shona replied, her eyes still fixed on the door. She couldn't understand her reaction to the man who'd escorted her betrothed to Creag Castle. Just looking at him had caused peculiar but not unpleasant sensations to ripple up her thighs and into very private places.

"Yer intended," her auntie explained. "He seems like a nice *mon*."

Shona swiveled her head back to the conversation. "He has one hand."

"Still, he's mature, not like the other two."

Shona had an urge to shriek. "Mature! He's old."

Jeannie bristled. "Weel, I'd wager he's not much older than me."

"Ye can marry him then," she retorted.

Her aunt stood, took her by the arm and led her away from the bed. "We're likely to wake Kendric with all this caterwauling. The Mackinloch is intended for ye, nay me."

Shona detected a sadness in the strange eyes. "Ye liked him."

Jeannie shrugged. "Aye, but that's neither here nor there. Ye're the one who's going to marry him and sooner or later ye'll have to reveal yer identity."

That much was true. Uncle Kendric would eventually awaken and the truth would come out. But the longing in Ewan Mackinloch's brown eyes taunted her. If there was a chance… "I liked the younger men better," she declared haughtily.

Jeannie scoffed. "Ye prefer a lad who canna speak to one with no hand?"

Shona pouted, aware her aunt knew exactly what she meant. "I was thinking of Ewan."

Jeannie snorted. "That's his name, is it? Cheeky bugger couldna take his eyes off ye."

"He doesna ken who I am. Probably thinks to pursue me."

"That's impossible and ye ken it."

Conflicting emotions swirled in Shona's heart. It *was* impossible, but she'd never been known for her obedience to authority. If she had to marry Fynn, she might as well explore her feelings for Ewan first. "My uncle has decreed I wed a Mackinloch. Ewan is of that clan."

"This deception is proving too dangerous. What ye propose might destroy a fragile peace."

"Aye. We need a new plan."

WE'VE BEEN TRICKED

THE UNUSUAL NUMBER of visitors to the castle obliged the ostlers to stable more than one horse to a stall. Two lads were lethargically grooming Liath and the other Mackinloch mounts. They left without hesitation when Ewan took their brushes and tossed them a coin.

He brushed Liath vigorously, hoping the restlessness fogging his brain might dissipate if he kept busy. "We need a new plan," he repeated when he was certain there was no one nearby to overhear.

Liath snorted.

Fynn's attention remained on checking Egil's hooves and he made no reply.

David nodded.

Guilt pressed on Ewan's temples. He'd not only landed himself in an impossible situation, he'd also made life difficult for two loyal men willing to accompany him to MacCarron lands.

Amid all the confused emotions swirling in his heart, he was certain of one thing. He wanted the golden-haired beauty.

Perhaps she'd consent to becoming his mistress if he had to marry Lady Lazy-Eye. The prospect left a sour taste in his mouth. He knew of many a married laird who kept a leman, but they weren't men who were generally respected, and such a rare beauty deserved a man who doted on her.

Exasperated, he raked a hand through his hair. Lust was filling his head with fanciful notions.

"Lovely lass," Fynn suddenly sighed, sounding more like a lovesick swain than a grizzled Highlander.

Ewan's gut tightened. "They both are."

"Aye," Fynn replied. "But yon Lady Shona is a fine woman."

"Won…won…won…wonky," David contributed, pointing to his own eye.

Fynn glared at him, jaw clenched. "And ye can barely talk, yet I warrant ye consider yersel' a fine *mon* nonetheless."

"Arguing is getting us nowhere," Ewan hissed. "And Lady Shona is promised to me, lazy eye notwithstanding."

Fynn scoffed. "But ye dinna fancy her."

"And ye do, I suppose," Ewan blurted out, immediately wishing he hadn't when the fire in his clansman's eyes betrayed the truth of the matter.

They glared at each other. Ewan opened his mouth but words refused to come. Gooseflesh marched across his nape when a loud snore from the neighboring stall interrupted the standoff.

Frowning, Fynn and David stood stock still. Ewan motioned them to stay where they were as he took a step into the narrow space that separated one row of stalls from the other.

He cocked his head to listen and decided the snoring rendered it unlikely they'd been overheard, but he had to make sure. He drew his dagger and crept stealthily towards the culprit.

He was tempted to laugh out loud when he peered around the splintered wooden frame. A shaggy-haired grey dog as big as a wee pony lay sprawled on the hay, sound asleep, tail twitching.

His amusement was short-lived when he realized a boy slept back to back with the deerhound. For a panicked moment he thought it was Andrew, but that was impossible. He was about to tiptoe back to his men when the boy rolled over and studied him with blue eyes wide. "Dinna worry," he yawned, sitting up. "Ruadh willna harm ye."

Nostalgia rose in his throat. The lad sounded like Andrew too.

"I'm nay worried," Ewan replied softly, not wanting to alarm the bairn. "What's yer name?"

"Robbie."

He hunkered down next to the beast. "Pleased to make yer acquaintance. Ewan's my name. I'm curious why the dog is called Ruadh? He's grey, not red."

"My auntie named him," Robbie replied, combing his fingers through the rough coat of the still-snoring dog, "because his mother was red, and the puppies were red when they were born, and she thought they'd always be red."

Ewan chuckled. "Seems reasonable."

"Aye," the lad replied, clearly at ease with a stranger.

"Yer auntie?" Ewan asked, wondering again about the complicated relationships among the MacCarron clan.

"Lady Jeannie. She's not really my auntie, but I call her that. Ye've mayhap met her. Mamie says I shouldna point out such things, but I think ye're new and might not ken who's who. She's the one with the lazy eye."

Evidently, sleep had dulled the boy's wits. "'Tis true we've only recently arrived, but isn't Lady Shona the lass with the peculiar eye?"

Robbie shook his head and laughed. "Nay, Cousin Shona is *bee-ute-i-ful*."

His laughter dragged the dog from his stupor. Ruadh raised his head and attempted a bark that emerged more like a muffled *woof* of greeting rather than a challenge. He yawned, revealing an awesome array of sharp teeth, then let his head fall back to the straw, apparently exhausted by the effort.

The fog slowly lifted from Ewan's befuddled mind. They'd been tricked. "Just to be clear," he said. "Shona's the fair-haired lass."

Robbie frowned. "Aye, but she's nay for the likes o' ye. She's promised to a cursed Mackinloch, if ye'll pardon my language."

†

SHONA OPENED THE door of Kendric's chamber only a crack until she was certain it was Moira who had knocked.

She inhaled the aroma of stewed rabbit as her maid carried in the tray of food.

"Quickly," Jeannie admonished, rising from her bedside chair. "I'm starved."

Moira obliged and bustled to the small table by the hearth. She removed the muslin cover with a flourish. "Cook sent a bowl o' broth wi' two drops o' laudanum for the laird as ye asked, and there's meat and gravy and parsnips for ye."

Shona wrinkled her nose. "Parsnips!"

Moira pouted. "Be grateful, my lady. Cook is trying his best to feed the visitors. The hall is full to bursting."

Shona couldn't help herself. "Are the Mackinlochs there?"

"Aye," Moira replied. "Since ye and the laird are absent, only the man with one hand sits on the dais, and he doesna look very comfortable."

"We should be in attendance," Jeannie retorted, chewing a mouthful of meat. "What will our guests think?"

Shona rolled her eyes. "We canna go down to the hall. The Mackinlochs will quickly discover our ruse when somebody blabs."

Jeannie sipped a spoonful of gravy. "I'll go mad if we have to stay in this oppressive chamber much longer."

Shona ignored her and turned to Moira. "The two escorts who are supping in the hall, does it appear they are still convinced I am Jeannie?" she asked.

"I suppose so, but only wee Robbie and that daft dog are sitting at the same table, and Mungo Morley is making no bones about stirring up old hatreds with rude comments."

Jeannie skewered a parsnip with her eating dagger. "Causing trouble. His favorite pastime. I'll take yer parsnips if ye dinna intend to eat them."

Shona pushed the trencher closer to her aunt. "At all costs, Mungo canna become our chief," she said.

A shiver stole over her nape. The one way to thwart the bully's ambition to become laird was to marry the one-handed Mackinloch.

"Aye," the others chimed in together, confirming her worst fear.

But it was a fate she resolved to put off as long as possible. The

Mackinlochs had promised to stay for a year and a day. Her brain might reason she was playing with fire, but her heart urged further investigation of her feelings for Ewan. "Ye must be our eyes and ears, Moira," she told the lass who knew more of her secrets than anyone. Born the same year, they'd grown up together. "Make friends with the escort. Find out what ye can."

Moira beamed a broad smile. "The bonnie lad?"

Shona had to nip that prospect in the bud. "Nay. He's too smart and will sense ye're prying. The other one."

A scowl furrowed Moira's brow. "The one who canna talk?"

"Aye. Him."

As the door slammed behind the pouting maid, Jeannie stirred the broth with the spoon. "Help me lift yer uncle. We must get sustenance into him."

Shona braced herself against the bed and struggled to raise Kendric's dead weight to a sitting position while Jeannie spooned broth into his mouth. Most of it dribbled down his chin, but then he slowly opened his eyes and swallowed.

"Good," Jeannie exclaimed. "Ye must eat, Brother."

She managed to get him to swallow a few more mouthfuls in between bouts of coughing before he turned bleary eyes to his sister and then to Shona. "What happened? Some sharp-toothed creature is gnawin' ma leg and ma hip."

His bulk became too much for Shona. She eased him down onto the bolster. "Yer horse threw ye during the hunt."

He blinked rapidly, as if trying to remember. "Spooked," he eventually mumbled. "Are ye wed yet?"

Aunt and niece exchanged a glance across the bed. "Tell him," Jeannie whispered.

"I'll nay wed until ye're better, Uncle," she said softly, but he'd already closed his eyes.

"Tell him," Jeannie urged again, then pursed her lips.

Shona nodded. "For the good o' the clan, I'll agree to yer wish that I marry yon Mackinloch—even though he has only one hand. But not quite yet."

"Aye," Kendric mumbled sleepily. "Asked for yer hand. Whats'er makes ye happy, lass."

EWAN NEVER THOUGHT he'd be glad of the company of a wee boy, a lazy dog and a stammering lad, but the atmosphere in the hall was decidedly unfriendly. He supposed the same might be true if a gang of MacCarrons were obliged to eat in the hall of Roigh Castle. However, he suspected Mungo wouldn't be hurling overly loud insults about the parentage of every Mackinloch since the dawn of time if the laird were present. It confirmed his initial impression of the man's cowardice. And the voice! He sounded like a petulant lass.

In the absence of The Camron and his close kin, Fynn sat in splendid isolation on the dais, adding to the murmurs of discontent, and providing fodder for Mungo's vitriol.

It was interesting that not everyone sided with the giant's insults. There were definitely two factions, but it was difficult to ascertain the identity of the second group's champion.

Amusing too were the varied reactions to Fynn's handicap. Some gawked at his ability to eat food without difficulty; others gasped each time he used his stump to dab his mouth with a napkin. Ewan had to admit the man had risen to the occasion and was playing his part well. There was whispered speculation about how he'd lost the hand and general agreement it had probably been in battle. No one seemed to work out that most battles fought by Mackinlochs in Fynn's lifetime were against MacCarrons.

Robbie had readily accepted the revelation that Ewan was part of the Mackinloch delegation. He'd politely apologized for his earlier remarks and now chatted on about all manner of things, though never with food in his mouth. "Mamie says it's bad manners."

Ewan cast about for some sign of the elusive Mamie, but no one seemed concerned about the lad.

Ruadh had evidently come to the conclusion that Ewan's booted foot was the most comfortable place to lay his enormous head, only lifting it slightly each time Robbie threw him a scrap or two.

The most curious thing, however, was that David had caught the eye of a pretty serving wench. The lass refilled his bowl of broth twice and ladled copious amounts of gravy on his meat. She even asked his name.

"David," he replied without a trace of a stammer.

"Moira," she breathed, smiling beguilingly and leaning forward in an obvious attempt to make sure the lad got a glimpse of her ample cleavage.

Not used to being ignored in favor of another man, Ewan felt an initial twinge of annoyance, but quickly realized he ought to be glad for the youth. Were it not for the speech problem, the fresh-faced David would make some woman a fine husband. Mayhap a lass who truly loved him wouldn't care about the stammer.

He leaned close to his kinsman's ear. "Ye should seek her out after the meal," he suggested, nodding to the servant as she made her way to the kitchens.

The young man blushed and shook his head.

"He's right," Robbie said. "Moira's a canny lass, according to Mamie."

Apparently, the lad had keen ears. "See," Ewan said.

"She's Lady Shona's maid," the bairn added.

A thought niggled in the back of Ewan's brain that it was odd for a lady's maid to be serving food in the hall, but he chose to ignore it. Perhaps she'd been assigned the duty because her mistress was tending a sick man. Besides, the more he knew about the real Lady Shona, the sooner he could plot his revenge for the subterfuge that had added an unexpected thrill to the pursuit. "Make friends with Moira," he muttered under his breath to David. "Find out all ye can about her mistress."

Robbie got up from the table at the same time and took David's hand. "I'll go with him, if I may be excused."

Ewan nodded, chuckling inwardly at the boy's good manners. As they walked away he called, "Dinna forget yer dog."

Robbie shook his head. "Ruadh is nay my dog."

Still pondering this conundrum, Ewan thought he should perhaps have warned David not to give away too much, but he quickly dismissed the worry. It was unlikely the shy lad would manage to say anything at all.

CAUGHT IN THE ACT

SHONA HAD TO force her aunt out of Kendric's chamber, and not only because she was reluctant to go. The woman was obviously about to keel over from exhaustion. "Ye're tired. Go to bed. I'll stay until the steward comes to keep vigil."

"Goodnight, then," Jeannie muttered in yawning agreement.

As she closed the door, Shona worried her aunt might not make it safely to her chamber, but she couldn't leave Kendric alone. He'd been restless since the meager meal an hour or so ago and she hoped the steward would remember to bring more of the opium potion in case it was needed during the night. The necessity of staying away from the hall and the other busy parts of the castle was becoming a nuisance. The ruse was turning her into a prisoner in her own home. How much simpler life would be if the appealing Ewan had turned out to be her intended.

Donald arrived a short time later, brandishing the vial of laudanum. "How fares The Camron?" he asked.

"He woke earlier and managed to sip a few spoonfuls of broth, but he's been restless since."

Donald peered at his master. "No sign of fever though?"

Shona swallowed back a yawn. "That's a blessing."

He pulled the chair closer to the bedside. "Go, my lady. I'll send for ye if needs be."

Donald had served as Creag's steward for nigh on twenty years and Shona knew she could depend on him. She pecked a kiss on her uncle's forehead. "Goodnight," she whispered.

After opening the door, she looked left and right before stepping out into the drafty hallway. Her chamber was a short distance away, but she'd walked only a few paces when she heard the familiar click of claws on stone. With his usual uncanny timing, Ruadh knew she was about to retire. His wet nose nuzzled her hand. "Clever dog," she said softly, turning to pat his head.

Gooseflesh swarmed over every inch of her body when she realized Ewan Mackinloch stood behind Ruadh, arms folded across his chest. An enigmatic half-smile hinted he knew something she didn't. His presence caused a peculiar but pleasant clenching in her nether regions, though an alarm sounded in her head.

"The hound seemed lost," Ewan suggested, "so I thought I'd best follow to see if I could find his master."

Fearing her trembling legs might not sustain her, she knelt beside Ruadh, hanging on to his neck like a shipwreck survivor clings to driftwood. "He's lazy and good for nothing; however, he's my hound and I love him."

Her heart raced when Ewan put his warm hand beneath her forearm. "Ye're obviously a tender-hearted lass, Lady *Jeannie,*" he replied. "Ye look tired. I assume the laird is sleeping? Will Ruadh object if I escort ye to yer chamber?"

When her mouth refused to form a coherent reply, she allowed him to help her stand, silently thankful when he held her steady.

Tongue lolling, Ruadh eyed him before trotting off down the hallway in the direction of her chamber.

"Yer dog seems not to mind," Ewan jested.

"He just wants to curl up in bed with me," she replied.

Gooseflesh turned to a liquid fire of embarrassment when she realized what she'd said. A betrothed woman didn't discuss sleeping arrangements with strange noblemen. But then, Ewan wasn't a nobleman, despite his bearing, and he didn't know she was the MacCarron bride. "I mean…"

"Dinna fash," he whispered closer to her ear than was proper. "I must seek my bed soon too."

She inhaled the aroma of leather and some elusive heady spice she couldn't name.

Ruadh gave them an expectant look when they reached her door.

Ewan laughed heartily. "He's a character."

The sound of his laughter did strange things to her insides. "Aye. Er…I trust ye were treated with hospitality in the hall…I mean ye and yer laird…Fynn, I meant…did ye get enough to eat? I apologize we…"

His kiss silenced her and stole away what little breath remained in her lungs. His lips brushed hers like a whispered caress.

She put a hand on his chest lest she sway into him. Disappointment surged when he stepped away and traced his finger down her nose. "Goodnight, Lady *Jeannie*. Ye're too tempting. I'll nay doot see ye on the morrow."

He reached down to turn the handle and push open the door. Ruadh trotted inside, jumped up onto her bed and sprawled across it. She teetered on the threshold, aware of nothing but the warm breath on her nape of the desirable man standing behind her.

"He keeps ye warm," he murmured.

She felt the heat of his hand on the small of her back and her wanton heart raced—he intended to follow her into the chamber.

A doleful whine from Ruadh dragged her back to her senses. She was promised to another.

She turned to face him, perturbed once again by the strange smile. "Goodnight, Ewan Mackinloch," she said firmly.

He bowed. "Sleep well, my lady," he replied. "With yer hound."

Safely inside the chamber, she leaned her forehead against the wood, listening to his footsteps receding down the hallway, trembling with the effort it took not to yank open the door and call him back.

As he made his way to Fynn's chamber, Ewan cursed his foolishness. Why hadn't he simply told Shona he knew who she was? His rock-hard tarse was of the mind he should have confessed his true identity.

His heart and loins insisted she was the woman for him. There was an alchemy between them he was certain she felt too.

Perhaps she was just a wanton woman who might surrender to lustful longings for any man she found attractive. What if he married her only to discover she was promiscuous? The prospect made him sick to his stomach. He'd be tempted to kill any man who even thought to touch her.

By rights, the chamber inside the castle was his, so he marched in on Fynn without knocking, then immediately wished he hadn't. His kinsman perched on the end of the bed, britches round his ankles, cock in his good hand. His embarrassment at being caught in the act flushed through the grey stubble on his face as he bent hurriedly to pull up his trews. "I was…"

Ewan looked up into the rafters, willing away the image of Fynn's impressive manhood. For all he was getting on in years…

His unannounced arrival had left the man in dire straits. "I dinna censure ye for it. I'll leave so ye can…er…continue."

"Nay. I apologize, my laird," Fynn muttered with uncharacteristic humility, sitting back down on the bed. "I dinna ken what's come o'er me since I set eyes on Lady Shona, I mean Lady Jeannie. I can think o' naught but bedding her."

Ewan had never considered lust could smite a tough Highlander like Fynn. "The eye doesna bother ye?" he asked.

His kinsman held up his stump. "Do ye really need to pose that question? She's a beautiful woman, though I get the feeling men make her nervous."

It was astonishing. Ewan had paid scant attention to Jeannie, repulsed by her one physical defect, yet Fynn the farmer had looked beyond that. "Mayhap she had a bad experience. Get David to ask his new lady friend."

Evidently uncomfortable, Fynn stood and paced. "But what good will it do to find out more? Jeannie's nay yer betrothed, but I canna woo her if ye dinna mean to honor the troth to Lady Shona."

At the mention of his true intended, Ewan's shaft swelled again.

"Dinna fash about that. I plan to pursue the blonde, but I've a mind to play with her first in revenge for her ruse."

Fynn stopped pacing and looked him in the eye. "Have a care. She's nay the only one playing tricks."

More preoccupied with thoughts of Shona curled up with Ruadh, he paid little heed to the warning. "Aye, weel, let's go find David in the stables and see what he's learned."

LYING ABED, SHONA touched her fingertips to her lips, daydreaming of Ewan's kiss. She remembered the texture of the woollen plaid draped across his solid form; the quality of the weave struck her as odd for a fleeting moment, but she quickly dismissed the notion.

She'd been kissed before, usually on the cheek, but had never experienced the thrill of longing sparked by the taste of Ewan's warm lips.

Only Mungo Morley had once dared plant a wet smooch on her mouth. The stink of whisky on his breath had been nauseating. Her darling father had warned him off, but Beathan MacCarron was dead and gone. She bit down on her knuckle, swamped by the pain of his loss.

Ruadh whimpered, then lifted his head when a soft tap at the door heralded Moira's return.

Shona blinked back the welling tears and sat up as her red-faced maid hurried to plump up the bolster behind her. "I sense excitement. What did ye find out?"

Moira stood beside the bed, hands clasped as if in prayer, eyes on Ruadh. "He's a bonnie lad, yon David."

Shona frowned. "I sent ye to spy on them. I trust ye didna give away our secret."

Moira's eyes widened. "Nay, my lady, I was discreet, but he seemed to enjoy talking wi' me. Hardly a stammer at all. And he has a lovely singing voice that could make a lass…"

She stopped abruptly and glanced briefly at Shona before returning her gaze to Ruadh, who cocked his head, seemingly as puzzled as his mistress by the revelation David could sing. "What I mean is, he sang a ballad about Jenny Shaw and let slip he was of that family."

"He's a Shaw? I thought he was a Mackinloch."

"The only time he stammered badly was when he struggled to explain why Ewan had told him to say he was a Mackinloch."

"Ewan?"

"Aye. He talked on and on about the *mon*. Scarcely a mention o' the fella who's yer intended. I got the feeling he hardly kens Fynn at all."

The temptation to giggle rose in Shona's throat as a suspicion planted itself in her mind. "There's more to this Ewan than we think."

Moira eyed her curiously. "And it sounds like ye wouldna have any objection if he turned out to be *the* Mackinloch."

Shona let the giggle fly free. "Ye ken me too weel, Moira Macgill."

Ruadh woofed softly in agreement.

SECRETS AND LIES

FYNN AND EWAN came upon David sitting on a bale of hay in the stables surrounded by a handful of young lassies arrayed at his feet. The sweetness of his pure voice caressed the air like a warm breeze, enthralling the women who listened to his song with rapt attention. Even sleepy-eyed horses had turned their heads to listen.

Ewan motioned Fynn to a halt just inside the door, but the moment David saw them he stopped singing and got off the bale. "I…I…I…"

The lasses, maidservants by the look of their apparel, scampered away.

"Sit," Ewan ordered, genuinely sorry he'd interrupted the lad's performance. "They were enjoying yer song."

David's face turned an even deeper shade of red when Fynn said, "Ye've a wonderful singing voice, laddie."

Ewan was as astonished as David at the remark, but didn't have the time or inclination to explain that the old warrior had fallen in lust, hence his newfound kindly nature. "Tell me of Moira," he said.

David smiled. "I like her."

He tamped down his impatience. "Aye, but what did ye find out?"

Puzzlement contorted the youth's face. "Ab…Ab…about what?"

"Lady Jeannie, o' course," Fynn hissed, reverting quickly to his usual hostile tone.

"Jee…Jee…Jeannie, or Sho…Sho…"

"Enough," Ewan shouted, causing several horses to toss their heads and stamp their feet, evidently annoyed they'd been deprived of

David's melodious singing. He pinched the bridge of his nose and lowered his voice. "Just tell us everything."

David sat down again on the bale. "Sho…Shona was wed afore."

Ewan clenched his fists, his fantasies about being the first to possess her going up in smoke. "What?"

"I mee…mee…mean the pretend Shona."

The knot in Ewan's gut loosened. "Ye're referring to Lady Jeannie? The real Lady Jeannie?"

"Aye."

Fynn gritted his teeth. "I kent a *mon* had hurt her. I'll kill him."

David swallowed hard, staring at the older man as if he'd lost his wits.

Ewan put a booted foot up on the bale and leaned forward. "Pay no mind. Go on with the tale."

"Ai…Ai…Ailig was his name. A cru…cru…cruel brute, they say. Ban…ban…"

"Banished?" Fynn asked.

David nodded. "But Moira thinks his bro…bro…bro…"

"Brother?" Ewan interrupted.

"Aye. Mungo aids him."

THE NEXT MORNING Shona hurried to Kendric's chamber, confident her aunt would have already ordered oatmeal from the kitchens to break their fast. Jeannie wasn't one to deprive herself of nourishment, though she never grew fat despite the copious amounts of rich food she consumed.

Shona had slept surprisingly well considering the terrible uncertainty about her uncle's injuries, the betrothal conundrum and Ewan's mind-boggling kiss. Had she not been awakened by the raspy lick of a wet tongue, she might still be abed.

Bathed, coiffed and dressed with Moira's help, she was bursting to share her suspicions about Ewan Mackinloch. Her maid hadn't been surprised by the revelations, and she was confident Jeannie would welcome the news.

Ruadh slumped down on the stone floor with a gruff growl when she refused him entry to the sickroom and shut the door behind her.

A quick glance at Kendric showed he was still asleep.

"He ate a little porridge," Jeannie explained, "and the laudanum Donald administered during the night is helping him rest easy."

Guilt poked at Shona. It might seem she wasn't showing much outward concern for the invalid, but her news had to be told. "I have something important to tell ye, Auntie," she began.

Jeannie took her by the elbow and drew her to the foot of the bed. "Wait! I have something to confess."

"Confess?"

"Ye canna marry Fynn."

The lines of worry on her aunt's face tempted Shona to reveal the truth, but it was too good an opportunity to tease. She feigned outrage. "Ye want him for yerself."

Jeannie blushed. "I do like the *mon*, but there's something not quite right about him."

Shona sniggered. "He has one hand."

"Nay, besides that."

Shona tapped a finger against her chin and arched a brow. "Ye mean he doesna act like a laird's son."

"Exactly."

"That's mayhap because he isna," she declared, hands on hips.

"How can that be?"

"I think Ewan is the Mackinloch who's come to be wed."

Jeannie scoffed. "Ha! Ye hope he is."

"Moira told me David is actually a Shaw. Ewan ordered him to claim he was a Mackinloch."

"But why pretend to…"

They stared at each other, then collapsed in a heap on the end of the bed, tipsy with laughter, sliding guiltily to the floor when Kendric groaned in his sleep.

Outside the door, Ruadh howled for the first time in living memory. It only added to their hysteria.

EWAN AND HIS kinsmen broke their fast in the hall. Fynn declined to sit alone on the dais. Between spoonfuls of oatmeal, the three kept a wary eye on the other men gathered there.

"Good…good…porr…porridge," David remarked, licking his lips.

Fynn agreed. "I hafta admit the food has been better than I expected. Nigh on as good as mine. Mayhap Clan MacCarron isna as impoverished as we thought."

Ewan suspected he was right and chuckled inwardly at the notion Fynn seemed to be a competent cook—if the breakfast trout was anything to go by. However, he was worried about what he'd learned concerning Mungo Morley. "When he leaves, I'll follow him, David, then ye come after me. My gut tells me he's up to no good."

"What about me?" Fynn asked.

"Keep up the pretense. Go pay yer respects to the laird. See how he fares."

Looking reluctant, Fynn scraped stunted fingernails through the stubble on his cheek.

Ewan punched his arm. "Look at it as an opportunity to see Lady Jeannie," he quipped.

Mungo and one of his gang rose from the table and headed for the kitchens, leaving no more time for argument. When they emerged a short time later, the giant was toting a small sack. He scowled at the Mackinlochs before exiting the hall.

Ewan waited a few moments before following the two men to a small outer door across the bailey from the stables. He paused and watched them glance around before ducking into a side entrance.

"They seemed anxious to stay out of sight," he explained to David when the youth joined him. "We'll follow at a safe distance after they exit the stables."

They waited until Morley and his man had ridden through the gates, then hurried to saddle Liath and Dubh. Five minutes later they headed out in pursuit.

Ewan said a silent prayer of thanks for fine weather that enabled them to see the dust cloud raised by the other horses. He resisted the temptation to increase their speed and kept to the cover of trees where possible. His caution paid off after about twenty minutes. The men they trailed reined to a halt, looked back the way they'd come, then left the path to enter a copse of hawthorns.

Ewan and David dismounted and pulled their horses into a clump of bushes on the opposite side of the trail. They tied up their mounts then scrambled back to the path and lay flat on the sloping bank.

"It's a meeting," Ewan rasped. "With his brother, I'll warrant. Bringing him food. Yer bonnie Moira had the right of it, I think."

David grinned. "Aye. Can…canny lass."

"I'd like to get closer, hear what they're discussing, but…"

"Noth…noth…nothing good," David whispered.

"That's for sure. It's clear they have designs on the chieftaincy and Mungo strikes me as the impatient sort."

His words gave him pause. He himself wasn't known as a patient man and David had every right to resent his impatience, yet he didn't react at all.

When voices drifted on the air they scrambled backwards into the bushes. Mungo and his man emerged and rode towards the castle.

It didn't take long for another rider to appear, Mungo's sack tied to his pommel. He looked both ways along the trail before urging his horse in the opposite direction.

When he was out of sight, Ewan and David retrieved their horses and led them out of hiding.

Grimacing, David traced a finger along his cheek as he mounted. "Does…doesna look like his bro…bro…"

"Nay," Ewan replied, straddling Liath. "Mungo's a red-haired mountain of a man; if that's Ailig, he's as tall, but dark and wiry. Half-brothers mayhap. That is a nasty scar. Looks like it almost took his eye."

"Up…up to no good," David observed as they regained the trail back to Creag Castle.

"Ye're right," Ewan agreed. He was preoccupied with what they'd witnessed, but the thought occurred that David must be getting more comfortable with him. The lad didn't seem to stammer as much. Or maybe he was just becoming accustomed to it.

COMPLICATIONS

Shona heard Fynn's voice out in the hallway before he knocked. From the groans of canine pleasure, it seemed likely the dour Scot was tickling Ruadh's belly. Jeannie hastily tidied away the empty porridge bowls. Laughing during the meal had resulted in hiccups, which made them giggle all the more.

When the tap came, they sobered and made an effort to tidy wayward wisps of hair and smooth rumpled skirts.

"Enter," Jeannie intoned. Her struggle to keep a serious look on her face while the eye twitched almost sent Shona into hysterics again.

She resolved not to look at her aunt when Fynn poked his head around the door, though it was tempting to blurt out they knew he wasn't the Mackinloch she was meant to wed.

"I came to see how fares the laird," he said solemnly.

Ruadh took advantage of the open door to slink in behind him. He trotted to the bed and licked Kendric's hand.

Shona gasped with delight when her uncle stroked the dog's head and whispered, "Good lad."

Jeannie clasped her hands to her mouth.

"They say animals can help folk recover," Fynn said.

"I think it's true, my lord," Jeannie replied, batting her eyelashes at the man like an infatuated maidservant. Trouble was, both eyes didn't blink at the same time. "Nothing does as much good as a beloved hound, and nourishing food."

Shona was about to point out that Ruadh was her dog, and her uncle had barely eaten a crumb since his accident, though her aunt had more than made up for it.

However, her companions ignored her as they withdrew to the window and became engrossed in conversation.

"Now food is summat I ken about," Fynn claimed. "I'm a fair to middling cook."

Jeannie flushed like the maiden she wasn't. "Oh, my," she gushed. "And I love to eat."

Shona rolled her eyes and groaned. "Ye'll make a perfect pair, then."

Fynn clenched his jaw and stared at her as if she'd told him he had two heads.

The truth struck her like a blow to the stomach.

He knew.

And what's more, this rough and ready fellow and her aunt *would* make a perfect couple. Jeannie deserved a good man, especially after Ailig's mistreatment. "Dinna fash, Fynn, we're wise to yer charade, as ye are to ours. I have to get out of this chamber and find yer master."

His look of confused shock lasted only a moment before he took hold of Jeannie's hand. "Forgive me, my lady, I'm nay the Laird Mackinloch's son, as ye've surmised, and I hope ye dinna mind me saying I'm glad ye're nay the woman Ewan is to wed."

His sentiments were the most convoluted confession of tender feelings Shona was ever likely to hear, but at least he'd confirmed Ewan was her betrothed. She headed for the door, anxious to be free to roam at will again.

"The Mackinloch has left the castle wi' David," Fynn informed her.

"Where have they gone?"

"I dinna ken. They followed yon Mungo."

"Why?"

"He's up to no good. Him and his brother."

The color drained from Jeannie's face. A tic seized her wonky eye. "Ailig? That's impossible. Shona's father banished him from MacCarron lands."

Shona glanced over to Kendric as a chill of dread crept up her spine. If her uncle died, Mungo and Ailig…

Reality stared her in the face. Her clan was suddenly in dire need of a strong man, a warrior like Ewan Mackinloch. She just hoped she hadn't alienated him.

Despite her trepidation at what the future might hold, her spirits lifted when Ruadh jumped onto Kendric's bed and lay beside him. As she exited, it occurred to her the dog looked like a lion rampant conveying the silent message that all would be well.

Though it went against his instincts, Ewan rode slowly, taking pains to arrive back at Creag well after Mungo. "I think it's time we reveal our true identities," he told David. "The Camron's accident has changed matters."

"True e…e…nough," his kinsman agreed.

"If Kendric succumbs to his injuries, there's nay doot in my mind the Morleys will make a bid for the lairdship. That wouldna bode well for Clan MacCarron, nor Clan Mackinloch."

"They m…mm…might not wait for him to die," David said.

Ewan discovered a new admiration for the youth. "Ye're thinking they might try to take over while he's lying injured."

"Or kill him."

Ewan thought back to the gatherings he'd witnessed in the hall, remembering the evil glint in Mungo's eyes; by all accounts his brother was also a brute.

Ice flooded his veins. There was danger to Kendric, right enough, but Shona would be the pawn in their deadly game. Even if they did away with Kendric, there'd be no guarantee the clan would accept Mungo as chief, unless he married the laird's blood kin.

Then there was the matter of the other faction, obviously opposed to Mungo, but on whose side?

"Ye're a smart lad, David," he said as he spurred Liath to a gallop.

Desirous of making a good impression on Ewan Mackinloch, Shona decided to comb her hair and wash her face before going in search of him.

Moira was on her knees in the chamber tidying a chest of rarely-worn gowns. She'd spread several garments on the carpeted floor. "I decided these could do wi' a good airing," her maid explained.

Shona stooped to pick up a dark green velvet frock and pressed it tightly against her ribs. "It's been so long since I wore this, it likely willna fit any longer."

"'Tis a shame. I like the material," Moira replied, leaning forward to feel the fabric. "Mayhap ye'll wear it again come winter."

Shona swished around the chamber clutching the dress to her breasts. "I might be much too fat by winter," she teased.

It didn't take Moira long to understand. "Ye hope to be round with a bairn?"

"Aye," Shona whispered, suddenly awed by the notion of bearing Ewan Mackinloch's sons. "I plan to reveal my true identity to the real bridegroom as soon as ye've helped me look my best."

Moira got off her knees just as someone rapped loudly on the door. "Hold yer horses," she complained.

Shona hesitated, fearing bad news about Kendric, but then reasoned she'd just left Jeannie; her aunt would have entered without knocking if the message was urgent. Pulling out the decorative hairpins that had once belonged to the mother she'd never met, she headed for the *boudoir*.

Humming, she arranged the hairpins so the little enamel butterflies were lined up in a neat row. Satisfied, she drew the comb through her long tresses, hoping her intended preferred fair-haired lasses. "Who was it?" she called, trying to decide if a single or double braid would be the best choice for the occasion.

Hearing no reply, she put down the comb and returned to the chamber. Indignant fear surged when she espied one of Morley's men with his arm around Moira's chest, a dagger pressed to the side of her neck. Mungo stood beside them, a strange smirk on his face.

"What's the meaning of this?" she demanded.

"There's to be a wedding," Mungo crowed. "Me and thee."

Shona scoffed. "Never."

"Then Moira here is a dead woman," he replied. "Such a shame."

Her instinct was to fight tooth and nail, but the terror contorting Moira's face gave her pause. She didn't have the strength to overpower two big Highlanders. "Ye're no different from yer cursed brother," she goaded in an effort to delay their departure.

To her dismay, he failed to rise to the bait. "We're going to walk out of the castle to the stables," he advised, taking hold of her arm. "One wrong move, and…" Grinning, he drew his finger across his throat.

She tried without success to pull her arm from his bruising grasp. "I understand ye only too well. Moira dies. Such a braw man to murder a helpless lassie."

She tasted bile when Mungo leaned close and breathed in her ear. "Aye, and if ye dinna please me, Wife, I might slit yer gullet as well. When I'm laird, I can do whate'er I please."

The other man chuckled, evidently as demented as his kinsman.

Dread surged as Mungo forced her to the door. If his dire plan succeeded, her life would be forfeit, and Mungo couldn't leave Ewan alive. The wrath of the Mackinloch clan would eventually fall on them all. MacCarrons would be massacred because she'd been too proud to accept a marriage alliance. Traitors had taken advantage of the confusion she'd caused.

Her abductor made sure the hallway was clear before signaling his man to bring out her maid. Shona winced when he twisted her arm behind her back and set them in motion. She thought to cry out if they passed her uncle's door, but he shoved her in the opposite direction. Fear for Moira paralyzed her voice.

Determined not to succumb to despair, she clung to a glimmer of hope. Mungo didn't know the identity of the true Mackinloch—and she still gripped a hairpin in her fist.

MISCHIEF AFOOT

E WAN LEFT DAVID to take care of the horses in the stable and hurried in the direction of the laird's chamber, perturbed not to find Mungo among the men gathered in the hall. He toyed with the notion of inquiring about the giant's whereabouts, but that might lead to an argument and he sensed there was no time to waste.

His fleeting presence caused a lull in the conversation, but no one followed him into the passageway.

Irritated to discover no guards keeping watch, he rapped on Kendric's door. The oversight would have to be remedied.

Adjusting his plaid and hoping he didn't look too much like a man who'd ridden hard for several miles, he smiled as the door opened, looking forward to some teasing and mayhap a wee flash of anger from Lady Shona's green eyes.

Jeannie quickly detected his disappointment. "My niece is nay here, my lord. But dinna look so crestfallen. She's gone to find ye."

Evidently, everyone's true identities had been revealed.

To his relief, Kendric lay propped up on pillows, Ruadh beside him on the bed. His eyes opened a crack when Ewan approached and cleared his throat. "Laird MacCarron," he said with a respectful bow, "I'm Ewan Mackinloch, yer niece's betrothed. I fear there's mischief afoot in the castle and I intend to root it out."

"Aye," Kendric rasped. "The buzzards are nay doot gathering. I kent ye'd be a strong *mon*. I thank ye."

Ruadh woofed as the laird drifted back into sleep.

Ewan spoke to Fynn. "How long since Lady Shona left?"

Jeannie frowned. "A fair while." She turned to look at Fynn who quickly put his arm around her waist. She leaned into him, clearly finding comfort in his support. It appeared things had progressed in a very short time.

"David and I were out riding," Ewan explained, suddenly feeling optimistic that Shona had decided to search for him. "Mayhap she didna think to look in the stables."

Fynn shook his head. "Nay, I told her ye'd followed Mungo."

The color drained from Jeannie's face. "It canna be true that Ailig has returned."

"Thin, dark-haired man, with a wicked scar down his cheek?" Ewan asked.

Jeannie closed her eyes. "Aye," she breathed. "A result of the fight with my older brother."

Fynn clenched his jaw. "I dinna ken what he did to ye," he declared, "but rest assured he'll nay live long."

"I'm of the opinion the Morleys intend to claim the lairdship," Ewan said. "I want a guard on this door at all times. Men ye trust, my lady."

Jeannie nodded, forcing a smile. "We perhaps shouldna worry too much. Knowing my niece, she likely went to her chamber to arrange her hair. She was afraid ye might be a wee bit aggravated and wanted to look her best."

Foreboding knotted Ewan's gut. "Lead the way there," he said.

SHONA HOPED THE desperation in her eyes would alert David as he came towards them in the stables. The blow from behind took him by surprise and dropped him like a felled tree. Moira wailed, but stopped when the dagger was pressed to her throat.

Shona had thought the man who'd struck David on the head was trustworthy. Watching him grasp the youth's ankles and drag him into an empty stall, she worried about the strength of Morley's support among the clan.

"Tie him up with the maid," Mungo hissed.

Relief threatened to buckle her knees. At least Moira would be safe.

"Simpler just to kill them both," his henchman said.

Shona clenched the hairpin tightly, wishing she held something more lethal than a hair adornment. Banking on Mungo's reputation as a superstitious dullard, she narrowed her eyes at him. "Best watch yer back if ye murder them. I'll haunt ye even after I'm dead."

He gnawed his lip. "Bind them," he repeated.

While his man bound and gagged Moira and David, Mungo hoisted Shona onto his saddle, then mounted behind her. "We'll meet at Conger's Rock," he declared, spurring his horse out of the stables and through the open gates.

He held her fast as they galloped away. The hairpin dug into her flesh. She relished the discomfort lest she scream out her terror.

THE DISARRAY IN Shona's chamber added to Ewan's fear she'd not gone willingly.

Jeannie confirmed his suspicions. "Moira would ne'er have left a chamber in such a mess. Look at all the lovely gowns strewn about."

Fynn emerged from the *boudoir*. "Empty. Just a hairbrush and a few pins."

Jeannie gasped. "I was right. She took down her hair."

Despite the uncertainty, Ewan felt a small surge of satisfaction. She had wanted to look her best—for him. The turmoil in his innards was a clear sign Shona meant more to him than just a young woman who might need his help. They'd shared only the briefest of kisses, but his heart knew.

He muttered an oath, filled with guilt that his stubborn determination to avoid the marriage had led to her abduction.

Be brave. I'll nay let ye down again.

He hoped Jeannie was strong enough to deal with the dire possibilities. "Mungo will try to force her into wedlock. Where will they take her?" he asked.

Fynn stroked her back as she sobbed into his chest. "I dinna ken, and if Ailig…"

Ewan raked a hand through his hair, frustrated he was in unfamiliar territory. "Think, my lady. A chapel. A priest who's nay too particular about the rules."

Jeannie looked up, tears rendering her strange eye even more peculiar. "The Morleys hail from Glen Nevis. Ailig may have been hiding there after his banishment. It's remote."

Ewan weighed his options. "A foray into a hostile village with only three of us doesna stand much chance of success, especially since we dinna ken the lay of the land."

"Aye," Fynn agreed. "And we canna leave the laird unguarded."

Ewan paced. "Seems to me there were a number of men in the hall who didna support Mungo."

Jeannie sat on the edge of Shona's bed. "No surprise. He isna well-liked."

"Do they champion another as the next laird?"

Jeannie dabbed her eyes with a kerchief Fynn produced from who knew where. "After my older brother died, Kendric took over, though reluctantly. As far as I ken, there's been only distant rumblings about Shona's husband succeeding to the chieftaincy when it became known she was to wed a Mackinloch."

"That's what Mungo's afraid of," Fynn said.

His words conjured an ugly suspicion. "This recent accident. How did it happen?"

"I dinna rightly ken. The men were out hunting deer to fill the larder for yer visit. My brother's horse threw him. Kendric might be able to tell us, though sometimes these things happen so fast."

"Was Mungo part of the hunt?"

The lazy eye was suddenly perfectly still as she stared at Ewan. "Nay, but he came soon after. Too soon mayhap. And there were likely other Morleys in the hunting party."

"Fynn, get back across the hall and bar the door of the laird's chamber. Stay there until Lady Jeannie returns with armed guards, then find me. I'll be looking for men willing to help me search for Shona."

Makings of a Good Laird

Mungo didn't blindfold Shona, so she was able to discern they were traveling south, following the River Lochy. She'd never heard of the rock he'd mentioned to his men and she lost her bearings once darkness fell. They seemed to veer away from the sound of the rushing river.

The night brought a welcome respite from his incessant chatter. She surmised he must be unsure of the terrain. She'd never known a man blather on so much about nothing. He would talk her to death if she was indeed forced into marriage.

They came at last to a clearing. Mungo dismounted and she was obliged to accept his help to stay upright when her numbed feet hit the ground. "I'm frozen to the bone, and hungry, ye big lout," she complained. "Not to mention I hafta see to my needs—in private."

"Dinna fash," he replied, herding her towards an enormous boulder. "Behind there. Go on. I'll leave ye be."

Determined not to lose her only *weapon*, she twisted the hairpin into her curls, then squeezed herself between the rock and prickly hawthorns. No possibility of escape there, and the scurrying of night creatures panicked her into completing the necessary task quickly.

She yanked her skirts off the thorns and emerged, glad to be out of the bushes.

"There's food and blankets in yon cave," Mungo said, pointing to some unseen destination up ahead in the dark.

She balked. "Cave? If ye think I'm spending a night..."

He put his hands on her bottom and pushed. "Cease caterwauling and climb."

It was difficult to see where she was going on the steep, overgrown trail. She lost her footing several times on the slippery pebbles and scraped her wrists and knees. Fingernails tore as she reached for gorse bushes lining the path.

When she feared her lungs might burst, Mungo took hold of her elbow and pushed her into an opening so small she'd have missed it. She crawled through, then shielded her eyes from the unexpected light of a campfire burning inside a large cavern. She wrinkled her nose at the pungent smell of charred meat.

Flames cast dozens of giant shadows on sheer rock walls. Her heart sank—she hadn't thought Mungo capable of mustering so many supporters. Making a run for it would likely result in being hunted down quickly, even if she made it out of the cave.

"Sit by the fire," Mungo ordered, dropping a blanket onto her shoulders. "And no more complaining, woman."

Shutting out the grunts of amused male agreement, she obeyed, glad of the warmth of the fire, but then one voice turned the blood in her veins to ice.

"They're born complainers, the MacCarrons."

Ailig.

She peered across the flames. There he sat, cross-legged, chewing on a bone, the scar on his face rendered all the more hideous by the orange glow of the fire.

"Ye're an outlaw on MacCarron lands," she hissed.

He spat into the fire. "These are Morley lands, lassie."

"Which are ruled by the MacCarron laird. My father banished ye."

He pointed the half-chewed limb at her. "The one who's dead, ye mean?"

She clutched the blanket more tightly, unnerved by the eerie sniggers of the other men and the evil glint in his eyes. "His ruling stands, and was confirmed by the present laird."

He tore off a chunk of meat with his teeth. "Ye're referring to the one who'll pass through death's door any day now," he said, his mouth full.

Hunger, fear and a feeling that there was more going on here than she understood combined to make her dizzy. Ailig Morley was well known for his vile temper. Arguing with him never led to a good outcome.

Someone thrust roasted meat into her bare hands. The greasy smell turned her stomach. Nevertheless, she forced herself to take a few bites.

As the hissing wood burned to embers, her eyes gradually became more accustomed to the half-light. Men drifted to shadowed recesses, but it seemed there were fewer than she'd at first thought. It was difficult to tell in the smoke-filled air. Six, maybe seven. Still too many to outrun, and the dainty weapon tucked into her hair would be useless against one man, let alone half a dozen.

She edged away as Mungo stretched out beside her, shaking her head when he patted the ground next to him.

"I'm nay likely to have my way with ye in a cave wi' my men looking on," he teased in his effeminate voice. "Lie down and I'll keep ye warm. Must look after my wee wife. Important day on the morrow."

She'd probably fall over if she tried to stay awake, so she obeyed, curling into a tight ball inside the blanket. She flinched when he laid a heavy arm across her hips.

"Just in case ye get a silly notion to run off," he quipped.

The dying embers hissed. Men snored. Horses occasionally nickered in the clearing below. An owl hooted. Shona listened intently for any sound of rescue, afraid to pay any mind to the small voice that said it was unlikely Ewan Mackinloch would pursue a bride who'd spurned him.

EWAN CLIMBED UP onto the wooden trestle table and surveyed the crowd of fifty or so men who'd answered his summons to the hall. Strictly speaking, the summons had been sent via Lady Jeannie, who stood beside the table, but he saw only curious looks on their faces, not scowls of hatred.

As he raised his hand to call for silence, an amusing truth struck him. He hadn't wanted anything to do with this clan, yet he felt a strange sense of being exactly where he was meant to be. These people didn't realize it yet, but they needed him.

"Ye dinna ken me," he began.

"He's the Mackinloch come to wed our Shona," Jeannie interrupted.

A few cursed—quietly mind you—others muttered, frowning in confusion. He supposed they wondered what had become of the man with one hand.

"Aye," he confirmed. "But yer lady has been abducted."

Now voices were raised in genuine anger. He shouted over them. "Mungo Morley has taken her. It's my belief he thinks to force her into marriage so he can be laird."

Shouts of *Never! Nay!* filled the air.

Then one voice was heard above the rest and the crowd parted as a tall clansman stepped forward. "I'm Walter Gilbertson. Kendric MacCarron is our laird. We dinna need a Mackinloch."

Silence ensued.

Ewan narrowed his eyes at the man who'd spoken. He recalled seeing him in the hall sitting among those opposed to Morley. "And it's my belief Mungo plans to kill Kendric."

"He canna be in two places at once," Walter countered.

Laughter.

"Nay. I suspect his brother will try to carry out the deed," Ewan replied.

Several muttered Ailig's name. All eyes turned to Jeannie. "Aye," she confirmed. "He has returned, and I trust what this young Mackinloch is telling ye. The Morleys plan to take advantage of Kendric's accident."

Ewan seized the moment. "I need two men to go with Lady Jeannie to guard the laird's chamber, and as many as possible to ride with me to find Shona."

Four or five stepped forward immediately and the laird's sister chose two.

Raised voices echoed off the rafters.

Has he taken her to Glen Nevis?

Where have they gone?

We wondered where the Morley gang had disappeared to.

Ewan raised his hand again, his heart troubled that, in truth, he had no idea where to look. "I need yer guidance. I was hoping to learn from ye where best to search for my bride."

The reaction wasn't what he expected. Folk stared, mouths agape, until Gilbertson broke the silence. "Are ye sure ye're a Mackinloch?"

Jeannie stood on tiptoe and beckoned him. Perplexed, he hunkered down to listen.

"Ye've the makings of a good laird," she whispered. "They're nay used to being asked for their opinions."

Perhaps the years of his father's influence had rubbed off, despite his best efforts to rebel. His pride was short-lived when a disturbance drew everyone's attention to the door. He leapt from the table to aid Moira. She struggled to support David. Both had rope bindings dangling from their wrists. The lad staggered like he'd been kicked by a horse, his ruddy complexion now ashen.

Pandemonium erupted as people swarmed around the injured pair.

"Mungo kidnapped my lady," Moira wailed, accepting a tankard of ale from another maidservant. "He and his men bound us but we finally got free. I feared David was dead."

David sat on a bench and accepted the ale from Moira. "Nay. But I've a fearsome headache."

Ewan eyed him, but there was no time to wonder about the stammer. Moira's declaration confirmed the plot and the crowd was clamoring for action. "Did they say where they were aiming to take her?" he asked.

"Conger's Rock," Moira replied. "But I've never heard of it."

"I ken where it is," Walter Gilbertson declared.

WILD DEER CHASE

SURROUNDED BY MEN and horses hurriedly preparing for departure, Ewan signaled when he spotted Fynn coming out of the keep with Ruadh lumbering along behind. They made their way towards him through the hubbub.

"If it's all the same to ye, I'll bide here," Fynn said as Ewan was about to mount Liath. "David canna travel in his condition and I'd best keep an eye on him."

Ewan hoisted himself into the saddle. He believed Fynn was genuinely concerned about the stammering lad, but suspected the decision had more to do with protecting Jeannie. "Aye," he replied. "No worries. These men want to fight their own clan's battle."

"True enough," Fynn agreed with a wink, "but they seem happy to have a Mackinloch lead them." He thrust a kerchief at Ewan. "Jeannie gave me this. It belongs to Shona. Teck yon hound. He'll know her scent."

Ewan held the delicate piece of material to his nose, inhaling the faint aroma of lavender. He should have known from the beginning that she was the one.

He tucked the kerchief inside the padded gambeson he'd donned under his plaid and bellowed his clan's war cry. *"Loch Roigh!"*

His shout was met with shocked silence, broken only by the neighing of excited horses and the wailing of over-wrought bairns.

Out of the settling dust clouds came Walter's voice. *"Aonaibh Ri Chéile."*

Ewan's apprehension fled. *Let Us Unite* was indeed a more appropriate call to action and boded well for the future.

"*Aonaibh Ri Chéile*," he shouted, fist thrust in the air.

He and Walter rode at the head of the MacCarrons as they embarked on their journey across the moorland.

"South," Walter pointed. "We follow the River Lochy."

Ruadh kept pace as the miles sped by, though he wandered off occasionally to investigate something or other. Ewan fretted over losing time when they slowed down to make sure the hound caught up. "Will we reach Conger's Rock before nightfall?" he asked Walter, not wanting to think about Shona being forced to spend a night with Mungo Morley. If the oaf harmed a hair on her head, he'd tear him limb from limb.

"So long as we keep this pace," Walter replied, "and naught untoward happens."

Ewan was relieved this stalwart warrior had decided to support his quest, but he was curious. "What changed yer mind, Walter?"

His companion eyed him, then smiled. "My son likes ye."

"Yer son?"

"Robbie."

So, the mystery of the boy's father was solved. But what of the mother who insisted on good manners? He was about to ask when Ruadh suddenly galloped off across the moorland at a speed Ewan wouldn't have thought him capable of. "He's caught the scent," someone shouted.

Ewan halted and turned his horse.

Walter reached for his reins. "But he's going in the wrong direction for Conger's Rock."

Ewan was conflicted as he watched Ruadh disappear into the distance, still running like a hound out of hell. "Mayhap they revised their plans and met up somewhere else."

Walter scratched his head. "Weel, if we hope to catch him we'd best start now."

They changed direction and pursued the dog, but the going was difficult. Potholes and bogs could cause even a sure-footed animal like

Liath to stumble and fall. They lost sight of Ruadh several times before picking up his trail again.

Ewan began to worry. They were traversing miles and miles of empty moorland, up hill and down dale, chasing after a dog known to enjoy a lazy life. In his experience, there was only one thing sure to get deerhounds moving the way Ruadh was, and that was…well…the scent of deer.

He cursed aloud when they finally caught sight of the hound bearing down on a big stag that was clearly laboring as it tried to make its escape uphill. Ewan suspected the dog had been hard on its heels for a good while.

"*Fyke*," Walter yelled as Ruadh launched his long body onto the deer's haunches. "Bluidy hound."

The stag faltered and crashed to the ground, but the terrain caused deer and dog to roll downhill. Once on its feet, the enraged animal would fight for its life and likely kill or maim Ruadh with its enormous rack.

"Typical deerhound," Ewan replied. "Naught for it now but to help him finish the deed."

They rode as close as they dared to the tangle of hoofs and paws before dismounting. A bowman ran forward and loosed an arrow that found its mark in the stag's throat. It grunted once then lay still. Steam rose from the carcass. Panting hard, Ruadh sat beside the dead deer—and yawned.

"He looks pleased with himself," Ewan admitted.

"As well he should be," Walter agreed. "That's a magnificent animal he's brought to ground. Ten point antlers. However, there's nay much hope now o' reaching Conger's Rock afore dark."

THE HAIRPIN

THE LONG RIDE and a night spent on cold rock took a toll on Shona. She felt stiff and sore as she supped oatmeal from a wooden bowl handed to her by one of Mungo's men. He'd provided no spoon so she did her best to lap the stuff up. It wasn't the best porridge she'd tasted, but its warmth brought comfort. It appeared Morley wasn't planning on starving her to death.

Despite her abductor's assurances, she'd lain awake all night worrying he might succumb to the male urges Jeannie had warned her about. She'd plotted a hundred ways to escape—all impossible. Now her head ached with the futility of it and her stomach was in knots. She put down the bowl and tried to stand, but the rock walls seem to close in on her. Mungo appeared and helped her up. "Eat hearty, lass," he advised with a grin. "'Tis yer wedding day."

The porridge rose in her throat. "I'm going to be sick," she warned.

He hurried her out of the cave. The cool morning air brought relief as she filled her lungs, but a grey mist hung over the rock, rendering it difficult to see anything beyond. She'd heard the rain during the night; droplets still clung to bushes and the rocks were slick.

Voices from below indicated some of the men had already gone down to ready the horses. "I wish to go home, Mungo Morley," she declared. "Yer plan will bring the wrath of the Mackinlochs down on all our heads."

"I'm nay worried about a greybeard wi' one hand," he replied.

She kept the truth to herself. The less he knew, the better. Despite her disdain for the idiot, she edged closer to him when Ailig appeared out of the mist. Mungo might be daft, but his brother was evil. She had few doubts this mad scheme was his idea and began to wonder about her uncle's accident. Last night's cruel words about her father's death played on her mind. Was it possible this perfidy went back further than anyone imagined?

"Take her and let's away," Ailig growled.

She squealed a useless protest when Mungo hoisted her over his shoulder like a sack of grain and slid down the path. He set her on her feet near the giant rock. "Go on. Two minutes before he comes."

Fuming and sick at heart, she edged behind the boulder and saw to her needs. The mist cleared as she emerged. Mungo led her to his horse. Just before he lifted her into the saddle, she felt for the hairpin. An involuntary sob broke forth when she realized it was gone.

As she had rightly surmised, six men rode with the Morley brothers. It confirmed her opinion the fools had no more sense than a lump of peat. Obviously, Ailig was ruled by a desire for vengeance and not by any reasonable plan to hold the lairdship of Clan MacCarron. However, if they succeeded in usurping the chieftaincy even briefly, people she loved might be killed in the confusion, and that didn't bear thinking about. Instead she fretted about the lost hairpin, one of the few precious things of her mother's she owned. It was preferable to dwelling on what might have been with Ewan Mackinloch.

As the morning wore on, Mungo's boasting about his suitability to be laird turned her blood cold. She closed her eyes and tried to imagine she was gathering heather on the sunny moorland. She might even have dozed, but was startled awake when the party reined to a halt outside a small ruined church.

Mungo lifted her down from the horse. "Here we are," he crowed.

She looked at the crumbling stone walls of the ancient church then back at him. "Are ye serious?"

But something else was wrong. It took her a moment to realize Ailig had disappeared. "Where's yer brother?"

"An errand," he replied. "None o' yer concern."

Ewan and his men dismounted in a clearing below Conger's Rock. They'd ridden hard since dawn, their dispositions not improved by having spent the night out in the open in the pouring rain.

They'd left five men to butcher the deer carcass, and Ruadh seemed content to leave them to it. Ewan had woken from a fitful doze in the middle of the night to discover the hound asleep against his back.

He hated the smell of wet dog, and damp wool bothered him even more, but it would be a good while before the early morning sun dried his plaid. He supposed he should be grateful the rain had stopped.

Walter went down on one knee in the grass. "They left their horses here."

The men fanned out to search for signs as to where their quarry had gone.

Ewan walked over to a large boulder, clenching his fists when he caught sight of a small piece of fabric caught on a thorn bush growing behind it. He reached in and pulled it free, fingering the tenuous link to Shona. "She was here," he shouted.

Walter nodded to a narrow path. "There's a cave up yonder. Probably where they spent the night."

Ewan felt better knowing Shona hadn't slept out in the rain, but… "Let's take a look."

They sprinted up the trail. The small opening Walter pointed out was easy to miss. They bent to crawl through and entered a large cavern. The smell of smoke and sweaty men lingered in the air, unsettling his empty belly.

Walter kicked over pieces of charred wood. "Campfire."

Ewan gritted his teeth as he surveyed the cave, anger boiling in his blood. He didn't want to think about what Shona might have endured here, far from home and alone.

A wet nose nuzzled his hand. Ruadh whimpered and pawed the ground. Ewan hunkered down to see what had caught the dog's attention. At first he saw nothing in the dim light, but then his fingers touched metal.

He traced a fingertip over the delicately enameled butterfly, then clutched the hairpin in his fist, filled with an urge to bellow out his rage against the man who'd removed the precious object from his bride's hair.

He took the kerchief from his gambeson and held it to the dog's nose. "This time we need ye to do it right, Ruadh. Where is she?"

He straightened and hurried after the hound when the animal bolted, praying they weren't off on another wild deer chase.

SIMPLETON

Some ruins that dotted the landscape were picturesque, but the overgrown exterior of the tumbledown church had nothing to recommend it. Shona suspected it had never been a substantial building and doubted anyone had worshipped there for decades. And why would they? It was in the middle of nowhere.

It had at one time likely been the cell of an abbey. But the monks were long gone. At least she thought so until Mungo ushered her inside and a robed figure shuffled out of the shadows.

"Meet Brother Horwich," her abductor announced.

Shona frowned, then quickly covered her nose to ward off the obnoxious stench emanating from the filthy wretch. Even Mungo stepped back. One look into the man's vacant eyes convinced her she was dealing with a simpleton. His hair imitated a monk's tonsure; his pate was bald, but the circular fringe of straggly grey wisps brushed his shoulders and hung like a frayed curtain over his gaunt face. His ragged robe may once have been brown, but time had faded it beyond description. A bony elbow and shoulder protruded where the fabric had rotted. A strong wind might whip it off his skeletal body entirely.

She looked around the dilapidated ruin, trying to ignore the scurrying and squeaking of what were probably rodents. There were signs of habitation—a meager blanket tossed in a corner, a stool tucked under a small, lopsided three-legged table, the fourth corner propped up on a stone from the crumbled wall. "Do ye live here, Brother Horwich?" she asked.

He tilted his head to one side, as if not understanding.

Mungo chuckled. "He doesna get to speak to women much."

Shona's heart filled with pity for the outcast, probably shunned by his village and forced to live out his days in isolation. She held her breath. "Are ye a hermit?"

Horwich beamed a toothless grin and tapped his chest. "Aye. Prior o' the cell. The last survivor."

She gritted her teeth and turned to Mungo. "This poor man is no priest. Surely ye dinna think…"

"Hush," he interrupted, forcing her arm behind her back. "Ye'll hurt his feelings." He pointed to one of his men near the door who held up a brace of plump hares. "Proceed, Brother, then ye'll get yer reward."

Horwich's eyes widened as he swiped a filthy hand across blistered lips. Shona wondered how long he'd been without a decent meal—or food of any kind.

She struggled to resist when another of Morley's men emerged from the shadows and tied a musty-smelling gag over her mouth.

Eyes raised to heaven, the simpleton lifted his hands in prayer and began chanting. She recognized a few Latin phrases and some Gaelic, but the rest was gibberish. After interminable minutes during which she thought she might go mad with anger and frustration, he paused and looked expectantly at Mungo.

"Aye," her abductor replied solemnly.

More babbling ensued then he paused again and looked at her.

Fearing her tortured arm might break and sweating with the effort of the fruitless struggle against Mungo's hold, she shook her head vehemently and voiced her refusal as best she could with the loathsome wet gag stealing away her breath.

Horwich smiled benignly and made an exaggerated Sign of the Cross over them—with the wrong hand. "Man and wife," he murmured with a heavy sigh. Humming, he wandered off into the shadows after deftly catching the hares tossed from the doorway.

Mungo laughed and scooped her up. "Come along, wee wifey. Off to bed."

FEARING THE HOUND had again led them astray, Ewan and his men finally caught up to Ruadh, surprised to see him napping outside a ruined building that may at one time have been a church. He got up and barked, wagging his tail as they approached.

"Mayhap he's cornered a deer in yon ruin," Walter quipped as they reined in their mounts. "A cell of Dunscar Abbey. Abandoned over a hundred years ago."

Ewan smiled wryly but as they dismounted he worried there was no sign of horses. "If they were here, I fear they've eluded us once more."

Twenty men surrounded the church as Ewan and Walter drew their daggers and shoved open what remained of the door. Hinges creaked, but there was no time to become accustomed to the darkness inside, nor to ponder the source of the aroma of roasting meat. A hooded figure scurried by, apparently fleeing the ruin.

Walter flung himself at the fugitive and they rolled together on the ground, but he got to his feet quickly and backed away. "*Fyke*, he reeks."

They covered their noses, staring in disbelief at a skeleton of a man scrabbling in the dirt like a starving dog for scraps of meat. He shoved grit-covered morsels into his mouth one after the other, glancing up fearfully now and again. Even Ruadh looked on in apparent disgust.

Ewan sheathed his dagger and swallowed the bile rising in his throat. "I dinna want to frighten him, but we need to know if he's seen Shona."

Wiping grease from his gambeson, Walter put his weapon away and hunkered down. "We're nay going to steal yer food," he assured the beggar.

A foreboding crept into Ewan's heart when he realized the man's rotting garb was an ancient monk's robe. "Look at him. He isna capable o' trapping his own food. Somebody brought it for him, but ye claim 'tis more than a hundred years since monks dwelt here."

"Nay," the beggar spluttered, sending a spray of food flying, "I'm Brother Horwich, the last prior."

Ewan and Walter exchanged a worried glance.

Others gathered round to stare, noses wrinkled in disgust as the outcast picked spatters off his filthy robe and popped them into his mouth.

"What kind soul brought ye the meat?" Walter cajoled.

"Canna tell."

Ewan was tempted to seize hold of the man, but the robe might disintegrate entirely and he truly didn't want to touch the fellow. "Canna or willna, Brother?"

"Swore I wouldna."

"Mungo evidently expected us to pursue them," Walter surmised.

Fearing the worst, Ewan narrowed his eyes. "So ye swore not to tell about the ceremony?"

"Aye," Horwich replied. "Man and wife. In nomine patri…son…holy…" His thin voice trailed off when he noticed Ruadh. "I like dogs," he murmured, scrambling on all fours towards the hound. Wisely, Ruadh backed away and ran off.

"I'll make sure Mungo dies a slow painful death for subjecting Shona to such a travesty," Ewan promised as he watched the beggar get to his feet and disappear into the ruin.

Walter shook his head. "I canna believe he thinks to claim what transpired here as a valid marriage."

"Who's to naysay him? Shona is the only one who knows the truth and I'll warrant he'll keep her silent until he's laird, and then…"

Feeling the need to pace, he tried to fathom what Morley might do next. The answer hit him squarely in the gut. "He's taken her back to Creag. We've fallen into the trap and left folk at the castle unaware of what's happening. We must ride back with all possible haste."

MUNGO DIDN'T REMOVE the gag until Shona stopped struggling, too exhausted to carry on the fight. The more she fought, the harder it became to stomach his foul odor. It occurred to her they were heading back in the direction of Creag Castle. The prospect brought renewed determination. Surely someone there would come to her aid.

She kept her thoughts to herself, resolved not to give her abductor the satisfaction of hearing her complain. He seemed to derive pleasure from her agitated movements on his lap.

She wondered if Ewan Mackinloch was still at Creag, or if he'd returned to Inverness, disgusted with the MacCarrons. Who could blame him? She felt his loss keenly, not only for herself but for her clan. Kendric wasn't a young man and his injuries were severe.

Her heart lurched. That's exactly what Mungo and his vile brother had counted on. In her state of frenzied indignation she'd forgotten Ailig and his *errand*.

She worried for Kendric and Jeannie and prayed fervently nothing untoward had happened to Ewan. She was becoming more and more convinced the Morleys had played a role in her uncle's accident, and probably her father's sudden demise. Ailig had never forgiven the man who'd sentenced him to banishment and inflicted the hideous scar, though he'd left her father no choice but to defend Jeannie against his brutality.

Laird Beathan MacCarron was a staunch supporter of the laws of the land and clan traditions. He defended a man's right to rule his wife, but was fond of boasting he'd never raised a hand against Shona's mother. He made no secret of his contempt for men who used their fists to control a woman.

His death devastated his family and his clan, but the possibility it hadn't been the mysterious accident everyone assumed made her blood boil.

She was anxious to reach Creag Castle, but her spirits plummeted when Mungo called a halt five miles from home near the abandoned fortress at Inverlochy.

Ailig rode out to meet them. "Welcome to yer lodgings, Sister," he crowed.

A pulse thudded in her ears. A burning desire to accuse him of her father's murder seethed within her, but she recalled one of Beathan MacCarron's favorite mottos.

Keep yer powder dry, lassie.

She lifted her chin and looked down her nose at him. "I am not yer sister, and I will lodge nowhere this night but in Creag Castle."

Narrowing his eyes, he leaned forward in the saddle to run a fingertip down her cheek. "Feisty bitch ye've wed," he said to his brother.

She flinched, disturbed by the naked lust in his gaze, but Mungo saved her by pulling his horse back. "And ne'er forget she's mine, Ailig," he warned.

The low menace in his normally strident voice sent a shiver through her, but she tucked away the knowledge of their jealous rivalry.

"Did ye get it?" Mungo asked.

Ailig spat, holding something aloft. "Aye. Yon steward is careless."

She stared hard at the small object he held, hoping against hope it wasn't the vial of laudanum Cummings had left for her uncle.

"Alas," Mungo said as he dismounted and lifted her down, "our bed in Creag will hafta wait one more night, my love. Ailig and I have business to attend to there, then I'll come for ye on the morrow."

Deadly certain they meant to murder Kendric with his own medicine, she surveyed the crumbling walls in the dying light. "Ye canna leave me here. This place has been deserted for nigh on ten years."

Surprisingly, Mungo seemed genuinely saddened by her plight. "Brian and Niall will bide here as weel. They've got blankets to warm ye, and there's bread and cheese left in…"

"Come on," Ailig urged, turning his horse. "Her comfort's of no consequence."

"She's my wife," Mungo retorted.

"For pity's sake, idiot. Keep yer eye on the prize."

Her *husband* shrugged, pecked a kiss on her forehead and remounted.

"No fires," Ailig shouted to the men left behind as the brothers rode away.

Scowling, Brian and Niall dismounted and led their horses towards the walls. Clearly they didn't relish a night sheltering in the eerie ruin either.

She considered making a run for it; in the daylight she'd find a ford across the nearby Lochy, and make her way home, but in the dark…

As if they suddenly realized they'd left her standing in the field, both men turned. "Get a move on," Brian shouted.

With no alternative, she traipsed after them into the keep. She'd never been inside Inverlochy when it was inhabited. The darkness rendered it impossible to see where the black passageways that led from the great hall went to. "Surely we can light a fire in here?" she grumbled, feeling her way across the cold stone mantel of the hearth.

"Ailig said not," Niall replied nervously.

It appeared she wasn't the only one afraid of the man.

But she couldn't let fear rule her. She was the daughter of a Highland chief and the two Morley henchmen left to guard her had best not forget it.

Resigned to another uncomfortable night, she yanked the blankets out of their arms and made a bed for herself in a corner where the hearth jutted out from the wall. "Keep yer distance," she snarled as the pair looked around for somewhere to sleep.

She curled up in the blankets, grimly satisfied she'd managed to intimidate them, but then if they were stupid enough to follow Mungo's mad scheme…

Nevertheless, she couldn't resist a parting shot. Why should she be the only one awake all night? "They say the Earl of Montrose still haunts this place, ye ken?" she said ominously.

STRICKEN WARRIOR

NIGHTFALL FORCED EWAN and his men to slow their pace, but he remained determined to push on to Creag Castle. Walter shared his foreboding that the Morleys intended to do away with Kendric. They hoped Fynn and David would realize the danger and protect the bedridden laird until they arrived.

Ewan chose to center his thoughts on the threat to Kendric, preferring not to think about what Shona was enduring. The ramifications of what might have happened to her during the time spent with Mungo loomed like a bottomless abyss. Even if the Morleys were dealt with, Duncan Mackinloch would never sanction his son's marriage to a woman who'd been violated, no matter how much Ewan might insist he still wanted her.

She'd be shunned by the MacCarron clan as well, through no fault of her own. If he'd not schemed to avoid the marriage, none of this would have happened. It came as a startling realization that he would willingly spend his life making up for the harm he'd inadvertently caused.

They came at last to the River Lochy. "No safe place to cross here," Walter shouted over the noise of the rushing water. "We'll go further along to the ford near the old castle."

"Inverlochy, I suppose?" Ewan asked, recalling what he knew of the region's bloody history. "Not too far out of our way, I hope."

Walter pointed. "Ye can see the towers in the distance. Falling into ruin now it's been abandoned in favor of the timber fort Cromwell built further south."

Ewan squinted into the gloom, just able to make out four squat round towers and a curtain wall, black in the weak light of the new moon. "It must be twenty years since Montrose routed Campbell's Roundheads there."

Walter scraped his beard. "I was a lad. About Robbie's age, I reckon, so that sounds about right. They say the ill-fated Earl of Montrose still haunts the place."

"Ye'd think he'd sooner haunt the MacLeod who betrayed him," Ewan quipped, though he'd prefer to be far away from the eerie ruin. It was a painful truth that his country was full of ancient castles stained with the blood of thousands of Scots.

"Tragic waste," Walter said, as if sensing his thoughts.

"Aye. Look at Montrose himself. Hanged, reviled, head stuck on a pike at the Edinburgh Tolbooth for years, then suddenly he's a hero. They dig up his bones, reassemble his body and bury him in the High Kirk."

They rode in silence for a few minutes, each preoccupied with his thoughts. Walter called a halt and looked back the way they'd come. "Havna seen the hound for a bit. Hope he tracks us to this ford."

Ewan too had become concerned. They'd traveled far and fast and Ruadh had fallen behind, or lost their scent. "Nay doot he can swim. We canna wait."

As they edged their horses to the water, the deerhound came bounding out of the darkness. Ewan's relief turned to irritation when the dog ignored them and kept on galloping towards the castle. "What the *fyke's* he after now?"

SHONA PEERED NERVOUSLY into the darkness of the hall, but couldn't see what was making the strange noise. It certainly wasn't a mouse, or even a rat. The loudly snoring guards clearly hadn't heard whatever it was. Perhaps Montrose did indeed haunt the place. But it sounded like a panting animal. Something with claws that clicked on stone. What kind of…

She backed as far into the ingle as she could when two eyes flashed briefly in a shaft of moonlight from a hole in the roof. Fear turned her blood to ice as the animal came closer.

She mouthed *Wolf,* but the alarm died in her dry throat. She almost laughed out loud with relief when, a moment later, Ruadh planted his paws on her shoulders and licked her face. "Hush," she cautioned when he whimpered his delight. His unexpected presence revived her flagging spirits.

She got to her feet, pondering how the hound had come to be here. One thing she knew for sure—he was too lazy to venture so far from Creag on his own. Men must be searching for her nearby. If she could get outside…

She guessed she was halfway to the door of the keep when rusted hinges squealed. Brian and Niall cursed, evidently awakened by the noise. Feet shuffled, daggers slid from sheaths. She had to trust that the men entering the ruin were not cohorts of the Morleys. "In here," she shouted.

"Shona?"

Euphoria soared. Ewan Mackinloch had led the search.

But her joy was short-lived when one of Mungo's men seized her arm and pulled her back from the door. "Two guards," she managed to yell before a hand was clamped over her mouth.

"Quiet, bitch," Niall hissed, but then howled when Ruadh sank his teeth into his leg. "Get this hound off me," he bellowed at Brian.

Shona struggled, trying to elbow Niall in the ribs and free herself from his grip, but he held on. She had no idea where Brian was, but evidently he wasn't helping Niall remove the growling dog attached to his leg.

The dark hall filled with echoes of running feet, loud shouts, swords crossed, Ruadh barking, shrieks of pain—then an ominous yelp. Niall loosed his hold and she collapsed to the stone floor, heart pounding. On hands and knees she felt frantically for Ruadh. Her worst fear was realized when her fingers touched wiry fur and came away sticky with blood.

Ewan had been in many a skirmish, often against MacCarrons and far greater odds than he faced now, but the stakes had never seemed higher.

The darkness, the barking, the shouting, his fear for Shona: all conspired to render him half-mad with rage and helplessness. He'd never forgive himself if he unintentionally harmed her with his dagger.

He held his breath and narrowed his eyes when the faint light of a sputtering torch finally flickered over the scene.

Two men lay on the floor—one dead by the look of it, Walter's blade plunged to the hilt in his chest, the other moaning, his trews torn to shreds, blood oozing from vicious dog bites on his mangled leg.

Grim-faced MacCarron men sheathed their weapons at Walter's command and more torches were lit.

Then he heard a noise that tore at his heart. Shona wept somewhere nearby. Frantic to make sure she wasn't injured, he grabbed a torch from one of the men and raised it high, handing it back abruptly when he espied her near the hearth next to Ruadh. He scooped her up and crushed her in his embrace. "Thank God," he murmured over and over as she put her arms around his neck and sobbed into his shoulder.

Walter knelt beside the hound. "The dog's wounded," he said grimly. "Badly."

Shona raised her head. "Is he...dead?"

"Nay," Walter replied, "but there's a deep gash across his shoulder, and a lot of blood."

Ewan braced himself for an argument. "I understand ye love him and he needs tending, Shona, but we canna delay. Mungo and Ailig..."

"I ken," she replied, rubbing her eyes. "They've gone to kill my uncle. They have his laudanum."

"I can leave men here if ye want to stay with Ruadh."

To his surprise, she grimaced and said, "Put me down."

He obeyed, expecting a tongue-lashing, but instead she stood on tiptoe and cupped his face in her hands. "Ewan Mackinloch, ye are a true hero for coming after me when I treated ye so badly."

Staring into tear-filled eyes, Ewan knew he'd lost his heart to this strong woman. "'Twas my fault, forcing Fynn into pretending to be yer intended. Forgive me."

"He's at risk too," she replied. "Mungo the Fool still thinks Fynn is my betrothed."

The need to question Shona about Morley burned in Ewan's heart, but he lacked the courage, fearing what she might have to confess.

Walter saved him. Gilbertson got to his feet and headed for the door, Ruadh cradled like a bairn in his beefy arms, the dead man's torn shirt tied around the wound. "We can stand about all night while the two o' ye blather on, or we can ride for Creag and save our laird. I'll carry this brave warrior."

Ewan smiled at Shona, then bent to brush a kiss on her lips. "Shall we, my lady?" he whispered.

"Aye, my lord," she breathed in response as he lifted her again and carried her out to his faithful Liath, vowing silently to make the Morleys pay dearly for every bruise and scratch she'd suffered.

PLAYING THE BUFFOON

SHONA'S RIDE TO Creag was nothing like riding with Mungo. Wrapped in the cocoon of Ewan's strong embrace, she found solace in his presence, strength in his firm thighs. She was covered in cuts and bruises, her clothing ruined. People she loved were in serious jeopardy. Ruadh was clinging to life in Walter Gilbertson's arms. Doubts about her father's untimely death churned in her belly. It was difficult to understand how she could place such implicit trust in a man she barely knew. He belonged to an enemy clan; she should resent him but instead was content to lean against his solid body and rely on his strength. His heat chased away the chill of fear.

It was hard to believe she was the same lass who never relied on any man, a woman who thought men were good for nothing but warfare, hunting and bravado.

Ewan barely spoke as they rode, unlike Mungo, but she savored every reassuring word he uttered, her inner turmoil soothed by his husky voice.

She sensed turmoil within him, too, but he seemed able to channel his nervous energy to the horse. The magnificent steed responded to commands Shona couldn't even discern. "What's his name?" she asked.

"Liath," Ewan replied.

She resisted the urge to retort that it was typical a man would name his horse after its coloring. "He *is* very grey," she conceded.

"Nay," Ewan replied. "He's *The* Grey."

She had to agree when the surefooted gelding carried them

through the darkness to within sight of Creag's lights, but she bristled that Ewan called a halt short of the open gates and stood in the stirrups. "Why have we stopped? We must enter," she insisted.

"If Mungo has taken over command, it might be a trap," Walter explained, shifting Ruadh on his lap.

Shona leaned over to stroke the dog's head, encouraged when he opened his eyes and whimpered. "Brave soul," she said.

"He's made it this far," Walter replied. "Perhaps the worst is over."

Regretting her outburst, she turned to look at Ewan as he sat back in the saddle. It was important to remember he was the son of a Mackinloch laird. That clan hadn't risen to dominance through impetuous acts. "What's yer plan?" she asked.

He smiled wryly. "I mean to wed Lady Shona MacCarron at the earliest opportunity and make her my wife in every way."

She appreciated his attempt to ease her apprehension, but his words nevertheless caused wanton feelings to spiral into her womb. She rose to the bait. "Would that be the Lady Shona with the lazy eye?" she teased.

"Saucy wench," he growled, intensifying her excitement.

It was clear life with Ewan Mackinloch would never be dull. He'd even managed to turn the dire situation they faced into a game. But he sobered quickly, his stern features letting her know he'd made a decision. "I dinna see any sign there's aught amiss in the bailey."

While she'd been posturing like a peahen, he'd been assessing the lay of the land.

"First off, we'll make our way slowly to the stables."

Walter nodded. "Any lads we find there can tend to Ruadh while we deal with Mungo."

Shona didn't like the idea of leaving her dog but acknowledged it had to be done. "Aye," she agreed. "They'll be able to tell us where the Morleys might be before we enter the keep."

Ewan shook his head. "Ye'll remain in the stables with Ruadh, my lady. I'll not…"

"This is my home," she retorted, swiveling to face him, "it's *my* family Mungo threatens. It was *me* Mungo dragged to hell and back, *me* he forced into a sham marriage. I refuse to sit fretting in the stables."

EWAN WAS PAINFULLY sure Shona had no notion the effect her indignant squirming was having on his manhood. Despite the uncertainty of what they might face in Creag Castle, he'd been unsuccessful in bringing his rampant cock under control during the short ride from Inverlochy.

He'd wanted a feisty lass, and that's exactly what he had in Shona MacCarron. Arguing with her would be a waste of precious time. The Morleys might at this very moment be threatening Kendric's life. "Very weel," he replied, easing her forward on his lap in a futile effort to end the pleasurable torture.

Apparently mollified, she sank back against him as they rode slowly through the gates, but he felt the rigid tension in her body. It increased his resolve to thwart Ailig Morley's scheme.

He dismounted in the bailey and lifted her down from Liath. "Ye're light as a feather," he rasped, holding her tempting body against his, then wishing he hadn't when desire once more heated his groin.

She rested her forehead on his chest. "Ewan," she whispered, "I thank ye for what ye're doing, in spite of all that's happened."

He clenched his jaw. The details of her ordeal would have to be dealt with, but not now. "Dinna fash," he replied. "All shall be weel."

The MacCarron men formed a protective circle around their lady, but no one challenged them in the bailey. Walter handed Ruadh down to Ewan. Shona held the hound's jaw as they made their way into the stables.

Suddenly, a boy bolted out and threw himself at Walter. "Da," he cried.

Walter scooped him into his arms. "Robbie! What are ye doing here this late at night? Why aren't ye home with yer Mamie?"

"She didna return yet from Auntie Margaret's and I was afraid for ye when I saw Mungo Morley come back."

Two yawning stable lads with lanterns emerged from the shadows, rubbing their eyes.

Ewan put Ruadh down on a pile of straw, relieved to see the bleeding had slowed when he eased away the makeshift dressing.

Shona knelt beside her hound. "Fetch something to cleanse the cut," she told the boys. "And find the ostler. He'll ken what to do."

"Aye, my lady," one replied as they hurried away to do her bidding, "though he might be three sheets to the wind."

She grimaced. "He'll sober quickly if I have aught to say about it."

Robbie wriggled out of his father's embrace and knelt by Shona, hands clasped in his lap as if afraid to touch the stricken animal. "Ruadh," he said hoarsely, "ye canna die."

Walter put a hand on his son's shoulder. "He's strong. He willna die, but we need to know where Mungo is."

Robbie swiped a sleeve across his eyes. "He came back with some of his cronies and went straight to the hall, bragging about marrying Lady Shona, but folk mocked him when he couldna explain where she was."

"He's a fool," Shona muttered.

"That's what they all said," Robbie replied. "There was a big argument when folk mentioned Moira had accused him of kidnapping her mistress—he swore up and down Lady Shona had gone with him willingly. He got angry and drank all the more."

"Did ye see Ailig Morley?" Ewan asked.

"Robbie might not remember Ailig," Walter cautioned. "He was just a wee bairn when the wretch was banished."

"Aye," his son confirmed, "but I've heard tell often enough of a *mon* with a terrible scar, and I didna see anybody like that."

"And ye're sure Mungo never went to my uncle's chamber?" Shona asked.

"Not that I saw."

"Where is he now?"

"He passed out in the hall. Right after he came back from the kitchens."

Ice trickled through Shona's veins as she scrambled to stand. Her trembling legs caught in tangled skirts and she would have fallen had Ewan not caught her. "The laudanum," she gasped, dread robbing her of breath.

Ewan held her tightly. "But he didna go to the laird's chamber."

She tried to pull away, desperate to make him recognize the danger. "He's clever in his idiocy. Ailig hid in the kitchens while his brother was playing the buffoon in the hall."

She saw the light of understanding dawn in his brown eyes. "They plan to lace Kendric's food with too much of the drug and have it delivered to his chamber."

She gripped his hand. "By an unsuspecting servant."

Ewan turned to Walter. "Stay here. Shona and I will take some of the men with us. Keep a sharp eye out for Ailig."

They hurried out and Ewan quickly organized the MacCarrons in the bailey. Once inside, they paused briefly in the hall, alarmed to find it empty, but left a handful of kinsmen there in case either Morley returned.

The men strode ahead as they entered the passageway to the laird's chamber. Shona ran to keep up, her heart in knots, but was relieved to see two guards still defending the door.

"Nobody has tried to force their way in?" Ewan asked.

"Nay," one yawned in reply. "A lass went in a short while ago with the laird's broth, but…"

Ewan put his shoulder to the door and burst into the chamber.

PLOT THWARTED

F YNN DREW HIS dagger and moved quickly to the open door.
David pulled Moira away to the window.

Ewan was only vaguely aware of these movements, his attention centered squarely on Jeannie who sat on the edge of the laird's bed, spoon in hand.

"Stop," he shouted, lunging to swat the bowl with the back of his hand. Broth spattered over the furs covering a gaping Kendric. Fynn hurried to save Jeannie from slipping to the floor in shock. The bowl flew across the chamber and came to rest at David's feet.

Shona strode to her uncle's bedside. "Poisoned," she explained. "Did ye eat any?"

Wide-eyed, he shook his head.

"Nay," Jeannie said, clinging to Fynn. "I was just about to give him the first taste. Thank goodness I let it cool first. God forgive me if I'd poisoned my own brother."

"But I brought the broth from the servery," the distraught maid-servant interjected. "How could it have been tainted?"

"Ailig stole the vial of laudanum. We believe he somehow got into the kitchens," Ewan explained.

Moira gasped.

The color drained from Jeannie's face. "Ailig is here? In Creag? I have to sit down."

Ewan exchanged a glance with Fynn as he guided Jeannie to a chair by the hearth. The glint of steel in his kinsman's eyes reassured him the man would fight to the death to protect Lady Lazy-Eye.

"I'm relieved to see ye safely returned, lass," Kendric rasped to Shona. "We feared the worst when Moira and David told us of yer abduction."

"'Tis an enormous relief to see they both survived the ordeal and I'm pleased to see ye looking better, Uncle," she replied, pulling away the broth-spattered covering. "Yon Mackinloch rescued me, believe it or nay."

"I had help from Walter Gilbertson, and Ruadh," Ewan pointed out.

Kendric narrowed his eyes. "Ye're too modest, laddie." He grimaced, shifting his weight in an apparent attempt to get more comfortable. "On another subject, Jeannie informed me o' the shenanigans ye young folk got up to." He wagged an accusing finger. "Pretending to be somebody else in order to avoid the marriage."

Shona paled, twirling a finger in the coverlet. "Aye, 'twas foolish."

Ewan agreed the deception was foolish, but knew his own father would be furious if he got wind of the escapade. His words were for The Camron but he looked into Shona's eyes as he spoke. "'Twas the act of a coward, my laird, and I'm nay a cowardly man. I'm ashamed of my behavior and regret it deeply."

"So now ye *want* to marry my niece?" Kendric asked.

He made no mention of the fact Shona had spent days and nights as Mungo's prisoner. Ewan decided he'd face that foe if and when it raised its ugly head. "More than anything. If she'll have me."

He'd never exposed so much of his heart to anyone, let alone a woman. He feared his lungs might burst as he held his breath, waiting…

Shona raked her gaze over him, from head to toe, as if considering the matter. Then she blushed beautifully, smiled broadly, and replied, "Aye. Ye'll do."

Ewan exhaled, took her hand firmly in his and brushed a kiss on her knuckles. When he raised his head, their gazes met. He narrowed his eyes in an effort to impart the silent message that she wouldn't always be allowed to tease him so brazenly, though he doubted that would prove to be true.

"Hurr...hurr...hurrah," David exclaimed, causing everyone in the room to cheer as well, though Kendric's cheer turned into a cough that became a groan.

"In that case," Shona's uncle declared when the pain seemed to ease, "I hereby appoint Ewan Mackinloch as interim laird while I convalesce. We're under threat and I can do naught to protect us if I'm lying here."

It wasn't the clan Ewan had hoped to lead one day, but the pride in his betrothed's green eyes confirmed it was the right one.

"I accept the honor," he replied, shaking Kendric's hand. "Ye can rely on me to rid MacCarron lands o' the threat in its midst."

A MAELSTROM OF emotions swirled in Shona's heart. The plot against her uncle's life had been thwarted. For now he was safe, though no one in Creag Castle would be completely free from danger until Mungo and Ailig were brought to justice.

She grieved for Jeannie in particular, threatened again by Ailig's reappearance in their lives. Her pale features betrayed a deep fear, despite Fynn's obvious determination to protect her. He wore his feelings for her aunt on his sleeve. The notion love had smitten Jeannie was akin to a miracle. Fynn was fortunate to have found a woman with such a generous spirit.

Heartening as well was the bond forming between David and Moira. The maid clearly wasn't bothered by the lad's speech problems, any more than Fynn and Jeannie cared about lazy eyes and missing hands.

She only hoped Ewan would be as tolerant of what had befallen her during the abduction. She had worried he wouldn't want her after the ruse and the kidnapping, yet he'd offered for her hand. Mayhap guilt had more to do with his reasoning, or, worse still, a desire to take over the lairdship.

She shoved aside her doubts, hoping what she'd glimpsed in Ewan's eyes was indeed genuine regard. The time would come when she'd have to confess what had happened, and trust he would believe Mungo hadn't raped her. Men were prideful creatures who were often quick to jump to mistaken conclusions. However, he was the chief her clan desperately needed.

And there was one more unthinkable horror that had to be addressed. She took hold of Kendric's warm hand. "I believe Ailig had something to do with yer accident, Uncle."

He nodded. "I've been trying to fathom how it came about. Jock is a good horse, steady and reliable. Something spooked him."

His suspicions gave her the courage to voice her deepest concern. "The Morleys were involved in my father's death too. I'm certain of it."

EWAN HAD PAID scant attention to the news that the laird of Clan MacCarron had died a few months ago. After the signing of the Clunes agreement to end the feud, there seemed little reason to worry about such matters.

Now he cared a great deal about Shona's allegations. If the Morleys had indeed murdered her father he would move heaven and earth to avenge his death. "Ye must have reasons for yer suspicions," he said softly.

"'Twasna so much the remark Ailig made about my father's death. 'Twas the way he said it. He was taunting me, making me feel he knew something I didna."

"He's capable of it," Jeannie murmured, staring into the empty hearth. "I dinna ken why I didna suspect something afore this. Beathan's death was so sudden."

"It took us all off guard," Shona whispered.

Anger seethed in Ewan's gut. He hadn't always seen eye to eye with his own domineering father, but the notion of someone murdering him couldn't be tolerated. His heart broke for his golden-haired beauty. If the Morleys had killed her only surviving parent, he'd make sure they suffered the consequences. "Tell me the circumstances," he said.

BITTER TRUTHS

Kendric patted the bed. "Sit here, lass," he said to Shona. "I'll tell the tale."

It was a relief not to have to recount the mysterious circumstances of her father's death, but she reached for Ewan's hand as she sat, needing his support.

She took comfort in the light touch of her uncle's finger twirled in a lock of her hair. The telling wouldn't be easy for him.

"My brother loved this castle," Kendric began.

Ewan grunted.

Her uncle bristled. "I ken the Mackinlochs have always claimed it belonged to them, but as far as we're concerned…"

Jeannie huffed impatiently. "For pity's sake, this isna the time to rekindle the feud."

Her brother growled, carefully shifting his position in the bed. "Weel, anyway, after his wife died, Beathan took to going up into the tower every night."

Shona wanted to make sure Ewan understood. "My mother died birthing me. They say Da took me up in the tower with him the day I was born."

He brought her hand to his lips, his eyes full of sorrow. She could happily drown in those brown depths.

Kendric continued. "As ye nay doot ken, the tower was added by the first MacCarron to take possession o' the castle after the Mackinlochs abandoned it."

Jeannie huffed again. "Saints preserve us from old men and their ramblings."

"I'm nay old," he retorted.

"Mayhap I should tell the rest, Uncle," Shona suggested, dismayed at the antagonistic turn the conversation had taken.

"Forgive me, laddie," Kendric told Ewan. "'Tisna my intention to alienate ye. Habits of a lifetime."

Ewan nodded. "Old hatreds die hard," he agreed.

Seemingly at the end of her patience, Jeannie approached the bed. "Weel, they'd best die here and now. The threat is from within, not from the Mackinlochs." She turned to Ewan. "As Kendric has rightly told ye, my brother Beathan went up to the tower every evening when he was home. For many a year he took his little girl with him."

Shona swallowed the lump in her throat. "He used to tell me about Ma," she explained. "He seemed to feel close to her up there. Mayhap if I'd gone with him the night he died…"

Her auntie cupped her chin in both hands. "Ye canna blame yerself. Beathan became moody and cantankerous as he got older." She cast her wonky eye in Kendric's direction. "Runs in the family."

Her brother bristled. "He just preferred the solitude. 'Tis the reason we thought he'd jumped off the tower when we found his broken body in the courtyard below."

Indignation flooded Shona. "I never believed that for a moment. An accident aye, though it was hard to fathom how such a thing could happen. The parapet wall is too high."

Ewan squeezed her hand. "And now we ken what likely happened."

"He was pushed off," Jeannie murmured.

FOR A MAN to embrace his betrothed in public wasn't acceptable behavior, but Ewan threw caution to the winds and pulled Shona into his arms, consumed by a hunger to warm her shivering body, to kiss away the tears and fill the void in her heart. "I swear to ye I'll avenge his death," he whispered, nibbling her earlobe.

He lifted her when she swooned against him. "This lass needs sleep," he told the others. "She's had a long ordeal."

Jeannie headed for the door, Shona's maid a few steps behind. "Follow me. Moira will help ye get her to bed."

"Just so we're clear," he said to Kendric. "I dinna intend to leave her alone this night. She's mine to protect. On the morrow we begin the hunt."

The older man sighed, exhaustion etched on his face. "Aye, laddie. Ye must do as ye see fit."

Fynn opened the door. "What do ye expect o' me and David, *my laird*?"

Ewan smiled at the one-handed warrior's knowing wink. "Go to the stables and inform Walter Gilbertson of what's transpired here. Put yerselves at his disposal. Tell him to post guards at every entry and exit. The Morleys are to be arrested on sight if they show their faces. I want to speak to the castle folk in the hall on the morrow an hour after dawn."

Satisfied he'd done all he could for the present, he followed Jeannie and carried Shona to her chamber, where he left her with Moira. "Go to yer apartment, my lady," he told Jeannie. "No harm will come to her as long as I draw breath."

She stood on tiptoe and pecked a kiss on his cheek. "Thank goodness ye came to us, Ewan Mackinloch. Shona's a lucky lass."

He smiled. "And, unless I miss my guess, ye are fond o' my kinsman. He's a Macintyre, by the way."

She giggled like a young maiden as a blush spread across her cheeks. "Aye. He confided as much. Who would have thought such a thing possible at my age?"

"Fynn is a good man," he reassured her as he opened the door and looked left and right. "I'll watch until ye're safely inside."

She hurried to her own apartment and waved before entering. He closed Shona's door and stood with his back to it, arms folded across his chest. Decorum dictated he leave. It was inappropriate to see his betrothed in her night attire, but he couldn't help himself.

Though she looked tired and pale when she emerged long minutes later, his cock saluted her beauty. Shrouded from neck to toe in a heavy linen nightrail with long sleeves, she was nevertheless the most alluring female he'd ever set eyes on. Moira had combed the tangles out of her hair and it caressed her shoulders like a shining cloak, reminding him of the hairpin hidden in his gambeson.

The necessity to discuss the circumstances in which he'd found the ornament sat like a lead weight on his chest. He would never cast blame on her for what might have happened, but didn't want to spend his life wondering. He needed the truth.

"Leave us, Moira," he said when Shona was tucked in bed.

The maid glanced at her mistress sitting propped up by the bolster.

"Ye can go," Shona whispered.

Moira hesitated only a moment before bobbing a curtsey and exiting. Ewan barred the door behind her.

"Should I be afraid?"

He perched on the edge of the mattress and took his betrothed's elegant hand, willing his hungry tarse to behave itself. "Ye need never fear me," he promised, slowly retrieving the hairpin, "and I ken ye're tired, but it's important I hear from yer lips everything that happened while ye were in Mungo's clutches."

SHONA STARED AT the treasured butterfly lying on the bedspread, afraid to look Ewan in the eye. "It belonged to my mother. Where did ye find it?" she asked.

"Ruadh found it," he replied. "In yon cave at Conger's Rock."

A snake wriggled in her belly. She'd done nothing wrong, but would he believe her?

"Mungo made me sleep next to him—by the fire. I must have lost it then."

Even to her own ears it sounded as if the worst had happened.

Ewan got to his feet and moved to the foot of the bed. He pressed his fisted hands into the mattress and leaned forward, ready to pounce. "Then?"

She inhaled to steady her breathing. "He put his arm across my hips."

She worried Ewan might break his teeth if he kept on grinding them together. "When I tried to move away, he wouldna let me."

Realizing he was close to losing control completely, she tried desperately to recall Mungo's exact words and the way he'd uttered them. "He told me, *I'm nay likely to have my way with ye in a cave wi' my men looking on.*"

Ewan's jaw fell open. To her surprise he burst out laughing. "Ye sound just like the brainless twit."

Relief blossomed and she continued her impersonation. "I think he feared Ailig was watching him. He explained the arm was *Just in case ye get a silly notion to run off.*"

She found herself standing beside the bed in Ewan's arms before she even realized he had moved. He rained kisses along her neck, nibbled her earlobe, cupped her bottom in his big hands and lifted her to his hard body. "The *mon* must be a eunuch if he slept alongside ye all night and didna have his way wi' ye."

She held her breath for a moment, worried his remark meant he didn't believe her, but his kisses and the thrusting of his hips carried on, igniting delicious feelings of yearning in private places as his manhood pressed against her body.

Holding her tight, he fell backwards onto the bed and turned her so they lay facing each other. He stroked her hair and trailed his fingers down her neck. Breasts swelled in anticipation, nipples tingled to be touched. She pouted, wantonly disappointed when he stopped.

"I want ye badly, Shona MacCarron," he rasped, "but when our bodies join 'twill be in our marriage bed as befits the daughter of a laird."

She nodded, awed by the reverence in his voice and the daunting promise of a physical union with him. "I'll try to be a good wife," she whispered, "but I had no mother to counsel me, and Jeannie…well…she suffered at Ailig's hands and would never speak of it. I confess I ken naught about pleasing a man."

He trailed his fingers gently over a breast. "Jesu, Shona, just touching ye pleases me."

Though his caress was featherlight, desire curled into her womb. She arched her back and cried out her need when he cupped her breast and brushed his thumb over her nipple. He smothered her cries with his mouth, coaxing her lips open with his tongue. She sucked on him like a babe at the teat, letting him breathe for her as he squeezed her nipple. He draped his leg over her thigh, drawing her closer to his body, then took her hand and pressed it against his manhood.

The notion of being abed with a man had always filled her with a dread of powerlessness. Instead, she relished the strength of Ewan's leg pinning her in place and surrendered willingly to the sensations caused by the rhythmic squeezing of her nipple. She responded in kind to the thrusts of his hips, delighting in the hard warmth of his manhood as it pulsed beneath her hand. She grew dizzy on the intoxicating taste and aroma of a powerful male.

A wild and hot wanting grew and grew in her female place until she tumbled into an abyss of bliss, vaguely wondering who was screaming so loudly.

SECRET FEELINGS

EWAN WATCHED DAWN trickle faint pink streaks across the sky. He'd moved the chair close to the window to lessen the temptation of crawling back into bed in order to ease his insistent arousal in the most satisfying way possible.

A rustling of linens caught his attention. Propped up on her elbows, Shona watched him from the bed. "Ye're awake," he said, resisting the urge to rush over and sift his fingers through her disheveled hair. One day soon he'd awaken with those glorious tresses wrapped around his sated body.

She stretched her arms over her head, resurrecting the pleasurable ache at his groin. "I feel different," she said.

Incapable of keeping his hands off her a moment longer, he walked to the bed. "That was just a wee taste," he said with a smug chuckle, cupping her face in his hands.

There was much more he wanted to say. He'd been awed by her innocent yet seductive response to his kisses and caresses. He hadn't touched her nether lips, yet she'd exploded like a firecracker before falling asleep in his arms.

He thirsted to taste that most intimate place; the waiting would be torture.

However, there wasn't time for sweet words and promises. He'd a duty to inform the folk of Clan MacCarron he was their interim laird and convince them to prosecute two of their own.

He stepped away from temptation and paced. "I've rehearsed over and over what to say to the people who are at this very moment gathering in the hall."

"Jeannie and I will speak in yer favor," she assured him.

"Walter too, I hope."

He paused when she threw off the linens and sat on the edge of the mattress with bare feet dangling. Nibbling those enticing toes would be...

He raked his hands through his hair and headed for the door. Mayhap he'd be better able to think if he wasn't distracted by her beauty. "I'll send Moira. Get dressed quickly. Fynn or David will come to fetch ye. Dinna open for anyone else. Ailig Morley seems to ken how to get in and out of this castle without being seen. We must be wary."

SHONA ENTERED THE *boudoir*, still daydreaming about Ewan's kisses and the explosion of euphoric sensations he'd caused. She saw to her needs and wandered back to bed, lazily pinching nipples that suddenly seemed permanently rigid.

She startled at the sound of Moira's voice outside the door and rearranged her nightrail, hoping the heat rising in her face wasn't too obvious. Ewan's touches had turned her into a harlot.

Moira let the bar fall across the stanchions after Shona let her in. She took one look at her mistress, narrowed her eyes and asked, "Ye slept weel?"

"Cheeky servant," Shona retorted, but then her joy won out. "Do I look different?"

Moira grinned. "Ye look happy."

It occurred to Shona as they entered the *boudoir* that Moira also seemed happier. "And what's made ye so congenial this morn?" She'd never seen her maid's face turn quite so red. "It's David, isn't it?"

"Aye," Moira whispered. "He's a canny lad. And his voice!"

They giggled and teased each other as the maid assisted her mistress to prepare for the meeting. They shared secret feelings about the men they were attracted to while Moira braided her hair.

Shona frowned at her reflection in the mirror. The linen frock seemed too simple. "Mayhap I should wear something more dignified. Folk might be angered at the notion of Ewan being made laird."

"Nay," her maid insisted. "They love ye, and they'll love him."

"Despite the fact he's a Mackinloch?"

"Aye," Moira replied after some hesitation.

PLEDGING VENGEANCE

Ewan vaulted onto the trestle table in the hall for the second time in as many days with a sinking feeling all might not go as well as he hoped. But then he hadn't really expected to be warmly welcomed as the interim laird. Discontented grumbling among the folk who'd gathered indicated they'd already heard the news and weren't happy about it.

He was glad of David's presence beside the table, and proud of his demeanor. The youth stood resolute, legs braced, head held high, but there wasn't a trace of fear on his face. Ewan hoped the same could be said of him.

He breathed more easily when Fynn entered with Shona and her maid. Clad in a simple linen frock, his betrothed seemed to bring a breath of fresh air into the stale heat of the hall. David's ruddy complexion flushed when Moira sent him a little wave.

It occurred to him Fynn didn't look pleased, but a member of a Mackinloch sept was perhaps entitled to feel uneasy in a MacCarron gathering. His attention was distracted from his kinsman when Walter strode in with several of the men who'd accompanied them on the rescue. Shona hurried over when she noticed one of them carried Ruadh.

Ewan chuckled inwardly. The lazy hound was making the most of the attention being lavished on him, but he was relieved to see the dog had survived his injuries.

The crowd turned its attention to the wounded warrior. Murmurs replaced grumbling. Taking advantage of the distraction, Ewan drew his sword and held it high. *"Aonaibh Ri Chéile,"* he shouted, recalling Walter's earlier plea for unity.

If the squeal of metal hadn't drawn attention, his war cry caused every head to swivel in his direction. A moment of stunned silence followed, so he plunged on. "Yer laird, The Camron, lies gravely injured, and canna lead the fight against a dire threat to all MacCarrons."

He scanned the faces, deciding to appeal to those who looked puzzled rather than angry. "Aye. Give full rein to yer anger when I tell ye the accident was no such thing. His horse was deliberately spooked by someone who wanted him dead."

"Nay!"

"Who was it?"

"Mayhap a Mackinloch."

David moved closer to the table, but Ewan refused to acknowledge the accusation. Some of the angry faces now look puzzled. Walter had hoisted Robbie onto his shoulders. Encouraged by the lad's smile, he searched the crowd for Shona until their eyes met. He lowered his voice and his sword. "Ye all ken I came here to wed Lady Shona MacCarron," he said softly.

An eerie silence fell as folk strained to listen.

"I hafta admit, I didna want to wed a MacCarron lass."

There was muttered acknowledgement. Clan rivalry and longstanding hatreds were something every clansman understood.

Ewan grinned. "Until I set eyes on her beauty. Then I couldna think of aught else but a wedding..." He risked wiggling his eyebrows... "and a bedding."

Laughter and some cheering ensued. His gamble that all men understood lust for a beautiful woman had hit the mark.

He held out his hand to beckon his betrothed to his side. She came with a smile on her lovely face that gave him strength. Eager hands helped her up onto the table. He put his arm around her waist and pulled her close. "Here and now I pledge to her my undying love and fidelity."

She turned wide eyes to him. "Ye love me?" she whispered.

He kissed her, murmuring *Aye* into her mouth.

The cheering increased as he lingered over the kiss, but then he schooled his features into a frown as he broke them apart. "But I also pledge to avenge the wrongs done to my bride."

Shona tensed in his arms, but there was no time to tell her he didn't intend to reveal she'd spent time with Mungo in dubious circumstances. "I told ye already of our suspicions about Kendric's injuries. Let righteous anger erupt when I reveal that Beathan MacCarron was murdered, pushed from the top of the tower."

Pandemonium broke out. Shona clung to his arm and laid a hand on his chest. "Ye didna give me a chance to reply, but I love ye too."

Feeling like the King o' all Scots, he smiled, brandished the sword once more and shouted over the noise. "Kendric has honored me. I am yer laird until he recovers. I pledge to do all in my power to bring the murderer to justice."

Confused shouts resulted, but the fury wasn't directed at Ewan. The demand was for the name of the traitor.

Walter nodded.

"Ailig Morley," Ewan bellowed hoarsely from his dry throat.

Outrage swept through the hall; more questions were raised, but pride heated his blood. He was confident he'd successfully established himself as laird, albeit temporary, of a hostile clan and he held the woman he wanted in his arms.

A scowling Fynn beckoned him.

"What's amiss?" he asked, bending to hear over the hubbub.

"I canna find Lady Jeannie."

SEARCH

Shona was whisked along the corridor to her chamber by what seemed like an army of angry men, one of them carrying Ruadh. She trembled with fear, despite Ewan's firm grip on her hand. Ailig Morley had somehow managed to infiltrate the castle again and he'd taken her darling aunt. She didn't want to contemplate the suffering the cruel coward might be inflicting on Jeannie—if she was still alive.

On first hearing the news of her disappearance, Ewan had protested he'd watched Jeannie enter her apartment. The color drained from his face when the truth dawned. No amount of reassurance could dissuade him he'd allowed the worst to happen. "The bastard was already there," he growled. "Just waiting."

She wasn't guiltless either. Ewan's preoccupation had been with her.

She sorrowed too for Fynn who strode alongside his laird, his face as grim as death.

Ruadh sighed his contentment when he was put down on Shona's bed.

Ewan bestowed a brief kiss on her lips once she and Moira were safely inside. "Bar the door. Ye're to remain here and open to no one but me," he told her, handing her his dagger.

She watched her maid drop the bar after he left, then stared at the heavy blade in her hands. "I canna move, Moira."

A gentle hand took her arm. "Come, lie down a wee while. We must pray all will be well. Ruadh will comfort ye."

"They have to be in the castle somewhere," she murmured as

Moira bade her sit on the mattress, took the dagger and eased off her shoes.

"Aye. Every entry and exit has been guarded since ye returned. They'll find him."

Shona wiped away a tear trickling down her cheek as she curled up with her beloved hound. "It's like he's a ghost."

WITH WALTER'S HELP, Ewan organized a thorough search of Creag Castle. Intuition told him the tower was the likeliest place to search. Ailig had apparently taken Beathan MacCarron by surprise there, which seemed strange since Shona's father obviously knew the tower well.

With Fynn and David, he combed through every stairwell, alcove, landing, storage room and chamber—twice. To no avail.

Exiting the door to the rooftop, they paced the length and breadth of it, peering into every sentry box, and opening the lids of every iron chest.

Nothing but rusted lances and arrows with decayed fletching. The defensive arsenals would need to be refurbished once the crisis was over.

Fynn seemed to retreat into his own private hell. Ewan understood. If it were Shona in Ailig's grasp again…

David wisely refrained from offering sympathy, simply expressing his solidarity with a firm hand on his kinsman's shoulder.

As arranged, they met up with Walter and his men in the Map Room, frustrated to learn the search had turned up no trace of Jeannie or her abductor. He was surprised to see Kendric slumped in a chair, a plaid thrown over his nightshirt, pain etched on his face. "I insisted they carry me here when I heard the news," he explained. "I felt useless in bed."

Unable to pace in the tiny room, Ewan's feeling of helplessness grew. He blurted out a question that was on everyone's mind. "And where the *fyke* is Mungo?" he thundered. "The Morleys canna just appear and disappear like phantoms."

He was at a disadvantage in a castle he didn't know at all. He was familiar with every nook and cranny of Roigh Hall, though the Mackinloch seat had been added on to by successive generations. He knew every hidey-hole and…

"Wait," he exclaimed. "The tower was built after the castle, right?"

"Aye," Kendric confirmed, "but that was hundreds o' years ago."

"Think back," Ewan exhorted the men crowded into the room. "Who were the masons of the clan at that time? Who designed the tower?"

"I dinna ken," Kendric replied, "and I doot anyone alive today kens that."

Ewan's hopes fell. "I was thinking mayhap if alterations were made that only certain folk had knowledge of."

Shona's uncle scratched his beard. "Weel, the whole castle was refurbished by the thirteenth chief."

Ewan tried to work out his place in the order of MacCarron chiefs. "When was that?"

"Funny thing," Kendric mused, "his name was Ewen."

The muttered agreement in the room did nothing to lessen Ewan's impatience. "And?"

"Aye," Walter added. "Ewen MacCarron of Lochisle. Fifteen hundred and something as I recollect. There's an escutcheon over the main door of the tower with the date the improvements were completed. Funny how ye see something every day and pay scant attention."

Ewan clenched his fists, not sure if this new knowledge was significant. "Not that long ago," he said hopefully. "Mayhap there were plans, sketches?"

He wondered if he'd spoken in Greek when silent stares greeted his question. Men scratched heads, chins, earlobes, even crotches. The air reeked of impotent worry.

"Didna end well for that chief," Walter muttered. "Executed for treason in Stirling after the Battle of Pinkie Cleugh."

Fynn broke the ominous silence. "Lady Jeannie is in the tower."

"But ye've searched," Kendric countered.

Ewan couldn't ignore the pleading look in Fynn's eyes. "How can ye be so sure?"

Fynn shook his head and swallowed hard. "When a *mon* cares about a woman, he kens things about her. The way she says things, what it means when she tilts her head or fidgets with her sleeves."

A murmur of agreement scythed through the gathering.

Kendric shifted his weight in the chair. "But what's that to do with the matter at hand?"

Fynn braced his legs. Ewan admired the dour warrior who had already disclosed more of his feelings than most men ever would, but sensed there was more.

"I'd recognize Jeannie's scent anywhere," Fynn declared.

Ewan knew exactly what he meant. "Ye detected her perfume in the tower?" he asked.

"Aye. Without a doot."

Ruadh's familiar doggy smell was comforting as Shona raked her fingers through the wiry fur. The ostler had stitched his wound and it seemed to be healing well. The hound sighed deeply as Shona scratched his belly. "Daft dog," she teased. "Did I thank ye for saving my life?"

He looked at her with soulful eyes as if to let her know he didn't mind the oversight.

"All in a day's work, I suppose," she whispered.

He startled, actually raising his head when Ewan's voice preceded a rap at the door. "Shona. Let me in."

Her heart stuttered at his grim tone.

She slid off the bed and went into his arms as he crossed the threshold after Moira lifted the bar. "No sign?"

"Nay," he confirmed, "we've searched high and low. It sounds unlikely, but Fynn seems to think he caught a whiff of Jeannie's perfume in the tower."

"Rosemary," Shona replied. "She uses it when she washes her hair; however, she hasna set foot in the tower since Da died."

His eyes widened. "That supports my theory there's a secret passage or concealed room in the tower."

She gripped his hands, almost afraid to hope. "Mayhap when they refurbished the castle in the last century."

"That's a possibility we discussed, but we have no records of the work that was done. I need Ruadh's nose."

"But he canna climb so many steps."

"I'll carry him," he countered. "Come with me to Jeannie's chamber and find something of hers he can track."

CLUES

Satisfied Shona and Moira were safe once more, Ewan set off with Fynn and David to meet Walter at the main door of the tower.

He set Ruadh down on the cobblestones when Walter beckoned him to examine the escutcheon.

"Look at this," Gilbertson said. "As ye'd expect, 'tis the ancient emblem of the MacCarron clan chiefs, an arm grasping a sword, encircled with a belt and buckle."

"And the motto ye taught me," Ewan noted.

Walter pointed. "Aye, but see the wee Viking ship carved into the scrollwork?"

Ewan and the men around him peered at the stone, barely able to make out the ship in the flourish bearing the date *Anno Domini 1536*. "Aye."

"That's a symbol o' the Morleys. They claim descent from Somerled's Viking pirates."

The fog began to lift. "The family worked on the renovations."

Walter nodded. "And wanted to leave their mark."

Fynn stepped forward. "So if there was a secret chamber, they would have kent."

"And pass...pass...passed it on," David said.

Ewan hefted Ruadh. The dog whined at being lifted, but began to wag his tail and woof when Jeannie's kerchief was put under his nose.

"He's got the scent," Fynn said, sounding hopeful for the first time.

Ewan led the way through the open doors, held his breath as he stepped over the grating covering the steps down to the cesspit, and began the ascent to the top of the tower.

He'd aspired to be a clan chief all his life, but had never imagined his first challenge would involve carrying an excited hound up a steep, winding staircase to find a missing woman.

"Something's bothering me," Shona told Moira.

"Yer incessant pacing was a clue," her maid replied. "Sit down for pity's sake."

"I canna. I keep thinking on what Ewan said about the refurbishments done in the last century by the ill-fated thirteenth laird."

"What of it?"

"Every MacCarron chief leaves a record of his time as laird. My father showed me where they're kept in the library. Some are musty old parchments that mostly tell of battles and feuds, I'm afraid, but mayhap The Camron in question wrote of rebuilding the castle. It was a momentous undertaking that took several years."

Moira knelt by the chest against the wall and opened the lid. "Weel, we've been ordered to remain here; we canna traipse off to the library. Mayhap I'll have another go at airing these gowns."

An inexorable premonition there was important information in the archives consumed Shona. If she stayed cooped up in her chamber much longer she'd simply fret about what was going on and begin to imagine all sorts of dire scenarios. Mind made up, she retrieved Ewan's dagger from the bed and strode to the door. "Stay if ye wish. I'm the daughter of a MacCarron chief and I refuse to hide in fear any longer. I'm for the library."

Moira scrambled to her feet and rushed after her as she exited the chamber. "The new laird willna be happy."

Shona tightened her grip on the hilt. "Desperate times call for action," she replied. "Ewan will understand I had to do whatever I could to save Jeannie."

She kept to herself the hope that Ewan Mackinloch was the kind of man who would want a courageous wife.

Head held high, she strode purposefully through the maze of deserted corridors leading to the tiny library. The MacCarron men were hunting for her aunt, but it pained her that Mungo and Ailig's treachery had rendered most folk too fearful to be out and about. The normally bustling castle seemed eerily empty.

"We must be wary," Moira whispered.

"Creag Castle is my home, the place I was born," Shona replied, refusing to pay heed to the deafening pulse beating in her ears. "I dinna intend to skulk around like a criminal." She winked at her maid and brandished the sharp dagger. "Besides, I have this."

Moira snorted. "And I can just see Ailig and Mungo Morley being intimidated by a lass wielding a blade."

Shona preferred not to consider that possibility, and was mightily relieved when they reached the small, arched door of the library.

"I often wondered what this led to," her maid confessed.

Shona wasn't surprised. Why would a servant who couldn't read need to know where the library was?

The bottom edge of the warped door dragged on the floor but, together, they managed to shove it open.

"I'd say folk dinna come here too often," Moira panted as they set their hips to the task of closing it behind them. Wood jarred on stone bit by slow bit until it was finally shut.

The odor of musty parchment and stale air assailed them. One hand over her nose and mouth, Shona fanned dust motes away with the dagger and peered into the gloom. The arrow-slit window on the far wall was encrusted with muck and bird droppings.

"'Tis smaller than I recall," she admitted, finding herself only inches away from teetering stacks of books and manuscripts.

"More like a wee cupboard," Moira agreed. "How do ye hope to find what we're seeking in this jumble?"

Fearing the next search might be for them if the hoard toppled over, Shona was afraid to move, let alone begin the hunt.

EVERY LANDING OF the twisting stone staircase opened to an alcove that led to a chamber or store room. Ewan worried that Ruadh seemed to have settled into his arms as if enjoying the adventure. He kept jostling the dog's head to make sure he hadn't fallen asleep. The increasingly heavy weight prevented him holding on to the safety rope attached to the wall. Sweating with the effort, he stepped into every alcove, then stepped out again when Ruadh showed no reaction.

"Mayhap this is a fool's errand after all," he muttered to Fynn as they stood in the third alcove.

"I'll carry him the rest of the way to the top."

Ewan looked up. "Nay," he replied. "We're halfway now."

He hefted the dog and began the climb again, out of breath when they reached the next alcove. Unlike the others, this one led nowhere. He was about to set off again when Ruadh became agitated, barking and squirming in his arms.

He tried again to leave the alcove and the hound howled.

Fynn inhaled. "Even I can smell the rosemary. Jeannie's here somewhere."

With some difficulty, Ewan handed the frenzied dog over to David and ran his hands over the back wall of the alcove. "It's solid. If there's a hidden chamber this isna the entryway."

Fynn leaned his shoulder against the stone and pushed—to no avail. He put an ear to the wall and shouted Jeannie's name, shaking his head when there was no reply.

At the outset of their journey, Ewan had never expected to care a whit about the kinsmen who'd accompanied him, but anger constricted his throat at the sight of Fynn's bereft face. Being a laird meant more than prestige. It brought with it enormous responsibility for the wellbeing of every member of the clan.

"I see no point going to the top," he said, determined to find Shona's aunt. "We'll look for clues from the outside."

SOMETHING ROTTEN

SHONA HANDED THE dagger to her maid. "Stay here," she advised. "Go for help if something happens to me."

Moira wiped her hands on her skirts and accepted the weapon, then leaned back against the door, the color draining from her normally rosy cheeks. "Since I canna read anyway," she said.

Though the words sounded flippant, Shona detected the edge of fear. "Aye, but promise ye'll nay waste time trying to dig me out if the pile falls."

Moira nodded, sniffling back tears.

Shona inhaled deeply and shuffled sideways into the stacks, then halted, momentarily distracted by distant shouts coming from the courtyard.

"Mayhap they've found Lady Jeannie," Moira suggested.

A voice in Shona's head confirmed she wasn't hearing shouts of victory. "I've begun now," she replied. "No turning back. The answer lies here somewhere."

Recollecting that the lairds' journals were stored on shelves at the rear of the library, she gingerly sidestepped her way through the stacks of parchments. Once things got back to normal, the archives would have to be sorted and kept in better fettle. She turned her head and fixed her attention on the window, afraid to look to the top of the piles lest she succumb to dizziness.

She didn't breathe again until she clamped a hand on the rough wood of the shelves. Her heart skittered against her ribcage when she recognized the red leather binding of her father's codex on the top of the cobwebbed pile.

Beathan MacCarron was a man of action, not letters, but he'd considered it his sworn duty to record the history of the clan. A vision of him laboriously penning entries filled her mind. One day she'd pluck up the courage to read what he'd written, but now she could only hope the thirteenth laird had been as conscientious.

Common sense suggested the codices would be in order. She moved one book after another onto a new pile, until she reached what she hoped was the correct book. Despite her best efforts not to hurry, dust danced in the air, tickling her nose.

Her sneeze brought a gasp from Moira.

"I'm all right," she muttered hoarsely when the stacks towering over her remained in place.

There was barely enough space to turn around, but she opened the brittle cover of the codex, relieved her assumption had been correct. Tilting the book to the window, she slowly leafed through page after page of notations about provisions, judgements rendered, minor repairs. The Mackinloch feud was mentioned many times. Ink blotches marred some of the sketches of children, battles, horses and the laird himself. Even one of the ill-fated Queen Mary.

"What about yer grand project?" she whispered, losing hope as pain lanced through her stiff neck.

She was more than halfway through when she found it. Dozens of entries about the rebuilding. Sketch after sketch, many of the tower. Not one showed any indication of a secret chamber or stairway.

She was about to slam the book shut in exasperation when she noticed an entry next to a drawing of the tower that mentioned the Mackinlochs.

Twitching her nose to ward off another sneeze, she read the bold script:

We live in dangerous times and hence need a safe place for my family to hide if the Mackinlochs come for me. As well there exists the ever-present threat from the godless king of the English. I am confident the stench will protect us.

She sighed heavily at the mention of the threat from the Mackinlochs. In the end, it wasn't the enemy clan that had claimed his life.

The English king must be Henry, since the entry was dated 1536, about the time the monarch had set aside his Spanish wife if she remembered her tutor's history lessons correctly.

But what was all this about a stench? She peered at the entry again, worried she'd mayhap misread the word, noticing for the first time a tiny drawing of a Viking ship in the flourish under the date.

She swallowed the lump in her throat. The Morleys boasted loud and long of their line of descent from Somerled, King of the Isles.

She closed the book, tucked it under her arm and edged her way back to the door. "I found something," she told Moira, "though I dinna ken what it means."

RUADH TEETERED GAMELY on all four legs, barking loudly at the tower. Peering up at the approximate location of where they'd stood inside the structure, Ewan tamped down his frustration. "There's no window, but I'm sure there's a hidden chamber. I just canna fathom how to get into it."

"I suppose that was the plan," Walter replied. "But if Ailig did indeed surprise Beathan atop the tower, there has to be a passageway leading up to the roof."

Fynn and David apparently overheard and disappeared back into the tower before Ewan had a chance to reply. He was about to follow when boisterous MacCarron warriors appeared in the courtyard shoving a prisoner ahead of them.

Mungo Morley.

Ewan resisted the urge to lunge at the fool who'd caused Shona and her family so much suffering. They forced him to his knees, then stepped away. The reports came fast and furious, everyone shouting at once.

Found him in the kitchens.

Stealing food.

String him up.

I'll make him talk.

None came too close. Mungo stank like a midden. "Where's Lady Jeannie?" he asked, thankful Fynn was scaling the steep staircase.

Sorely shrugged. "I dinna ken. What have ye done with my wife?"

Ewan fisted his hands, glad when Walter spoke first. "Ye canna hope to claim 'twas a legal marriage betwixt ye and Shona. I myself saw the poor excuse for a priest ye bribed."

Muttered agreement rose from the crowd.

"Shona is *my* betrothed," Ewan growled.

Mungo stared in disbelief. "Ye're nay the man wi' one hand." Then he shook his head. "What matters is we exchanged vows and I bedded her first, so I'm her husband, and ye're an adulterer. Not welcome in Clan MacCarron."

Fury boiled in Ewan's veins. Morley was lying, but the wretch had made serious accusations that couldn't be ignored. The wrinkles of doubt on many a brow indicated as much. "Take him to the hall," he ordered, "and ask Laird Kendric to convene a hearing. We'll settle once and for all who's fit to be chief."

At all costs, Shona had to be protected. At least she was safely away from the imminent proceedings.

The prisoner was hauled to his feet and escorted into the keep by men who seemed to have lost some of their fervor. Dismayed Mungo may have swayed opinion to his side, Ewan lingered to wait for Fynn and David. He was reluctant to impart the news, especially when they confirmed they'd found nothing on the roof.

"Only a grate covering the air vent for the cesspit," Fynn hissed.

David waved his hand in front of his nose. "Sti...sti...stink," he stammered.

THE WOMEN HURRIED along the corridor, intending to go to the tower, but the noise of folk gathering in the hall drew their attention.

Shona paused to consider what to do next. She leaned back against the wall, glad of the cold stone and a chance to catch her breath. She hefted the codex that seemed to be getting heavier by the minute.

"Summat's going on in the hall," Moira panted, holding out the dagger, hilt first. "Give me the book."

"Nay," she replied, reluctant to refuse the weapon but unwilling to hand over the codex. "We'd best see what's going on."

She approached the hall cautiously, signaling Moira to stay behind her. Clutching the book to her breast, she peered around the arched entryway, puzzled to see a large, agitated crowd.

"What's happening?" Moira whispered.

Shona's heart hammered when she espied Mungo Morley in front of the dais. She could only see his back but there was no mistaking who it was standing head and shoulders above the mob. "They've captured Mungo," she replied, ready to rush into the hall with her precious book. But something made her hesitate. "Uncle Kendric is sitting on the dais."

"Do ye see Lady Jeannie?"

"Nay, nor Ailig."

"Mayhap they're holding a trial to make him tell where they are."

She nodded, but her belly churned when Ewan mounted the dais, his face a mask of fury. "Something's wrong," she murmured.

Her fears were confirmed when her grim-faced uncle called for silence and declared, "I convene this court to look into the matter o' the alleged consummation o' the marriage o' Mungo Morley and Shona MacCarron."

TRIAL

Ewan's certainty that Shona would be spared the humiliation of the proceedings blew away like chaff on the wind when she stormed into the hall, clutching a large book. He might have known she wouldn't remain in the safety of her chamber.

Without his prompting, Fynn and David moved to clear a path for her.

"There was no marriage," she shouted breathlessly.

Ewan burned to jump off the dais and take her into his arms, but Kendric was presiding over this court, not him. It would be foolish to jeopardize the outcome in any way.

Shona glared at her accuser with undisguised loathing. For the briefest of moments, Ewan wondered if she hated Morley because he'd raped her. He quickly doused the flame of suspicion. He had to trust she'd told him the truth.

"If I was The Camron," Mungo whined, looking too smug, "I'd enforce the clan rule that women are nay permitted to speak at a court."

Shona narrowed her eyes and scanned the crowd as a murmur of agreement with Mungo's assertion rippled on the air. "So, it seems a MacCarron lass is nay allowed to defend herself against calumny." She nodded to Fynn and David. "And apparently I must rely on Mackinloch kin to defend me from my own clan."

Kendric cleared his throat. "I'm sorry to say that Morley has the right of it, lass. Ye canna speak."

Ewan hoped she would turn her head to look at him and be assured he would speak for her.

SHONA HAD NEVER seen a volcano, but her father had told her about the discovery of the ruins of Pompeii when he was a boy. She seethed now with molten anger against all males and their stupid rules. Surely her clansmen wouldn't believe Mungo simply because he was a man, but even as the thought occurred she acknowledged the reality of the way things were.

She sought Ewan's gaze. Perhaps he could intercede. His clenched jaw and tightly folded arms told of his fury, but his eyes spoke of calmness and trust. He would speak for her.

She held up the book briefly, then gave it to Fynn. "A clue," she whispered.

He carried the codex to Ewan who nodded to her as he accepted it. She willed him to open it, to find the passage, but he put the tome down on the head table.

"Speak yer piece," Kendric told Mungo.

She noted with some satisfaction that Morley was staring at the codex and didn't look quite so smug.

"Me and Shona got wed," he declared.

She snorted.

Walter pushed his way to the front. "He bribed a simpleton squatting in the old Dunscar Abbey cell."

"I'll call for witnesses shortly, Walter," Kendric said wearily, scratching inside the top of his cast. "Carry on, Morley."

"Then I took her to Inverlochy and we did the deed."

Shona fisted her hands, heedless of the fingernails digging into her palms.

"Mungo wasn't at Inverlochy when we rescued Shona," Walter shouted. "He left her with two guards. One of them is in the infirmary now suffering with dog bites. Ask him."

Mungo shifted his weight. Sweat broke out on his forehead. "The witnesses aren't supposed to speak yet," he protested.

Kendric glowered. "How could ye have done the deed, as ye so indelicately put it, if ye left her wi' guards?"

Mungo scratched his head. "I was mistaken. We did it before."

"Before what?"

Shona snorted back her amusement. The idiot had just talked himself into admitting he might be a rapist. He was tying himself in knots with his lies.

"In the cave at Congers Rock," he muttered.

Shona met Ewan's gaze as he stepped forward. "If Morley has finished his testimony, my laird, may I speak?" he asked Kendric.

Admiration blossomed in her heart. Ewan's calm voice gave away nothing of his inner turmoil.

Kendric nodded.

Every face turned to listen to the next tantalizing revelation.

"My betrothed told me of her imprisonment in the cave."

"She's nay yer betrothed," Mungo insisted.

Kendric huffed. "Quiet. Ye've had yer say."

"She was understandably afraid, but Mungo told her, *I'm nay likely to have my way with ye in a cave wi' my men looking on.*"

His mimicry of Morley's ridiculous voice was so astoundingly perfect, she had to bite on her knuckle, but some didn't hide their amusement.

Mungo hunched his shoulders and glared at Ewan.

"He did put an arm across her hips but explained it was *Just in case ye get a silly notion to run off.*"

Many laughed out loud, enjoying the impersonation. Shona felt more hopeful. She reminded herself Morley didn't command much respect among the majority of MacCarrons anyway. Her betrothed had realized it and was capitalizing on the knowledge.

Ewan's voice deepened. "I told Shona that the *mon* must be a eunuch if he slept alongside her all night and didna have his way wi' her."

It was a confession of a very personal and private nature, but it seemed to endear Ewan to the onlookers and they guffawed at

Mungo's expense.

"Always suspected there was summat wrong wi' Morley," someone shouted, eliciting more crude remarks about Mungo's sexual prowess.

The giant's ruddy complexion turned an alarming shade of crimson.

"We'll see smoke come out of his ears soon," Moira whispered beside Shona.

Ewan placed a casual hand on the codex. "Mayhap we should ask Ailig what transpired," he shouted over the din.

"Aye," Mungo replied. "Er...nay...I mean."

A hush fell over the crowd, though a few whispered of Ailig's banishment.

"Which is it, *mon*?" Ewan asked. "Do ye deny ye've aided yer brother in his nefarious schemes?"

"Nay...aye...I've aided him wi' food and shelter, but..."

"He's an outlaw."

"Aye...nay...his banishment was unjust."

"And ye hated Laird Beathan for it."

"Aye...nay...we..."

"He's likely to make himself dizzy wi' all the nodding and shaking of his head," Moira muttered.

"So ye murdered him," Ewan thundered.

"Nay...I'm nay a murderer...'twas Ailig."

Ewan narrowed his eyes. "He pushed the laird off the tower."

Mungo studied his feet. "Aye."

"And caused Kendric's horse to bolt."

"Aye."

Kendric struggled to stand, brandishing his crutch. "Ye *fyking* miscreant. Wait till I get my hands on ye..."

Peacefulness crept into Shona's heart, despite the ruckus that exploded around her. She'd never accepted the notion her father had taken his own life. He'd been vindicated, the murderer exposed. A plot to overthrow the hereditary lairds of Clan MacCarron had been thwarted. But where was Ailig and what had he done with Jeannie?

EWAN WASN'T FINISHED. There could be no question left in anyone's mind about Shona's innocence in all this. He pointed an accusing finger at Mungo Morley. "Before us stands a criminal, a liar, a murderer's accomplice. Can we believe his accusations against our Shona?"

"Nay," everyone shouted.

He looked into the tear-filled eyes of his betrothed. "I swear before all o' ye, I look forward to the day I wed Shona MacCarron, for she is the purest and loveliest lass I've ever met."

"Aye," came the resounding response.

He turned back to Mungo. "Now what have ye done wi' Lady Jeannie?"

"I'll nay betray my own brother," he whimpered.

Ewan pointed to Fynn, simmering nearby. "Tell us or I'll nay intervene while my kinsman here persuades ye. He's a mite worried about her."

"Wait," Shona cried, hurrying to the dais. "The codex. I'm sure the thirteenth laird has given us a clue, but I dinna ken what to make of it."

She leafed hurriedly through a few pages, blowing away puffs of dust, then pointed to a drawing. "Here."

Ewan read and re-read the bold script, understanding some but not all of the cryptic message.

"What does it say?" Kendric asked.

"It talks about the need to build a place to hide…from the Mackinlochs."

Folk groaned.

"From the English king too," Shona added.

Muttered opinions were exchanged as to which English king it referred to since every last one was considered a thorn in the side of all

Scots.

Ewan was none the wiser. "Aye, but he talks about a stench. I dinna…"

He looked up and noticed Mungo's red face had turned ashen.

Suddenly, everything fell into place. The stink that clung to the wretch, the grating at the foot of the staircase and another on the roof. "The cesspit," he declared.

"What?" Walter asked, scratching his head.

"We get to the hidden chamber by way of the cesspit."

THE TUNNEL

Ewan grasped Shona's hand. There was no possibility he would allow her anywhere near the cesspit. As the indignant crowd surged out of the hall, sweeping Mungo along in its midst, he opened his mouth to tell her so.

"I'll nay stay here," she said before he could speak.

The determination in her gaze quickly persuaded him it would be useless to argue. "Come on then," he replied lifting her down from the dais, "but only as far as the tower."

She grinned. "Aye. The cesspit's a job for menfolk."

He chuckled as they hurried to follow the crowd. "Ye're a feisty lass, Shona MacCarron, and I love ye for it."

When they reached the tower they discovered Fynn had already lifted the grate off the opening at the base of the stairway, despite his handicap. "Steps," he told Ewan, nodding into the blackness.

The foul smell normally masked by the cover sapped some of the enthusiasm from the mob. They hung back, evidently content to wait and see what happened next.

"The Camron said the stench would protect them," Shona said.

The stink made his belly roil, but Ewan accepted his responsibility. "I'll lead, with Fynn. David will take three men up to the roof. Walter, watch over Shona. If aught happens to me…"

"Nay," Fynn replied, one foot already on the top step. "I claim the right to go first."

Accepting that he was unlikely to win an argument with his stalwart kinsman, Ewan kissed Shona, then leaned his forehead against hers. "We'll find her," he whispered.

"Just make sure ye come back to me," she replied hoarsely.

"I will," he promised. "Though I may not smell so sweet when I return."

The breath hitched in her throat as she stepped back to stand with Walter.

David quickly chose his men and started up the main staircase.

Ewan inhaled deeply, accepted a torch from a bystander, and followed Fynn into the slippery abyss.

"HE'S A DECISIVE man," Walter rasped. "He'll make a good laird."

Shona couldn't form a reply. Ewan thought she was feisty and courageous but, in reality, fear held her in its grip. She doubted they would find Jeannie alive, and dreaded even contemplating a future without the man she'd at first done her best to thwart.

Two MacCarron warriors arrived carrying a chair on which sat a very red-faced Kendric.

"Put me down here," he shouted, brandishing his crutch. "I'm a useless old *mon*. Have to be carried everywhere. Better if I died."

Shona hunkered down next to her uncle and took his hand. "Ye'll survive this ordeal," she reassured him, "and those responsible for it will be punished."

"Nay doot about that," he replied, snarling at Mungo who'd been forced to his knees near the door.

"Ewan and Fynn have gone down into the pit," she told him, swallowing the lump in her throat. "David is making his way to the roof."

Kendric grunted. "So if he's still in yon tower, Ailig is trapped." He glared at Mungo. "*Is* he still there?"

"Aye," Morley admitted sheepishly. "I had to leave to get food for Lady Jeannie. That woman eats like a horse."

A spark of hope sprang to life in Shona's heart. Mayhap her aunt was still alive.

EWAN HELD THE torch high, though the fetid air had robbed it of much of its flame. He wished there was a rope to hang on to as he followed Fynn down a dozen or so slippery steps. The alternative was to lean his shoulder against the slimy wall. Mayhap it was just as well since his other hand kept his plaid clamped firmly over his mouth and nose. The familiar smell of the wool was preferable to the stench. It was regrettable but the beloved plaid would have to be burned with the refuse once this escapade was over.

He thought to make some flippant remark about not expecting to be creeping cautiously into a cesspit when they'd left Roigh, but that would necessitate taking a breath, and he doubted Fynn was in the mood for jests. The descent was difficult enough with two good hands.

He risked inhaling when his kinsman announced they'd reached the last step. "Looks like the tunnel divides into three up ahead," Fynn growled.

Even with the failing light of the torch, it was possible to make out that the two passageways veering off to the left had been constructed much later than the black hole that likely led down to the cesspit. "I'll wager the steeper one leads to the hidden chamber," Ewan said. "The other likely ends up outside the walls."

The mystery of the Morleys coming and going undetected was unraveling.

Fynn didn't hesitate and after a few paces along the steeper tunnel they arrived at another winding staircase, scarcely wide enough for a man.

Ewan blew on the torch to rekindle the flame when it threatened to flicker out. "We might end up feeling our way," he growled.

"Aye," came the reply. "But there is a rope affixed to the wall here. On the right—luckily."

Once again Ewan had to give his dour kinsman credit. Even in dire circumstances he could make light of his handicap.

They climbed the staircase, drawing their daggers when they heard a commotion above them. "He's heading for the roof," Fynn exclaimed.

Hampered by the narrow confines of the stairwell, they hurried as fast as they could to an uneven landing, where a small wooden door stood open. Sweating and out of breath, Ewan suspected Fynn was correct and didn't hold out much hope of finding Lady Jeannie, at least not alive, but he entered the small, windowless chamber nevertheless.

Blankets lay scattered about. The only furniture was a small table and a couple of stools. The stale air in the confined space reeked of human waste, rotten food and rodent droppings, but it was a relief not to discover a corpse. Still, his hackles rose. It was no fit place to imprison a lady.

"She's not here," he said, but suddenly realized he was talking to himself. Fynn was already on his way to the roof.

He tossed away the useless torch, sheathed his weapon and climbed up the remaining steps, heaving himself through the small grate just after his kinsman. Daggers drawn, they scanned the empty battlements, panting hard. "He's up here somewhere," Fynn growled. "The grating had been removed."

Ewan worried there was no sign of David and his men. "We'll check the sentry boxes. Ye go to the right, I'll go…"

"There she is," Fynn yelled, pointing to the parapet on the east side of the tower. "The bastard's going to push her over."

Ewan's heart raced. Wrists bound and mouth gagged, Jeannie perched atop the wall, wedged between two crenellations, her backside out in space.

Ailig was nowhere in sight.

"Wait," Ewan cautioned, but Fynn paid no mind and rushed to save Jeannie. She shook her head vehemently, the wonky eye focused on something out of sight.

Suddenly, Ailig stepped out from a dilapidated sentry box and swooped towards Fynn, prodding his chest with the point of a sword, forcing him to walk backwards to Jeannie. "She'll ne'er belong to a freak," he menaced.

Ewan suspected Morley hadn't seen him in his rush to attack Fynn. He crept forward cautiously, afraid his kinsman and the woman he loved would fall to their deaths before he could reach them.

His heart leaped into his throat when David surged from behind one of the iron chests. Bellowing a war cry, the youth unsheathed his sword and took a mighty upward swipe at Ailig's extended arm.

The evil grin left the wretch's face as his severed hand and the sword flew over the battlements. Shouts of warning followed by a loud gasp rose up from the crowd below.

Fynn lunged, skewering Ailig with his dagger. The brute's eyes crossed as he collapsed to his knees and died in a gurgling heap at Jeannie's dangling feet.

David put up his sword and secured Shona's aunt while Fynn removed the gag and slit the rope binding her hands. She slumped into his embrace, weeping.

Ewan slapped David on the back. "Well done, lad. Ye saved the day."

SUPERFLUOUS

EVERYONE HURRIED TO step away when two missiles came over the parapet; one landed with a clatter, the other with a strange thud. Once it was deemed safe, they surged around, curious to see what had come flying off the tower. Shona wished she'd remained in ignorance when she set eyes on the gory sight.

Her belly roiled; the only good thought filling her mind was that she didn't recognize the dented weapon. She prayed fervently Ewan wasn't the one who'd been maimed, but if the worst had happened she would do everything she could to aid him. After all, Fynn…

A cry from the battlements jolted her from the macabre possibility. "Lady Jeannie is safe."

She looked up, elated to see Ewan waving both arms in the air. "Ailig's dead," he shouted.

Already on his knees, Mungo bent his head to the dirt and wailed.

"Take him to the cells," Kendric ordered. "We'll deal wi' him later."

A resounding cheer rose up from folk who brandished fists as Mungo was hauled to his feet and dragged away by two burly MacCarrons.

Shona hugged Walter and hurried to the stairway before he could prevent her. However, when she lifted the hem of her skirts and peered into the malodorous black hole that led down to the cesspit, she decided patience was sometimes a virtue.

Feeling he'd been superfluous to the outcome of events atop the tower, Ewan offered to carry Jeannie down to safety, but his one-handed kinsman was having none of it. Indeed, Shona's aunt steadfastly refused to loosen her grip from around Fynn's neck.

They used the main stairway, but the descent was still tortuous. David preceded them, a solicitous guide every step of the way.

Jeannie remained silent throughout, and clung to Fynn even when he finally set her upright in the courtyard.

Shona rushed to embrace her aunt, raining tearful kisses on her face and stroking her hair.

"'Twas David saved us all," Fynn declared hoarsely before a broad grin split his dour face. "Fitting ye should cut off his hand, laddie."

The news spread quickly and folk clustered around the red-faced youth, offering congratulations and words of admiration. Moira hung on his arm, beaming with pride. His stammered protestations at being treated like a hero were dismissed.

With help, Jeannie eventually walked to Kendric and bent to kiss his cheek. "I feared never to see ye again, Brother," she murmured. "Ailig murdered Beathan. He boasted of it in the hidden chamber."

The laird gritted his teeth, obviously having difficulty controlling his emotions. "Aye. There'll be a dire punishment for Mungo, I guarantee it."

Standing alone, Ewan watched the tearful reunions, the boisterous congratulations, the back slapping. He supposed he should feel the outsider, yet it pleased him that MacCarron folk were happy for Mackinloch kin as well as for their own.

Shona finally came to embrace him. "Thank ye," she whispered, leaning her head against his shoulder.

He hesitated to put his arms around her. "I dinna smell very wonderful," he said.

She looked up at him and smiled. "Hug me anyway."

He willingly obliged, feeling life return as she pressed her slender body against him. Her warmth chased away the chill of fear he'd felt in the tunnel. "Ye should be thanking David," he said. "I did nothing."

She pulled away and stared at him. "Rubbish," she said. "Ye're the one who provided leadership and gave everyone courage and hope. Ye worked out the clue in the codex and found the way to the secret chamber. Ye're intelligent and brave. What more could a clan ask of its laird?"

SHONA POUTED WHEN Ewan suggested she go to Jeannie's chamber. "I want to stay with ye," she protested. "Fynn has accompanied her there."

"I'd like nothing more," he replied, "but there are matters requiring my attention. Ailig's body, for one. The crows will have a feast if we leave it atop the roof."

She privately thought it a fitting end for the monster, but kept the barbaric opinion to herself. "I suppose ye'll have need of yer kinsman's help."

He put his hands on her waist and gently turned her before patting her derrière. "Aye. Go to yer aunt."

She went reluctantly, knowing he was right. Jeannie would need a woman's shoulder to cry on, but she relived the intimate touch of Ewan's hand on her bottom as she made her way to the hall to first retrieve the codex.

She was surprised to see Moira standing by the head table, staring at the old book, hands fisted in the folds of her skirts. "It willna bite ye," she said with more sarcasm than she intended.

Her maid startled and stepped away from the table. "I was just..."

Shona picked up the heavy tome with both hands. "I'm sorry. It's been a long day. I didna mean to upset ye."

Moira shrugged, but Shona well recognized the feigned indifference the lass often used to hide her true feelings. "Would ye like to learn to read?"

Her maid's frown caused her to think an adamant refusal would be the response, but then doubt crept into her eyes. "I'm nay clever enough."

"Nonsense. Anyone can learn letters. We'll see to it."

Moira's broad smile made her wonder why she hadn't thought of the notion before. Servants who could read would be more useful to the castle and the clan. She handed the book over to her maid, filled with a sense of optimism about changes she and Ewan could bring about. It would be a new era. One in which old feuds were forgotten and life improved for everyone.

IMPORTANT MATTERS

KENDRIC BRANDISHED HIS crutch and chattered loudly as his bearers carried him into the keep. "The day's events seem to have served as a tonic," Ewan said to David and Walter.

"He does loo...loo...look better," the lad agreed.

Gilbertson chuckled. "Kendric is strong. He'll recover, though he still complains of pain in his hip."

Ewan clamped a hand on David's shoulder. "Now, hero of the hour, we have the unsavory task of bringing down Ailig's body."

"That's nay...nay...a job for a laird," his kinsman retorted. "I'll fi...find men to aid me."

Ewan at first thought to insist, but perhaps it was wiser to let the youth take charge of an important, if gruesome duty. "Fine," he replied. "Walter can likely provide names."

Walter nodded. "I suggest we take the body down to the ice vaults. There's likely still a goodly amount of snow hauled from Ben Nevis last winter."

Ewan indicated his agreement. "We also need to clean up the filth in the secret chamber."

"Not much use having a secret chamber now the Mackinlochs are aware of it," Walter quipped with a wink.

Ewan acknowledged the irony. However, as Walter and David quickly organized a group of willing men to carry out the distasteful tasks, he remained convinced a hidden refuge was a good thing to maintain.

He went by way of the hall to retrieve the codex, and assumed

Shona had taken it when he discovered it was no longer atop the head table. She evidently knew where the clan's annals were kept. He looked forward to investigating the history of her clan from the MacCarron point of view. No doubt the accounts of clashes with the Mackinlochs would be very different from those kept in Roigh Hall.

Confident that matters needing immediate attention were in hand, he toyed with the notion of seeking out his bride and wiling away the rest of the afternoon with her. His body heated at the prospect of whispered intimacies.

He shook his head. A laird couldn't always do what he wanted, no matter how great his desire to seek reassurance in the arms of his beloved that he had survived the first major test of his temporary lairdship. His duty was to meet with Kendric to discuss the future of Creag Castle and Clan MacCarron.

STILL CARRYING THE codex, Shona tiptoed into her aunt's chamber, having dispatched Moira to prepare a bath and fresh garments for the evening meal in the hall. Jeannie lay on the bed, seemingly asleep between the sheets. Fynn rose from the chair, a finger pressed to his lips. "Her maid bathed and put her to bed," he whispered. "She didna want to speak of her ordeal."

Shona worried Jeannie couldn't bring herself to reveal the harm Ailig might have inflicted, but Fynn looked like a man reborn now the woman he loved was safe. She didn't want to cast a shadow on his happiness. "I'm glad my aunt found ye," she told him. "Ye're a good man and she deserves happiness."

He clenched his jaw. "I swear I'll take good care of her," he rasped.

Shona nodded. "But now Ewan needs ye. I'll stay here."

He bowed slightly then tiptoed out. She suspected it had been many a year since the proud warrior had bowed to anybody. His respect was humbling. Mayhap she did have the makings of a good laird's wife.

She put the codex down carefully and crept to the bed, surprised to see Jeannie had both eyes open. "Ye're awake."

"I was pretending," she confessed. "Fynn insisted I sleep, but how can a woman sleep when all she can think of is ripping the *mon's* clothes off?"

Shona laughed. "Auntie!"

Jeannie sat up. "My biggest regret when I feared Ailig meant to murder me was that I hadna lain with Fynn. In the way a woman lays with a man, if ye get my drift."

"I get yer drift, right enough," Shona managed to reply, despite the laughter constricting her throat. But then she sobered and took her aunt's hand when the words sank in. "Ye believed he'd kill ye?"

"I was certain of it, especially sitting atop yon tower wi' my arse in the wind."

Jeannie would probably regret these unladylike outbursts. "I think yer fear has got the better of yer tongue," Shona said softly.

Her aunt shook her head. "From now on I plan to say what I like, and take what I want. And I want Fynn Macintyre." She averted her strange eyes. "If he'll have me."

"I'm sure he will. He doesna care if..." She stopped abruptly, ashamed of what she'd been about to imply.

Jeannie snorted. "Dinna fret, pet. Ailig and his weasel of a brother didna have their way wi' me. Ailig takes his pleasure wi' his fists, and I doot Mungo knows what to do wi' a woman, despite his never-ending boasting."

Shona was torn between laughing and crying. "Did he hurt ye?"

Jeannie shrugged. "The bruises will heal."

ON HIS WAY into Kendric's apartments, Ewan collided with a red-faced Cummings.

"Stubborn old man," the physician mumbled.

"I assume ye're referring to the laird," he replied with a grin.

Cummings rolled his eyes. "He willna listen to my advice that he stay in bed. Wants to sit in the chair."

Ewan shrugged, reminded of his own obstinate father. "In my experience with men of his ilk, 'tis a waste of time to argue."

Cummings smiled resignedly. "Aye."

Ewan closed the door behind him, confident there was no longer a need to drop the bar for security.

Kendric beckoned. "Come sit by me," he said. "We've important things to discuss."

Espying nothing else to sit on, Ewan carried a footstool over to the chair and perched on it, hoping it wouldn't give way under his weight. "The date of my marriage to Shona, for one," he said.

Kendric raised an eyebrow. "Weel, that wasna the first thing on my list, but I suppose we must settle the details of the hand-fasting."

Ewan shook his head. "I'm nay interested in hand-fasting. I want her for my forever wife."

Kendric chuckled. "Good, good. I suppose we'll need time to publish the notices, though we sent out messengers with news of the agreement with yer clan sennights ago."

Ewan reckoned Shona would be his in two to three weeks, but the mention of the agreement brought up an unavoidable topic. "We must discuss the payment of the installments yer clan promised to mine."

Kendric squirmed. "That wasna even on my list, but ye can see to that now ye're laird."

Another obstacle out of the way. "What to do with Ailig's body?"

Shona's uncle stared at him. "Is this a long list ye intend to trot out before I can address my concerns, laddie?"

Ewan didn't know how to respond, but Kendric saved him the trouble. "Donald tells me Niall Morley will soon be sufficiently recovered to return to Glen Nevis, though he'll walk with a terrible limp after Ruadh feasted on his leg. Punishment enough, I warrant. He can take Ailig's body back with him."

Satisfied with this solution, Ewan pressed on. "I believe my kinsman will seek permission to wed Lady Jeannie."

Kendric's florid face reddened further. "By heck, o' course. Fynn is a grand lad. Aught else?"

Ewan hesitated to bring up another point. Kendric clearly had something important on his mind. "David and…"

"Aye, another good match, but now I'll have no more delays so we can discuss what's worrying me. Do ye have a plan for the stag yon dog tracked?" He slapped his uninjured thigh. "Who'd have thought Ruadh capable of bringing down such a prize?"

RESPONSIBILITIES

After Jeannie fell asleep, Shona sat in the armchair for a while, leafing through the old codex. It made for interesting reading and increased her resolve to speak to her uncle about ensuring he left a written history of his tenure.

When her aunt's maid came to see if she was needed, Shona left her to watch over Jeannie and the book.

She was anxious for a bath and fresh clothes, but she'd been remiss in not making sure Ruadh had been comfortably settled in the stables after his part in the rescue.

His wagging tail thumped when he caught sight of her. He managed to struggle to all fours for a moment but she knelt beside him and eased him back down onto the straw. "Rest," she urged, rubbing his head. "Ye've earned it."

"He's glad to see ye," remarked one of the lads forking hay.

Ruadh growled contentedly deep in his throat as she stroked his belly, noting the wound was clean and the stitches seemed to be healing. She massaged his jaw for a while—something he always loved—but then became aware of the lengthening shadows. "Time to go," she whispered, kissing his cold, wet nose. "I'll come see ye on the morrow."

He raised his head, dark eyes full of indignation, and whimpered. As she walked towards the door, the whimpering became louder. She turned around. The whining stopped; the tail wagged again.

"He doesna want ye to go," the lad said.

She shook her head. "I ken what he wants. A nice comfortable bed in my chamber."

She considered the stable hand. He wasn't a big youth, but he looked capable. "Can ye carry him indoors?" she asked.

Ewan assured Kendric he knew exactly the person who would happily take care of the stag. He left the chamber and returned to the courtyard, glad to find Fynn there among a group of men gathered around Ailig's body laid out on a litter. Their boisterous laughter intrigued him and he soon understood the reason for the amusement. Fingers gripped tightly around the bloody wrist of the severed hand, a grinning Fynn held it up alongside his own mutilated arm.

It struck Ewan as macabre, but the MacCarrons seemed to find it funny. Another gleeful fellow brandished Ailig's badly dented sword which hadn't fared well from its encounter with the stone courtyard.

A hush fell when they gradually realized he had joined them. Fynn hastily bent to place the hand atop the corpse. The smile disappeared and he became again the sour-faced clansman. Ewan hoped he wouldn't always be seen as a negative presence. "Naught wrong wi' a bit o' fun," he said with a smile. "Especially after a day like today."

The tension eased as men muttered their agreement.

"However," he announced, "The Camron has decided Niall will be allowed to return home and he's to take the body with him. Let's get it down into the vaults."

Men immediately stepped forward to pick up the litter and carry it away, leaving him alone with Fynn. "I'd say Morley wasn't well liked."

"Goes back aways, apparently," his clansman replied. "The Morleys of Glen Nevis have been at feud wi' the MacCarron chiefs on numerous occasions in the past."

Ewan tucked away that bit of clan history. It was essential a laird know who could be depended upon to stick by him through thick and thin. It was gratifying to be sure that Fynn Macintyre would be one such compatriot.

He slapped a hand on his clansman's shoulder. "Now, my friend, Kendric has decided to give ye the special responsibility of aging and roasting the stag Ruadh brought down."

He was suddenly reminded of the day he'd given Andrew the toy sword. He thought the beaming Fynn was going to smother him in an embrace as the bairn had done. "Can ye handle it?" he asked.

"I havna seen it yet. I hope they waited a day afore they butchered it. The meat'll be tough otherwise. I assume they've stored it somewhere cold, but not too cold, mind. Do they have a spence? Of course. Every castle has a larder, although mayhap the MacCarrons…I'll hafta make sure. Can David assist me? Wait!"

He finally took a breath, but resumed his monologue and set off walking at the same time. "Two, mayhap three weeks until it can be roasted, ye ken. I hope The Camron doesna mind waiting. Important not to cook venison until 'tis well-aged, especially a big stag. How big is it?"

Tired of trying to keep pace, Ewan grabbed his arm. "Stop. Do ye even ken where ye're going?"

Fynn frowned and looked at Ewan as if he were the one who'd gone a bit daft. "To find the spence."

"In answer to yer question, The Camron wants the venison served at a wedding…or two. So three weeks works well."

Fynn gaped. "Two weddings?"

Ewan winked. "I assume ye can convince the lovely Lady Jeannie to wed with ye afore then?"

Fynn puffed out his chest. "Aye, laddie, that'll be no trouble at all."

"That's settled then, but leave the larder for the morrow. Time now to bathe and dress for dinner in the hall. 'Tis a night for celebration."

He held the edge of his plaid as close to his nose as he dared. "This is fit for naught but the rubbish heap, and ye dinna smell too sweet yerself."

"I'll remove my things," Fynn said as they entered the guest chamber.

"No need," Ewan replied. "They'll find separate quarters. We'll share until then."

When scullery lads brought kettle after kettle of water for the bath, it was a relief to strip off his soiled garments, though he fretted over the beloved plaid.

His dismay must have been apparent on his face.

"Mayhap the laundresses can salvage it," Fynn suggested, gathering up the discarded clothing. "I'll teck it down to the laundry, and fetch yer belongings from the stable."

Ewan privately thought leaving his and Fynn's raiment for the maidservants to pick up was a more practical idea. However, he did need his second plaid. His kinsman seemed to prefer absenting himself while his lord bathed, so he said nothing as the man left.

He sauntered into the *boudoir* where he found a cake of Castile soap. Inhaling the aroma of the unexpected luxury, he stepped into the wooden tub, content to discover the water was still pleasantly warm. He lay on his back and ducked his head, which necessitated bending his knees in the too-small tub. Resurfacing, he rubbed the soap in his hair, wishing Shona's long fingers were massaging his scalp, then ducked down again and rinsed off the lather.

He lay back in the tub and lazily trailed the soap over his chest and belly. The pleasing notion of his betrothed's hands on his manhood produced the predictable result as he cleansed the intimate parts of his body. He chuckled at the memory of Fynn's consternation when he'd come upon him easing his needs. Perhaps it was as well the man had left.

He heard the outer door open and close as he was getting out of the tub. Assuming it was Fynn, he grabbed a drying cloth, started rubbing his hair and walked into the chamber.

He resisted the temptation to cover his obvious arousal with the towel when he almost walked into Walter.

Gilbertson's reaction wasn't what he might have expected. There was no embarrassment in his undisguised assessment of Ewan's body.

"Yer pardon, my laird," he said, without a hint of subservience. "I knocked but there was no answer. I took the liberty of bringing this."

Ewan's gut clenched. A MacCarron plaid? It went against every instinct.

Walter nodded to Ewan's groin. "'Tis clear ye'll make a fine husband for our Shona as far as yer bodily endowments are concerned, and ye've proven yerself a courageous leader this day, but if the feud is ever to truly end…"

The frank exchange should have been fraught with tension and uncertainty, yet in that moment Ewan recognized Walter as a true friend, a man he could count on to give him honest advice. He reached for the plaid and draped it over his shoulder. "How do I look?"

Walter grinned. "Like a Mackinloch pretending to be a MacCarron."

Ewan threw the wet towel. Still smiling, Walter caught it handily. Colin had never been one to indulge in horseplay, but suddenly Ewan had a brother and it was a heady feeling.

"I'll wear it on one condition," he said. "It'll be pinned with the Mackinloch clan brooch."

"Fair enough."

FEELING REFRESHED AFTER Moira helped her bathe and dress, Shona patted Ruadh's head. "Ye're spoiled, dog, but I dinna care if it helps ye heal faster."

The hound woofed his agreement without bothering to raise his head from the mattress and seemed not to mind at all when she and her maid exited the chamber.

To her surprise, Jeannie met them in the hallway. There were faint bruises on her aunt's cheekbones she hadn't noticed before. "Ye should still be in bed," she cautioned.

Her aunt linked her arm. "I nearly died this day, Shona. I dinna intend to spend my life in bed." She winked the good eye. "Unless o' course I'm with…"

Moira's cheeks flushed and she hurried ahead.

Shona held up a hand. "Enough. I get the message. Ye are in lust with Fynn Macintyre."

Jeannie squeezed her arm. "Aye. Do ye think he'll ask me to marry him? Mayhap we can be wed the same day? He's perhaps a confirmed bachelor. Even if he doesna ask me, I'll willingly be his leman."

Shona called a halt and put her hands on her aunt's shoulders. "Of course he'll ask ye to be his wife. He's an honorable man, like Ewan."

"And ye're sure ye love this Mackinloch?"

"With all my heart," she replied, knowing it to be true.

They resumed their walk along the same hallways where fear had held sway just hours earlier. "'Tis wonderful to have our home back to normal," she said.

"Aye," her maid sighed in reply.

She'd thought Moira too far ahead of them to hear and hoped she hadn't heard Jeannie's remark about becoming Fynn's leman. It wouldn't do for servants to gossip about such things.

When they entered the hall, Moira bobbed a curtsey and went off to sit at a servants' table.

Shona was startled when everyone in the hall got to their feet and cheered. The show of love and respect was a vindication. They were letting her know they believed Mungo Morley had lied. She inhaled deeply as a weight lifted from her shoulders—one she'd carried since her father's death. It hadn't dawned on her before that the clan also bore the burden of uncertainty surrounding his fall from the tower, but they knew the truth now—Beathan MacCarron had been murdered and they could grieve his loss appropriately.

They cheered for Jeannie too, and she waved her thanks, looking younger than she had for years. The lingering fear of Ailig had been taken away.

Shona was surprised to see her uncle seated at the head table, though he looked pale and tired, and not very comfortable with one leg still completely encased in a cast. She thought to scold him as she and Jeannie took their places at the head table but her aunt touched her arm. "He wants to be here," she whispered. "'Tis his right to celebrate with the clan."

As folk regained their seats at the benches, the chatter gradually resumed, but many besides Shona kept turning to the entryway, including Jeannie and Moira. Expectancy hung in the air.

Her uncle enveloped her hand in his big paw. "He'll come," he assured her.

Impatience to see Ewan again was evidently written on her face. Small wonder with so many intense longings coursing through her body. A hush fell over the crowd when he and his kinsmen finally appeared. They hesitated only a moment before Ewan strode to the head table.

Shona's heart raced as a fever swept over her body. Mayhap she'd fallen foul of some noxious disease lingering in the musty library. Her fellow clansmen and women were evidently as gobsmacked as she was. It took them a moment but soon benches scraped on stone as they stood and cheered loudly. The son of the laird of a clan they'd been at war with for generations, marched through the hall of their stronghold wearing a MacCarron plaid.

Almost dizzy with happiness, Shona risked a glance at her uncle, the only person still seated. Fists clenched atop the ancient table, he smiled broadly, his eyes moist.

The cheers grew to a crescendo when Kendric beckoned Ewan to the head table and he took his place next to Shona.

"Thank ye," she whispered hoarsely, aware of the cost to his pride of wearing her clan's plaid.

He took her hand. "I suppose I'll get used to it," he replied with a wry grin, nodding to acknowledge the applause.

Curious stares greeted Kendric's next gesture. He beckoned Fynn to take his place beside Jeannie. When Macintyre obeyed and took his lady's hand, it gradually dawned on the crowd what was happening. The cheering began again, accompanied this time by the banging of tankards on tables. It was clear Fynn was held in high esteem, which would certainly make life easier for Ewan. The most important thing though was the glow of happiness that lit her aunt's face.

Kendric held up a hand and the din slowly subsided. "I have one more happy announcement," he declared. "It seems Lady Shona's maid and Laird Ewan's kinsman intend to wed."

All eyes sought the pair, who both blushed deeply. Shona worried David might not yet have asked for Moira's hand, but he grinned, swept Moira into his embrace and kissed her lustily. She entwined her arms around his neck and kissed him back with equal fervor. The rafters echoed with the cheering and whistling that ensued.

MARKING TIME

I N THE DAYS that followed, Ewan spent countless hours in meetings with Kendric and the clan elders, but Shona was never far from his thoughts. He enjoyed sharing an account of the deliberations with her on the rare occasions they had time to themselves. They'd agreed it would be deemed inappropriate to meet alone in their private apartments, so a quiet corner by the window of the sickroom became their trysting place. They sat in separate chairs until they were sure her uncle was asleep, then she moved to sit on his lap.

The warmth of her lovely bottom pressed to his arousal was sweet torture, but it was better than no contact at all. It seemed like the day of their wedding would never arrive.

"Yer uncle is a more reasonable man than my father," he admitted in a whisper, but acknowledged privately that was perhaps just the way of the world. Kendric's ready acceptance of many of his ideas for the future of Clan MacCarron caused him to wonder. Had Duncan Mackinloch deliberately rejected some of his suggestions because he was afraid his second son might plot to usurp Colin's right to succeed as laird?

While Ewan hadn't seen eye to eye with Colin and knew in his heart he'd make a better leader, he would never have challenged his brother's birthright.

"We settled on preliminary plans for the improvement of defenses and the refurbishment of the hidden chamber," he told his betrothed. She laughed when he mentioned discussion on both topics was liberally sprinkled with good-natured jests about the diminished threat of the Mackinlochs. Her genuine amusement warmed his heart and caused him to realize Kathleen's tittering seemed false in comparison. Shona enjoyed his company, and they shared a similar sense of humor. Gratifying, too, was her interest in matters concerning the future wellbeing of the clan, and she wasn't shy about offering suggestions.

"Tempers frayed during discussions regarding raising money to pay the agreed-upon installments for the purchase of Loch Alkayg," he conceded.

His frustration ebbed when she replied, "Is there a Highlander anywhere who doesna balk at the prospect of spending coin?"

She grimaced at the news they'd discussed improving all the castle's cesspits after it came to light the entire drainage system hadn't been cleaned in living memory.

In an obvious effort to change the subject she asked, "Did ye remember to bring up the library?"

He nodded. "The elders looked at me curiously when I spoke of it. It was clear some had never set foot in the place and others admitted they didn't know of its existence."

She rolled her eyes. "I'm nay surprised. It's a well-kept secret."

"Weel, they ken about it now. Kendric mumbled a promise to be more conscientious about recording recent events."

She lowered her voice. "Ye should have pointed out he has time at his disposal now he's lying injured."

All in all, he was pleased with the way the Clan Council supported him taking Kendric's place until he recovered. Mayhap when the older man passed on, the clan might consider naming him The Camron.

He chuckled at his own folly. As if the MacCarrons would choose a Mackinloch.

RUADH LOVED A lazy life, yet he soon insisted on hobbling about on unsteady legs. Shona worried he might loosen his stitches, but the ostler assured her he'd be fine. In his opinion, exercise was good. She laughed when the dog gave the old man a baleful look, as if he'd understood the word *exercise*.

She appreciated his company when she went for a walk in the kitchen gardens.

Ewan was involved in many discussions with Kendric and other clan elders and she deemed it a good omen for the future that he shared his impressions of the meetings with her. He respected her. It never occurred to most of her fellow clansmen that a woman might have worthwhile opinions.

Rumor had it Ewan, Fynn and David were spending many hours watching over the aging of the deer meat and assembling the ingredients and equipment needed for the cooking.

"It sometimes seems the three bridegrooms are more interested in the food to be served at the banquet than in the ceremony itself," Jeannie complained one day as she watched the seamstresses working on yet another fitting for Shona's wedding gown. "Mackinlochs must think the MacCarrons have never roasted a deer before."

They fell into the habit of taking turns with dress fittings. As soon as the lasses were satisfied with the progress on one gown, they moved across the hall to the next fitting, Ruadh dawdling behind.

Kendric declared it was more appropriate the maid's marriage to David take place the day before Shona's wedding. "Her family will want to be in charge of those festivities," he pointed out. "It's their right."

Moira was openly relieved by the decision.

The laird's health improved. Cummings cut away the top part of his cast and he was able to walk a few steps each day with the aid of crutches tucked under both armpits. He didn't conceal his frustration with the crutches, but conceded they were a necessary evil. He still complained of pain in the hip and the physician acknowledged it might never go away. "*Fyking* Morleys," Kendric often muttered. "I suppose we'll have to convene a trial for Mungo soon."

Shona suspected he was delaying the inevitable until he could preside without anger getting the better of him. She toyed with the notion of suggesting Ewan act in his stead, but her betrothed wasn't exactly impartial when it came to Mungo Morley. Still, she felt the matter should be resolved before her wedding. She didn't want to be worried about it during the festivities, but was reluctant to raise the issue with her future husband.

Donald assigned servants to clean every nook and cranny of the hall. Banners were taken down, aired and repaired when necessary. Boys crawled along rafters on hands and knees sweeping away cobwebs. Hunting trophies, shields, swords, tapestries: all were removed, cleaned and put back in place. The hearth and chimney were scrubbed and pumiced. Ivy was ripped from the castle walls and festooned from the rafters.

The laundresses worked overtime. Apparently, every MacCarron wished to wear clean garments to the nuptials.

Extra scullery workers were hired on from the village and Cook had them scrubbing every dish, pot, utensil and plate. Jeannie remarked that the man seemed relieved not to have to worry about the venison.

All this feverish preparation for her wedding thrilled Shona. She thought the day would never arrive. The memory of the intense sensations Ewan's touch evoked was never far from her thoughts. His promise there were more delights in store haunted her dreams. Still, deep in her heart, a worry gnawed that she had no notion of how to be a good wife. She prayed her betrothed was a patient man.

EWAN ENJOYED PARTICIPATING in the preparation of the stag. He'd never taken much interest in such things before and discovered Fynn was an endless source of lore regarding the aging and roasting of venison.

Even the spencer seemed impressed by his insistence on keeping the larder neither too cold nor not cold enough. Ewan deemed it overzealous to check the degree of coldness several times a day, but wasn't about to argue with the expert.

Cook deferred to his judgement as to which parts of the deer he might use for pies and stews and grudgingly contributed a goodly amount of costly allspice.

David hung on Fynn's every word and made it his mission to track down some of the more elusive ingredients his kinsman required. His elation was evident when he returned from finally unearthing a store of juniper berries in the castle's undercroft. Cummings insisted on holding back part of the supply for medicinal purposes and warned William the Butler would be livid at the loss of fodder for his still. Though it was hard to believe, some clansmen apparently preferred gin to whisky.

On the journey from Roigh, Ewan had been afraid David and Fynn might end up coming to blows, and was pleased to see the camaraderie developing between them.

The stag also kept the men busy and out of the way of their womenfolk.

Every clan member was agog with news of the grand preparations for the roasting, pie making, boiling and stewing, slated for the day before the wedding.

That was also the day of David's marriage to Moira, scheduled early in the morning so he could spend the afternoon assisting with the *great work*.

UPS AND DOWNS

Upon hearing of Niall's departure with Ailig's remains, Kendric finally appointed a panel of three elders to decide Mungo's fate. "More humane to get it o'er wi'," he muttered, "now he's said his goodbyes."

A worm wriggled in Ewan's belly. "Goodbyes?"

"Aye. Mungo asked for a last chance to pay his respects to his brother before the body was returned to Glen Nevis, so I sent word for it to be taken to his cell."

Ewan hesitated to let his annoyance show. Surely it was for him to decide if Mungo's request be granted or not. "I'd have thought the cadaver would be frozen."

"Weel," Kendric replied, "Mungo didna care about that since he'll ne'er see his brother again. We may not understand why, but he loved Ailig. I deemed it the right thing to do. And in any case 'tis chilly in the cells too."

A macabre vision of Mungo bidding farewell to a thawing corpse made Ewan shudder, but there wasn't much he could do about it now. "Can we at least hold the trial in the Chart Room in order to spare Shona the further stress of a public spectacle?"

Kendric agreed wholeheartedly, and summoned the judges to gather with Ewan as his representative. They convened quickly and dispatched guards to fetch the prisoner.

Ewan shared Shona's relief that judgement would be rendered before the ceremony, but he drummed his fingers on the table while he waited. He would not be part of the deliberations, but his gut twisted at the prospect of once again setting eyes on the wretch who'd caused his bride too much pain and sorrow.

David's wedding was to take place in two hours, and Fynn already had most of the chunks of deer meat skewered on a spit. Stews were simmering in the kitchens and Cook had pies in the ovens.

"Shouldn't take but an hour to reach a verdict," Ewan muttered, annoyed he'd spoken at all. He couldn't be seen to be interfering.

They'd been waiting too long when one of the grim-faced greybeards remarked, "I didna think the cells were so far distant."

No sooner had he spoken than the guards appeared at the open door. It was clear from their hesitant posture neither wanted to be the first to cross the threshold. Ewan clenched his fists and glared. "Weel?"

One pushed his comrade inside. Bile rose in Ewan's throat when the man held up Ailig's severed hand. "Mungo isna in the cells," he rasped, his gaze fixed on the mutilated limb. "We reckon…"

Ewan leapt out of his chair, unable to contain the anger boiling in his belly. "He's not in the cells because he's ridden to freedom strapped to the back of a donkey."

"Aye," came the whispered reply. "'Twould appear so."

The three scowling elders came to their feet. "He changed places with his brother?" one asked.

"Aye. Ailig's body is still in the cell. It was covered by a blanket, and when Mungo didna waken for his meal last night…"

"The jailers assumed he was asleep," Ewan roared, shoving his way past the two men wedged in the doorway.

"Nay," came the rejoinder. "They thought he was grieving."

Ewan snorted his disbelief and hurried to the cells, the three judges trailing behind. It appeared others in the castle had heard the news and soon Fynn and David joined the procession. Clad in a bloodstained leather apron borrowed from the cook who was three times his girth, Fynn's scowl showed his indignation at being torn way from his labor of love. David's hair and beard had been trimmed and he wore his best plaid.

"I canna believe this," Ewan told his kinsmen. "It seems the jailers helped carry out the *body* and strap it to the donkey."

"Mun…Mun…Mungo's tw…tw..twice the size of Ai…Ailig," David said.

"Probably too drunk to ken what they were doing," Fynn replied. "Mayhap they're the gin-drinking idiots."

"Remind me to recruit new men for the job," Ewan shouted as he reached the bottom of the steep steps leading down to the cells.

He was actually relieved the guards responsible for the fiasco had disappeared. He was afraid his fury might have gotten the better of him. Prisons never smelled wholesome but here the stench of death was unmistakable. "Find them right quick and tell them they'd best dig a grave for this stinking corpse now," he growled. "Hand and all."

He gritted his teeth and leaned his palm against the damp wall. "We must hunt Mungo down."

Fynn scratched his grey stubble. "Our David is getting wed this day, and me and thee on the morrow. We dinna ken where they've gone. It could take days. And then there's the deer."

Ewan gritted his teeth. "Aye," he rasped, dreading the prospect of telling Shona her abductor was on the loose again. Postponing the weddings was out of the question, as was expecting Fynn to abandon his mission.

"*Fyking* Morleys," he mumbled, sounding too much like Kendric for his liking.

SHONA TURNED HER head this way and that in front of the mirror, trying to see if Isobel had tucked the butterfly hairpins into her braided hair correctly. She considered it a good omen that Ewan had recovered the one she'd lost in the cave, otherwise the set would be incomplete.

"I hope ye like the way I've done it," the lass whispered politely. "'Tis my ambition to be a lady's maid, but I havna had much practice, so I appreciate Cousin Moira recommending me, my lady."

The child's face reddened considerably as she rambled on. Shona sought to put her at ease. "Looks wonderful. How old are ye?"

"Fourteen," Isobel replied.

"Weel, I'm glad of yer help while Moira's staying at her parents' cottage, and, of course, she'll be gone for a few days after her wedding."

Isobel steadied her new mistress by the elbow as she slipped on her shoes. "'Tis generous of ye to allow her the time. I've heard some clans dinna give their servants any holidays."

Shona smiled, unsure of how to reply. She hadn't thought twice about allowing Moira time to enjoy her new status. "Mayhap yer cousin can take ye under her wing. She'll need yer help when she falls pregnant."

A grin split Isobel's face. "I thank ye, my lady, and ye'll soon require more maids yerself when the bairns arrive."

A thrill of excitement surged up Shona's spine. She'd been preoccupied with the notion of being a wife and hadn't given much thought to the prospect of soon becoming a mother. Jeannie was the only mother she'd known, but her aunt had set a loving example.

She was impatient for her betrothed to arrive soon to escort her to the chapel, but when the rap on the door came, it sounded too urgent and insistent to be him.

Isobel opened the door. The hesitant scowl on Ewan's face caused Shona's heart to lurch. "What's wrong?"

He took hold of her hands and looked into her eyes. "Forgive me. Mungo has escaped."

She swayed, glad of his strength when he steadied her in his embrace. "Escaped?" she parroted.

Even after he explained what had happened she didn't believe it. "How could they be so stupid?"

"Aye," Isobel whispered, wiping away tears.

Despite her own turmoil, it occurred to Shona the lass had a caring heart that would stand her in good stead.

Ewan inhaled deeply. "Walter is already in pursuit. I swear we'll track him down, but for today we've a wedding to attend."

She nodded, forcing a smile. "Aye. We canna let this setback interfere with David and Moira's special day."

Ewan kissed her knuckles. "Ye're a brave lass, Shona MacCarron. Are ye ready?"

Leaning heavily on his arm, she allowed him to escort her to the chapel, determined not to give another thought to Mungo Morley.

Moira's family and friends were already in attendance. They bowed and curtseyed respectfully when she and Ewan entered, followed by Jeannie and her escort—Kendric hobbling on crutches supported by Donald and a servant.

Shona took a moment to offer her congratulations to the bride's mother. "I'm confident they'll be very happy."

Arms folded across her expansive bosom, Mrs. Macgill raked a critical gaze over Ewan and complained, "He's one o' this lad's lot."

Shona was tempted to laugh when her beloved replied politely, "Nevertheless, he's a good man."

"Aye," the woman conceded, turning away to greet Kendric and Jeannie.

Ewan grinned and whispered, "Notice she has no problem with the stammer, just his clan."

He walked over to shake hands with the groom who stood near the altar, Fynn by his side. It was difficult to tell which of the two looked more nervous.

"Moira's father has been generous," Shona whispered to her betrothed when they had taken their seats. "He's given David a tocher of a dozen sheep and several acres of his holding."

It occurred to her as she spoke she hadn't wondered about her own dowry; surely her father had left some provision? However, Ewan seem more worried about David becoming a farmer. "We'll have to work that out. I never thought I'd say this but I still need him close. He's loyal to a fault."

It was a reminder that the road ahead might not always be smooth. Current events had endeared Ewan to her clan, but old hatreds could simmer for years. On the morrow she was to wed a man who would need every smidgen of the love and loyalty she had to give. It was an awesome responsibility, but the alchemy between them reassured her.

She watched Moira enter the small chapel on her father's arm. The simple blue linen frock suited her maid and Shona knew only too well the look of love radiating from her smiling face. She squeezed Ewan's arm. He covered her hand with his and whispered, "Not long now, Shona MacCarron."

The promise in his husky voice confirmed she'd found the right mate.

THE PRESS OF Shona's tempting breasts against Ewan's bicep was arousing in its innocence. He closed his eyes and listened to David make promises to Moira, pondering what he would say to his bride on the morrow.

Not in the chapel—the Kirk required adherence to the wording of its liturgy, and he fully intended to honor those vows.

He also looked forward to whispering sweet nothings at the banquet.

However, the emotions filling his heart would have to wait for the privacy of their bridal chamber. Then he'd be free to offer up his soul to the woman he loved.

Immersed in his reverie, he didn't notice the ceremony had ended until Shona nudged him. "I hope ye willna fall asleep on the morrow."

A blur of blue rustled by as a broadly-smiling David escorted his bride out to the hall. Ewan helped Shona rise. "I was dreaming of our union," he said softly.

She smiled then faltered slightly, evidently understanding his deliberate *double entendre*. He caught the unmistakable aroma of a woman aroused when she swayed against him. The memory of her response to his touch remained fresh. "Aye, Shona lass, I plan to make all yer dreams come true."

COOK DISHED UP venison pie at the luncheon, but no one expected the choicer pieces of meat to be served. Many of the guests contributed food and drink in the time-honored tradition of the penny wedding.

Wrapped up in wanton thoughts of Ewan's promises, Shona had no appetite. Jeannie finished off her leftovers.

Fynn and David were anxious to return to the kitchens, but stayed to watch the brides-cake ceremony. Everyone cheered and congratulated the groom when the seed-cake broken over Moira's head crumbled to pieces.

David looked puzzled, as did Ewan.

Shona explained. "It's our tradition. If it breaks into many pieces they'll have a happy marriage with a home full of healthy bairns."

"Weel," he shrugged, "I dinna need a cake to tell me it'll be the same for us."

When she arched a quizzical brow he took hold of her hand under the table and pressed her fingertips to his hard maleness. "See," he whispered, grinning wickedly.

Suddenly, they were the only two people in the hall. No other voice penetrated her hearing. His clean masculine scent filled her nostrils. The heat from his body made her skin tingle.

The rest of the celebration passed in a blur and, before she knew it, she was back in her chamber and Ewan was kissing her goodbye. "Get some rest," he crooned, "I'm off to see if there's any news of Morley. Keep the door barred until I return."

Isobel rushed in as he was leaving. She bobbed a curtsey then hurried to help Shona remove her shoes. "'Twas a lovely wedding," she sighed. "I hope I find a good man like David."

Shona sensed a little too much fondness for her cousin's new husband in the maid's words, but then young lasses tended to become infatuated with handsome swains. "Aye," she replied, trying to put a stern edge on her reply, "off ye go and keep Moira company while David's busy."

She dropped the bar after Isobel left, and curled up with Ruadh, trying to recall events after Ewan's brazen gesture.

She may have nodded sympathetically when Jeannie complained at Fynn's early departure. She must have uttered her agreement when Moira's mother nagged about roasting a stag being more important to her son-by-marriage than staying with her daughter. She had a vague memory of wiping pie crumbs off her uncle's beard before he was carried back to his apartments.

She yawned and closed her eyes, hoping she'd at least thought to embrace Moira and offer her congratulations.

OFF HIS HEAD

EWAN CAME CLOSE to colliding with Donald at the door of the keep.

"I was on my way to find ye," the elderly steward panted. "Walter's back."

The news came as a surprise and raised his hopes. "Already? With Morley?"

Donald shook his head. "Only Niall. Hands tied to the pommel of a donkey. Looks done in. Just now arrived in the bailey."

Ewan hurried out, wondering if Mungo was dead, but the grim look on Walter's face quickly dispelled that notion. "Where did ye find him?" he asked.

Gilbertson dismounted. "Not far distant. Tied to a tree." He poked Niall's arm. "I'll let him tell the tale."

When the bleary-eyed wretch looked up, Ewan saw that his nose was badly broken, his swollen face smeared with blood. He frowned at Walter who shook his head. "Not my doing."

"The *mon's* a lunatic," Niall rasped.

"Mungo did this to ye?" Ewan asked.

"After we made good our escape, he blathered on and on about taking Ailig's body with us."

"The ruse wouldna have worked then," Ewan said.

Walter cut the rope binding Niall to the pommel and slid him from the donkey. Off balance, Morley touched the back of his hand to his nose and winced. "I said as much, but he whined on and on, insisting we had to come back. So I told him he'd have to return alone."

Ewan had an inkling what was coming next. "He wanted the horse."

Niall coughed and spat out blood. "Aye, and when I refused, he attacked me like a wild thing, punched me in the nose and tied me to a tree with the same rope we used to secure him to the donkey. He's my kinsman but he's nay right in the head. I regret the day I chose to follow him. He's nay the *mon* his father was."

Ewan almost felt sorry for the wretch. "Weel, my friend, many's the Highlander who's followed the wrong path because a kinsman demanded it of him."

Walter seized Niall's shoulder and pushed him into the arms of two of his men. "Take him to the infirmary."

Gooseflesh marched across Ewan's nape as he watched the warriors hoist Niall under the armpits and drag him away. While everyone had been distracted by the wedding, Mungo had probably infiltrated the castle. "Morley may already have discovered Ailig's body is no longer in the cells. Question is, where is he now?"

A LOUD BANGING on the door jolted Shona and Ruadh awake. Her heart calmed. It was Ewan's voice demanding entry. She patted the hound's head when he tried to get up. "Lie down, it's all right, though it doesna sound like there's news of Mungo."

She lifted the bar and opened the door, startled anew when Ewan gathered her into his embrace and leaned his forehead against hers.

"I had to make sure ye were safe," he growled. "Mungo is here."

A chill raced across her nape. "In the castle?"

"He's gone completely daft. Tied Niall to a tree and came back for Ailig's body."

She struggled to understand. "But…"

Ewan tightened his grip around her. "Aye. It's been buried, though I dinna ken where. Might even have been thrown in the cesspit."

It was no surprise he wasn't aware of the clan's burial ground. The

MacCarrons preferred the Mackinlochs not get wind of the location close to disputed territory. "Likely in the communal grave in the cemetery near Loch Alkayg," she revealed. "But if he finds out, what will he do?"

"No telling with a lunatic."

Shona shivered as a horrible memory assailed her. "I suspected he was mad when we were in the ruined church."

Alarm clogged her throat when hurried footsteps sounded in the corridor. Ewan drew his dagger and turned to protect her, sheathing the weapon when Moira and Isobel rushed into the chamber, clinging to each other. Red-cheeked and panting hard, both lasses looked like they'd run a considerable distance. Moira's lovely blue wedding frock was disheveled, the hem torn and dirty. Grey smudges had replaced the happy glow on the new bride's face.

"The village," Isobel sputtered hoarsely. "Fire."

EWAN STALKED TO the window, alarmed to see smoke billowing outside the gates. "This is Mungo's handiwork. Two, possibly three cottages alight."

Shona shouldered her way to stand beside him and gasped. "Oh no, looks like Walter's might be one of them."

"Aye," Moira confirmed, "we were on our way back to Mam's when we espied the smoke. We raised the alarm in the bailey. There's men on the way with buckets."

"Stay here, all of ye," he ordered, heading for the door.

"Nay," Shona exclaimed. "Members of the clan might be hurt. It's my responsibility to be there. We'll go by the Still Room and fetch salves and supplies."

"I'll come with ye. Where is yer aunt?"

"I dinna ken. Mayhap with Uncle Kendric."

As he was crossing the hallway, Jeannie came out of Kendric's chamber, her eyes wide. "Fire," she exclaimed.

"Aye," he confirmed. "We think Mungo set it. Stay here with the door barred."

"Morley's here?" she asked.

"No time to explain," he replied.

She nodded and returned to the chamber.

Confident she was safe, Ewan beckoned the women and led the way to the Still Room where they quickly gathered what they needed. It irked that he was playing nursemaid when he should have been fighting the fire, but leaving Shona alone was out of the question.

They hurried out of the castle and down the hill. A grim-faced Donald came to meet them. "The flames are mostly out," he said hoarsely.

Ewan surveyed the scene. Women and whimpering bairns huddled together, their faces pale and drawn. Shona and her maids hurried to offer help. Men with smoke-blackened faces and torsos tossed water on smoldering piles of rubble, but the chain of clansmen who'd formed a bucket brigade was breaking up, Fynn and David among them. He saluted his recognition of their help. He heard no weeping and wailing, which he took as a good omen. Cottages could be rebuilt. Lives lost were another thing entirely. "Damage?" he asked.

"Two homes partly destroyed. The thatched roof has collapsed on the third. Walter's. Appears to have started there."

He scanned the area for Gilbertson, perturbed when he saw Shona running towards him. "Come quickly," she shouted. "Walter's going mad, trying to get inside his cottage. He canna find Robbie."

Ewan headed in the direction of the commotion, his heart bleeding for the man who'd become a staunch friend and ally. To lose a son…

Bellowing Robbie's name, Walter struggled with several villagers trying to restrain him near the doorway of the smoldering ruin.

A lass Ewan assumed was Walter's wife knelt on the ground, weeping, her face buried in her hands. Shona caught up and knelt beside her, pulling the distraught woman into her embrace. She looked up at Ewan, green eyes brimming with tears.

He stood nose to nose with Walter. "Ye canna go in there."

Gilbertson gritted his teeth. "My son is buried 'neath the roof."

Ewan glanced inside the ruin. The thatch was gone but heavy beams still hung precariously. "And if I let ye go in and ye dinna come out, what will become o' yer wife?"

"Wal...ter," the woman wailed.

Glowering, Gilbertson shrugged off his neighbors and knelt to console his distraught spouse. Taking advantage of the distraction, Ewan squared his shoulders and entered the smoke-filled ruin, turning a deaf ear to Shona's shriek of protest.

SHONA'S INSTINCT WAS to follow Ewan. But she had a duty to comfort Walter's wife in this time of dire uncertainty, just as Ewan had answered the call to save Robbie. She loved him for it, but what was he thinking?

For long minutes, there was no sound except the shouts of men extinguishing the last of the flames and women consoling frightened bairns. Then, suddenly, timbers crashed and smoke billowed from the doorway. Shona feared the worst, but Ewan's shout calmed the snake writhing in her belly. "I'm all right," he yelled. "Just a beam."

He emerged a short time later, dirty, coughing and bleary-eyed, but without Robbie. Jaw clenched, Walter tried to push past Ewan. "I thank ye, but I'll find him."

Ewan blocked his progress. "Are ye sure he was at home? There's no trace of him inside."

Walter looked to his wife.

Heather clenched her fists in her lap, avoiding her husband's gaze. "I left for a little while. Just to go for water. I stopped to chat with Kirsti. He was playing...I thought..."

"He was outside?" Ewan asked.

Heather nodded.

"Then where the *fyke* is he now?" Walter thundered.

A shout from Fynn drew everyone's attention as he approached with two men. Shona thought she recognized them, but they were filthy, and her nose soon let her know they were the workers who'd begun cleaning out the cesspits.

Evidently aware of their stench, Fynn bade them halt while he came close. "I was on my way back to the kitchens to see about the stag when I ran into these men. They encountered Mungo as they were coming up the steps from the cesspit."

Ewan drew his dagger. "He's gone up to the secret chamber."

"But why?" Shona wondered. "He'll be trapped."

Fynn shifted his weight, looking uneasy. "He'd a boy with him. He told them he'll exchange the lad for Ailig's body."

"He's a dead man," Walter hissed, as he and Ewan started back towards the castle.

All heads turned to the tower. Shona gasped at the sight of the red-haired giant standing on the roof, waving like a conquering hero. "He truly is mad," she murmured, narrowing her eyes at something Mungo had lowered over the side of the tower. "What's he got hanging…"

The words died in her throat as Heather scrambled to her feet and set off at a run. "Robbeeeee!" she screamed.

ARE YE DEAF?

EWAN AND WALTER halted at the foot of the tower where a small crowd had gathered, everyone craning their necks to see the boy dangling helplessly from the top. Many gasped, covering their mouths as Mungo reached for the rope with both hands and set Robbie swinging.

Women hurried to console Heather when she arrived, Shona not far behind.

"Be brave, son," Walter yelled.

Robbie looked down and nodded, but didn't cry out.

"Canny lad," Ewan remarked, wracking his brain for a strategy that would save the bairn's life. "Mungo's got both hands free. He must have the rope tied to something."

"And looped around my son's chest," Walter replied through gritted teeth. "But he'll slash it if we rush him."

"Nay, nay," Heather sobbed.

Walter embraced his wife. "Robbie's smart. I've told him often enough to always keep his wits about him, and he will."

He regained his place beside Ewan when Fynn and David arrived, laden with blankets. "We can make a softer landing if he drops," Fynn suggested. "We'll need men with two good hands," he added with a wry grin.

Several volunteers eagerly sorted the biggest and best, and stretched it out below the dangling boy.

Mungo pointed his dagger at Robbie. "I'll cut his throat if I dinna see my brother's body right soon."

The men holding the blanket looked to Ewan for instruction. He waved them to stand to the side as an idea struck him. He cupped a hand behind his ear. "What did ye say?" he said to Mungo in a normal voice.

A man behind him started to speak. "He said…"

Ewan swung round and glared. "I ken what he said. I want him to think I didna hear him."

Folk nodded as the plan dawned on them.

He turned back to the tower. "I canna hear ye," he mouthed, careful to make no sound.

"Are ye deaf? I want Ailig's body," Morley bellowed.

Keeping his eyes on Mungo, Ewan spoke to the crowd. "Shrug as if ye canna make out what he's saying."

"They're playing their parts well," Walter told him a few seconds later.

Ewan cupped his hands to his mouth. "Ye're too high up," he said softly.

Mungo copied his gesture. "I canna hear a word," he yelled.

"He's losing his temper," Shona warned, coming to stand by Ewan.

"I want his attention off Robbie," he explained. "I need to convince him to let me get up there to parlay."

Tears welled. She didn't want him to go, but the resignation in her eyes told him she knew he must.

He turned to Walter. "Is yer lad strong enough to climb up the rope?"

A glimmer of understanding flickered in Gilbertson's eyes. "Aye."

Ewan shrugged and pointed to himself, then skyward. "Hopefully he'll allow me to the top."

"Nay," Mungo bellowed, pressing the blade to the rope. "Ye're not coming up unless ye bring what I want."

Shona leaned close to Ewan's ear. "On the one hand he's not as daft as we think. On the other, how does he plan to escape with a corpse if ye take it up into the tower?"

He slapped his palm against his forehead. "He hasna thought that far ahead, but ye've given me an idea. We need a body."

Shona wasn't the only one who at first didn't understand what Ewan meant, but David stepped forward right away. "I...I...I'll do it."

Moira gasped and leaned into her mistress. "Has he nay done enough already?" she murmured with a sniffle. "We're newly wed this day."

Conflicting emotions swirled in Shona's heart. Her maid deserved happiness, but Robbie…

Fynn came to the rescue. "Better a one-handed man play the role, lest he demand proof. I came to Creag pretending to be a laird, surely I can be a convincing corpse."

Even Walter smiled at the grim humor.

Ewan took charge. "Go get yerself shrouded then, laddie."

Fynn, David and a few others hurried away to the keep.

Shona worried. "He's a mite bigger than Ailig."

Ewan put a comforting arm around her shoulders. "We have to hope the idiot willna notice."

He looked up at Robbie again then turned to the men holding the rescue blanket. "Keep a wary eye on the boy. Ye might have to get into position quickly if the rope gives way. I dinna trust Mungo to have secured it properly."

Time dragged as they waited. Shona wandered over to Heather. "The sound of yer voice might keep Robbie's spirits up," she suggested.

The woman walked closer to the wall but the vacant look in her eyes was disconcerting. "It's like she's in a trance," Shona whispered to Ewan.

As if sensing his wife's distress, Walter stood behind her and put his hands on her waist. "Talk to him."

She nodded and finally looked up. "Dinna worry, Robert."

Walter nuzzled her nape. "Louder," he urged.

Heather clenched her fists. "They've gone to fetch Ailig and then Mungo will let ye go. Ye've always been a good bairn and God willna let aught bad happen to ye."

She slumped backwards into her husband's arms, a forced smile on her face.

Robbie made no reply but Shona could have sworn Mungo wiped away a tear as he peered over the wall. "He's like a child," she murmured to Ewan.

He smiled grimly as he gathered her into his embrace. "Aye, but a dangerous one."

WHILE THEY WAITED, Ewan thought back over the tumultuous events that had taken place since his arrival. "It's possible none of this would have happened if we hadna come," he whispered to Shona.

"Nay," she replied. "Ailig was a snake lying hidden in the grass, waiting to strike. The news ye were coming might have prompted him to act against Kendric sooner, but it's evident he and his brother have been plotting to usurp the lairdship for a long while. They murdered my father before our betrothal was settled."

He hoped she was right. "Some of yer clan willna see it that way, especially if we fail to save the bairn."

"Ye willna fail," she reassured him.

He inhaled deeply, wondering how he had come to deserve the loyalty and trust of such a woman. "Just having ye close makes me stronger," he whispered, wishing he could crush her body to his and simply soak up her love. "But here comes the *corpse*."

She kissed his cheek then moved away and watched with him as David and another man approached the tower. They bore a litter on which lay a shrouded body.

Ewan beckoned them to bring it closer. The notion his grizzled kinsman lay beneath the shroud suddenly struck him as comical, especially if he still wore the cook's apron. "'Tis hard to believe ye're dead, Fynn Macintyre," he lamented.

"Dinna make him laugh," Shona cautioned.

Swallowing the nervous laughter bubbling in his throat, Ewan gestured to the litter and looked up. "Here's yer brother," he shouted. "What do ye want us to do with him?"

Walter glared angrily. "Ye'll get him riled up if he believes ye're making fun of him."

Evidently he'd failed to hide his inexplicable amusement. "Sorry. I dinna ken why it seems so hilarious."

He sobered when Fynn sauntered into the courtyard. "Naught funny about my demise," his kinsman rasped with a sly grin.

Puzzled, Ewan looked again at the corpse on the litter. It was impossible they'd dug up Ailig's body, but the whole situation suddenly seemed even more comical. He feigned a coughing fit while he controlled his hysterical need to laugh out loud. Shona slapped him on the back.

Mungo's high-pitched voice made it worse. "How do I ken it's Ailig?" he asked.

Ewan clenched his jaw. "How many dead men do ye reckon we have lying around here? Come down and see for yerself."

"I'm nay that daft."

Ewan avoided Shona's gaze, sensing she was also close to losing her composure.

"Show me the hand," Mungo demanded.

Ewan wiggled his eyebrows. "The moment of truth is at hand," he quipped under his breath.

David winked as he fished about in the folds of the shroud and pulled out the severed limb.

It was a gory mess.

Folk in the crowd gasped in horror.

Ewan peered more closely. The bloodied end of a deer's leg bone protruded from a ragged sleeve.

"We squa…squashed ju…ju…juniper berries over it, for good measure," David explained.

Ewan composed his features, then looked up. "Satisfied?"

THE CORPSE

Shona shaded her eyes to look up. "He's mad, but he isna stupid," she whispered close to Ewan's ear, not wanting to dash Heather's hopes.

An audible gasp rose from the crowd when Mungo hauled Robbie back to the safety of the parapet. He put an arm around the lad and shouted, "Secure my brother's body to a horse. And I'll need one for me and the lad."

Ewan arched a brow and shrugged. "He's evidently shortsighted as well as dimwitted."

As soon as Mungo disappeared, Walter dispatched two men to the stables.

Fynn and David lifted the *corpse* off the litter. "The antlers were too much of a challenge," Fynn explained, "but we managed to get the rest o' the carcass stuffed in."

Shona stared incredulously. "The head as weel?"

David nodded. "Too ba...ba...bad."

"Aye," Fynn agreed with a sigh. "We could have made all manner o' useful things wi' yon bones."

"No better use than saving a child's life," Shona replied.

"Speaking of which," Ewan said, "we canna let him ride out of here with Robbie. Walter, come with me."

They entered the doorway to the tower. Difficult as it was to watch him go, Shona accepted it was in Ewan's nature to risk himself for others. His courage was what she admired most about him.

"Where are the horses?" Heather cried impatiently. "It willna take him long to come down."

Shona put an arm around her shoulders. "Hopefully, he'll never make it to the ground."

Heather slumped against her as the men from the stables appeared at the run leading a roan and a donkey. "But he'll kill my son if they challenge him."

"Without Robbie, he has no means of escape."

She hoped she was right as Fynn and David lifted the bag of bones onto the reluctant donkey and quickly secured it with rope. If she hadn't known what was inside she'd have believed the beast's burden was a corpse—which she supposed it was, in a way.

EWAN AND WALTER encountered Mungo part way down the central staircase. He'd slung Robbie over his shoulder like a sack of grain. The bairn's feet were unbound, but it was impossible to know if his hands were tied. He made no sound and Ewan worried he might already be dead, though there was no blood in evidence on the dagger Mungo gripped. That didn't mean he hadn't strangled the boy.

"Robert Gilbertson," Walter said sternly, evidently plagued by the same uncertainty, "I'm proud o' ye. We'll soon have ye safe, do ye hear me?"

"Aye, Daddy," came the brave reply.

Walter exhaled. "Let my son go," he hissed. "Take me instead."

Mungo scoffed. "Nay, the lad's smaller. Ye're too much of a handful."

"*Fyking* coward," Walter mumbled under his breath.

"Get out o' my way," Mungo shouted, waving the dagger, "if ye dinna want me to harm the bairn."

"We've few options in this narrow stairwell," Ewan muttered to Walter. "Let's wait until we get to the courtyard."

Walter gritted his teeth, but nodded his agreement. They felt their way backwards towards the steps to the outside, never taking their eyes off Mungo and his precious burden.

A TERRIBLE HUSH fell over the crowd when Ewan and Walter came out of the tower without Robbie.

Heather sobbed in Shona's arms, but she shrieked her son's name when Mungo emerged carrying the boy like a sack of grain.

"I'm all right, Mamie," the lad shouted, eliciting compliments about his bravery from bystanders.

The scowling giant paused, scanning the scene. Shona hoped his gaze didn't linger overlong on the *corpse* lashed to the donkey. The animal stomped and brayed, clearly uncomfortable with its burden.

"I asked for a horse, nay a donkey," Mungo protested, but didn't pursue the matter when no one replied.

He inched his way towards the beasts, keeping a wary eye on Ewan and Walter. "Everybody move away," he yelled.

Heather gripped Shona's arm as the crowd slowly obeyed. When Mungo got close to the roan, Robbie began to squirm and kick.

"I told him of Ailig's burial," his mother whispered. "He kens that's nay the body."

She shrieked when Mungo swatted the lad's bottom with the knife-wielding hand.

"Be still," the giant growled, but Robbie kept on kicking.

Shona glanced across at Ewan who had taken advantage of the distraction to edge closer.

Evidently rattled by the boy's sudden resistance, Mungo paid scant attention to the *corpse*, took the reins of the donkey and mounted the roan, then drew Robbie down into his lap. "If ye try to hunt me, I'll make sure the boy suffers," he threatened.

Walter growled.

Heather wailed.

Anger threatened to choke Shona.

Ewan's gaze darted here and there, searching for a means to stop the brute leaving. He rolled his eyes heavenward when Ruadh sauntered into the courtyard.

THE PACK

Ewan groaned. It was doubtful the hound's presence would help matters. Mungo hardly seemed to notice, too busy looping the rope binding Robbie's hands to the pommel. The lad kept on squirming, forcing his captor to clench the dagger between his teeth to free up his hands. However, the blade still posed a danger.

Ewan's heart sank further when Ruadh trotted over to the *corpse* and began sniffing the shroud.

"Come away," Shona cajoled, patting her thigh.

"Geroff," Mungo shouted at the hound, then took the dagger from his mouth and swore, spitting blood.

Ewan cursed, even more determined not to be bested by a complete idiot. "Leave the dog be," he shouted to Shona when a spark of an idea flickered. Ruadh was a deerhound after all.

As he hoped, the dog sank his teeth into a corner of the shroud and pulled, putting more effort into it when his prize refused to budge. His whining, or mayhap the smell, attracted the attention of several other dogs who joined the fray, trying to pull the *corpse* from the donkey.

Soon they were snapping at each other. The donkey brayed and kicked, alarming the roan. Mungo's face reddened considerably as he strove to control his mount and screamed for it all to stop. In his confusion he dropped the reins of the donkey. The braying beast bucked around the courtyard in a futile attempt to dislodge its unwelcome burden. The dogs were relentless in their pursuit. Most dodged the hooves successfully, others yelped and fell by the wayside when they weren't so lucky.

"We mayhap tied it too well," Fynn mumbled to Ewan.

"The uproar is clearly unsettling Mungo."

"Ye'd be unsettled too if 'twas yer brother about to be eaten by dogs," his kinsman replied.

Ewan conceded he wouldn't wish that fate on Colin, much as he disliked the man.

Mungo eventually caught up to the frenzied donkey, but when he leaned over to grab hold of the reins, Robbie shoved him hard and he fell to the ground. Then the brave lad dug his heels into the roan's flanks and yelled, *"Siuthad."* The beast responded and trotted away from the melee. Walter ran after him. The donkey took off towards the stables, the pack snapping at its bucking hind legs. The bag of bones was, by now, dragging on the ground.

Ewan ran to Mungo before he had a chance to get to his feet. He grasped the wretch's shoulders and turned him over. Lifeless eyes stared into nothingness. Blood trickled from a twisted mouth. The fool had impaled himself on his own dagger.

Ewan went down on one knee and closed the unseeing eyes.

Shona came to embrace him as he got to his feet. She stared at the dead man. "This was inevitable I suppose, and perhaps for the best." She kissed his cheek and whispered, "Thank ye."

The warmth of her body pressed against him calmed the fear and dread that had coursed through him since he'd seen Robbie dangling from the tower. "I'm nay the hero," he replied. "Robbie saved himself, with help from yon hound."

"But ye knew Ruadh would provide a distraction," she insisted.

Resounding cheers drowned out his protestations when Walter returned to the courtyard carrying Robbie. The smiling boy waved shyly to the admiring crowd as his weeping mother threw her arms around him.

THE CHEERS GRADUALLY died down. A peculiar silence settled on the courtyard. Shona recognized many capable clansmen, young and old, who gazed about, as if none quite knew what to do now that the threat had been dealt with.

Even Walter seemed content to simply cling to his wife and bairn.

It was Ewan who took charge. Within minutes he'd sent Fynn back to his labors, dispatched servants to prepare chambers for the Gilbertsons, organized a work crew to begin restoring the burned-out cottages, appointed a burial detail to take care of Mungo's body, and set off for the stables with David to sort out the dog and bone issue.

Soon only Shona and Mrs. Macgill remained in the strangely quiet courtyard.

"Mayhap they're not a bad lot after all, yon Mackinlochs," Moira's mother conceded before flouncing off.

Heart bursting with pride, Shona looked up to the top of the tower. "Dinna fash, Daddy, the clan's in good hands," she whispered before hurrying off to see to the provision of a bath for the Gilbertsons.

※

EWAN WAS PLEASED with the progress being made on the various tasks that needed to be dealt with. He didn't deserve credit for saving Robbie and ridding the clan of the threat to the lairdship, but there was no doubt many of the MacCarrons he came into contact with as the afternoon progressed treated him with greater respect.

Once he and David had pacified Ruadh and his pals with a few choice bones, he sent his kinsman back to Fynn with the remainder of the carcass.

When he made his way to the village, some of the men toiling there seemed surprised when he solicited suggestions for the speedy reconstruction of the cottages. Reticent at first, they soon offered their ideas for the organization of the work. They attacked the filthy task with enthusiasm when he gave his approval and began helping clear out the debris in Walter's ruined home.

They'd made some progress when the Gilbertsons made their way down the hill from the castle. The trio had clearly bathed and changed clothes. Heather shyly tucked strands of wet hair behind her ears. Ewan was fairly sure he'd seen the gown she wore on the floor of Shona's chamber on the terrible day he'd discovered Mungo's treachery. Walter wore trews and a shirt, but no plaid. Robbie squirmed out of his mother's grip and headed for the ruin.

"He'll nay stay clean long," Walter lamented, peering inside his cottage.

"Neither will ye if ye go in there," Ewan replied.

"But it's my responsibility," his friend pointed out.

Ewan showed his blackened hands and beckoned him away from the grime. "Nobody expects ye to help with this now, and it's my wedding day on the morrow. Soon enough ye can help with the rebuilding."

Walter clenched his jaw. "Aye, about the wedding. Since yer kinsman is getting wed the same day, I had thought to offer myself as yer second, but the laundresses are overwhelmed. They reckon it will be days before my only plaid can be cleaned and repaired." He nodded to the ruin. "The rest of our raiment went up in smoke."

Ewan was humbled. "I'd offer ye my hand, but it's a mite dirty. I can think of no one I'd rather have as my second, Brother. And I ken where there's a spare MacCarron plaid that a good friend once lent me."

Walter offered his hand. "'Twill be my honor, and naught wrong with a wee bit o'dirt to seal a deal."

Ewan proudly accepted the gesture, but Walter grimaced when Robbie ran by seconds later, his bright eyes two white circles in a mucky face. "Now all we have to worry about is keeping yon bairn clean."

Heather hurried after her son. "Impossible," she remarked.

TWO WEDDINGS

THE NEXT DAY, Ewan stood before the minister in the chapel, but all his attention was on the smiling woman whose warm hand he held. His gaze wandered up her slender arm, tightly clad in fabric that exploded in a puffy riot at her shoulder. Strangely, it drew the eye to the décolletage that provided a tantalizing glimpse of pouting breasts he hoped soon to be suckling.

The fitted bodice clung to her shapely figure then flared into copious skirts that seemed to float as she walked.

He couldn't have named the fabric used to fashion her luxurious gown, but the vibrant reds and golds matched the fire burning in his heart.

He thanked whatever force of nature had deterred him from offering marriage to Kathleen.

At the risk of offending Shona's clan, he'd decided to wear a Mackinloch plaid. He was marrying a MacCarron and would strive to heal the deep divisions between their clans, but Mackinloch blood ran in his veins and they would have to accept that. His bride and her uncle supported his decision.

The significance of Walter's stalwart presence at his side wasn't lost on anyone. Only he and Ewan knew the history of the plaid he wore.

Fynn and Jeannie also stood before the minister. Ewan could scarce believe this was the same rough and ready farmer who'd accompanied him from Roigh. A casual visitor might have mistaken him for a proud Macintyre laird. The smiling woman responsible for the transformation looked radiant in a green gown. To Ewan's eye it was nearly identical to Shona's, except it revealed less of her bosom—as was perhaps fitting. Fynn was likely pleased since his bride had kept her girlish figure despite her appetite.

Another unforeseen miracle was David's presence as Fynn's second. Two men who'd set out with little in common, not even mutual respect, had forged a unique bond.

The minister cleared his throat. Ewan nodded his readiness to repeat vows he was contentedly certain he would keep.

He looked into the green depths and saw his own soul. "I, Ewan Mackinloch…take thou, Shona MacCarron…to my espoused wife…as the law of the Holy Kirk requires…and thereto I plight thee my troth."

His bride tightened her grip on his hand, took a deep breath and repeated her vows. "I, the said Shona MacCarron…take ye, Ewan Mackinloch…to my espoused husband…as the law of the Holy Kirk requires…and thereto I plight to thee my troth."

The sincerity in her steady gaze told of vows honestly spoken. Ewan had an urge to strut about the church like a rooster. His wife loved him despite the foolish trick he'd set in motion to avoid marrying her. She'd seen strengths in him he hadn't seen in himself. Of course, she'd conspired to trick him as well. He chuckled inwardly, grateful the Fates had persevered to bring two reluctant soul mates together.

Shona flounced out of the chapel like the Queen o' All Scots. She was regally dressed—after all a lass only got married once, so what was the point in scrimping on a gown—and the king of her heart was her escort.

The brief physical liaison they'd shared still evoked tingles in unmentionable places and promised a marriage bed filled with sublime delights.

The most wonderful day of her life might never have happened if her scheme to avoid marrying a Mackinloch had worked. Fortunately, the Fates had thwarted the plan and she'd shared the ceremony with her beloved aunt, thus doubling her happiness.

All that remained now was the banquet, about which she had mixed feelings. The castle was agog, but the excitement had more to do with the venison than the happy event. Fynn had confidently taken Jeannie to wife without blinking an eye, but questions about the roasting of the stag seemed to render him a nervous wreck with a stammer to rival David's.

Those fortunate to sample the pies served at David and Moira's wedding plagued others with tales of the mouth-watering treat in store.

Able to walk now with the aid of two arm crutches and the ever-faithful Donald, Kendric led the wedding procession into the hall and took his rightful place at the head table. Beaming, he gestured Ewan and Shona to sit to his right, and Fynn and Jeannie to his left.

Folk applauded as they took their places, but the cheering rose to a crescendo when Walter led in Ruadh and ushered him to a blanket in front of the head table. Everyone acknowledged the dog had earned the right to the first morsels of venison.

He sat regally, tongue lolling.

"Look at him," she whispered to Ewan, "eyeing his court as if he's King of the Castle."

They both chuckled when he yawned, evidently bored when the minister appealed to everyone to bow their heads and thank God for His goodness.

Instead, the hound looked with anticipation to the kitchens as servants emerged bearing serving trays.

Every head followed Ruadh's lead and not the minister's.

"He isna the only one salivating," Ewan pointed out as they sat.

Though Shona's chair was four removed from Fynn's, she sensed his nervousness. Jeannie leaned forward to exchange an exasperated glance with her niece.

Seated at a table with his new bride's family, David fixed his worried gaze on the servants as they delivered trenchers of meat and vegetables to the head table and one to Ruadh.

The dog got to his feet and made short work of the treat, then wagged his tail, lapping up the loud cheering.

Fynn and David unclenched their jaws.

"Seems Ruadh approves," Kendric shouted over the din. "The festivities can begin."

EWAN SAVORED THE venison, but particularly enjoyed feeding his new bride the best morsels from his trencher. It took resolve not to lick the juices from her tempting lips and kiss her senseless. He suspected the crowd half-expected him to do so. A hush fell over the gathering every time he leaned towards her.

He'd readied himself for some antagonism among Shona's clan. After all, he was a Mackinloch and had just played a role in the deaths of MacCarron kinsmen. There were a few scowling faces, mostly among the more elderly folk but, all in all, he was confident the majority favored the marriage, if grudgingly.

He deemed it fortuitous that much of the attention had shifted to Fynn whose culinary triumph had made him famous. The majority of the raucous toasts were offered to him and his helper, and to the dog. Opinion was unanimous it was the best venison anyone had ever tasted. The man responsible steadfastly refused to reveal his secrets.

"There's a lesson to be learned here," Ewan whispered to Shona.

She turned to listen. The happy smile, the wide-eyed innocence, the blush spreading across her breasts caused him to lose track of what he planned to say next. His cock ruled his thoughts.

"A lesson," she prompted, eyeing him curiously.

"Er…aye. The way to a clan's heart is through its belly."

She nodded thoughtfully, but didn't seem to appreciate the witticism. He took a quick swig of the wine to hide his disappointment.

The blackberry wine was excellent, rich and fruity, but he didn't intend to over-imbibe and was glad Shona took only the occasional sip.

Kendric, however, drank heartily. Jeannie and Shona both cautioned him softly that laudanum and wine could be a potent mix. He waved away their warnings. "If a *mon* canna celebrate the wedding of his niece and sister on the same day…"

A fit of hiccups followed, causing Jeannie to slap him heartily on the back.

He belched, then continued. "Anyway, I sipped only a wee dram o' *dwale* today so I didna have to worry about the laud'num."

Shona gasped, but Ewan gently restrained her when she tried to get out of her seat. "Leave him be. I'll keep an eye on him."

"But *dwale*," she protested. "He's determined to stick with old ways and doesna realize it can be more dangerous than laudanum. Cook has had more to worry about than how much henbane he put in the *dwale*."

He patted her hand. "He'll suffer for it on the morrow, but I'll warrant his worst affliction will be a pounding headache."

A few minutes later he hoped he was right when Kendric struggled to his feet, swayed alarmingly on his crutches and raised a goblet. "Falls to me to say a few words about…"

He scanned the hall, seemingly recollecting his thoughts until his gaze settled on Ewan. "About this union of our feuding clans."

The smile faded from Shona's face as a knot of apprehension tightened in Ewan's gut.

"Aye," Kendric continued, "all o' ye gathered here well remember what happened at the Battle o' the Ninth Inch."

Utter silence reigned.

Ewan felt sure everyone else must have noticed the drunken slip of the tongue that had rechristened the *North* Inch.

Only Fynn shrugged as they exchanged an amused glance.

If anyone else caught the error, they apparently decided to overlook it in favor of resurrecting old grudges.

Frowns replaced smiles. Eyes narrowed. Jaws clenched. Ewan shifted uncomfortably in his chair when Shona's fingernails dug into his thigh. Surely the laird wasn't going to drag up a battle between the Mackinlochs and the MacCarrons that had taken place three hundred years before—definitely not in living memory.

"Aye," Kendric declared, "when our clans refused to settle the dispute, the *trial by combat* was decreed by King Robert hisself. He was there, ye ken. Witnessed the bloody massacre of MacCarrons by the cursed Mackinlochs."

NINTH INCH

"On a Monday morning in late September the clans marched through the streets of Perth to the sound of the pibroch and armed with bows and arrows, swords, targes, knives and axes, to the western banks of the River Tay."

Shona wished for an axe so she could bash her uncle on the head. Determined to keep the smile plastered on her face, she scanned the crowd, many of whom mouthed the same words, so well did they know the tale. In mid-chew, her auntie stared in disbelief at her brother.

Shona dug her fingernails deeper into Ewan's thigh, not only to ease the tension she felt in his muscles, but to settle her own agitation. A celebration that had begun with great promise threatened to turn into a brawl if Kendric's drunkenness led him to open up old wounds.

Another voice took up the tale. "They put up barriers on three sides o' the island to keep spectators off the battlefield, with the Tay on the fourth side."

Ewan's leg began to twitch uncontrollably. She didn't need to look at him to know his jaw was clenched, though she also sensed something had amused him.

"The Dominicans' summerhouse was turned into a grandstand for the King and his entourage," someone shouted.

The retelling of the tale had taken on a life of its own and Shona acknowledged with a heavy heart there'd be no stopping it.

"Aye, but then they discovered the Mackinlochs were short one man," Kendric exclaimed.

"Twenty-nine, nay thirty as agreed," many yelled.

"Coward deserted," others accused.

Shona feared her nails might draw blood if she dug them any deeper, but Ewan remained in his seat even after this insult to his clan, though she suspected he burned to challenge the accusation.

"Just when it seemed that the battle would have to be abandoned, a volunteer stepped forward," Kendric continued. "But only because the Mackinlochs offered him half a crown of French gold."

Raucous derogatory laughter broke out, but came to an abrupt halt when Ewan pushed back his chair and stood.

Determined to demonstrate loyalty to her husband, Shona probably still looked like a happy bride. Inwardly, she prayed fervently that she wouldn't be widowed on her wedding day.

EWAN RECOGNIZED HE faced a crisis. What he did next would perpetuate the feud or bring it to an end. The temptation to respond with his fists was powerful, but for the sake of both clans and for Shona and the bairns they would bring into the world, it had to end.

He scanned the crowd, then smiled. "Small in stature and a bandy-legged fellow he was, this braw *mon*, this volunteer."

Mouths that had been on the verge of saying the very same thing fell open. He'd achieved his first goal and taken them unawares. If they thought only Clan MacCarron repeated this tale over and over, they were in for a surprise.

"Aye," someone shouted. "Henry Smith."

"Hal o' the Wend," Ewan replied.

He wasn't sure, but he thought Shona swallowed a chuckle as the nickname was repeated in hushed tones; or mayhap she just coughed. He didn't risk looking at her, but glanced at Kendric instead, taken aback when the laird winked at him.

He attributed it to the man's state of health and inebriation, but then The Camron went on with the tale. "The king's trumpeters sounded the charge."

A few who'd evidently also overimbibed made trumpeting sounds, eliciting general titters.

Ewan's hopes lifted. Perhaps he would get to spend his wedding night with his virgin wife after all. The prospect spurred him on. He braced his legs and tucked his thumbs into the waistband of his trews. "The pipes screamed, maddening the combatants who started forward, slowly first, then at the run."

Somewhere at the back of the hall a piper began a lament.

Fynn got to his feet. "They met in the center o' the field," he recited, his husky voice raising the hair on Ewan's nape, "crashing upon each other like a storm surge upon the rocks."

"Blood flowed," Ewan bellowed, warming to the task, "men groaned and screamed in pain and fury."

Walter stood. "The furious wail of the bagpipes could still be heard above the tumult, urging the warriors on."

As if inspired to play more boldly, the piper gave his instrument full rein.

"Then the pipes sounded a retreat," Kendric yelled hoarsely above the din, brandishing one crutch.

Ewan was certain the laird would topple over, but Donald appeared out of nowhere and propped him up.

Evidently confused by the new instructions, the piper faltered.

David thrust his fist in the air. "Twenty men lay dead on the field," he sang, his melodious voice adding poignancy to the bitter words of the age-old ballad.

"Arms and legs cleaved off," a baritone voice intoned.

"Heads cleft to the chin," David sang.

Ruadh howled.

Ewan was astonished. It was as if both clans had sung the same gruesome story for three hundred years. He didn't consider himself a good singer, but nevertheless joined Fynn and David in the second to last verse.

The fray resumed,
but at the end
eleven Mackinlochs remained,
including Hal o' the Wend.

They stayed silent when every male voice in the hall belted out the inevitable conclusion.

One MacCarron still lived
A terrible cost.
He surrendered victory.
The contest was lost.

It was sorely tempting to add that the last surviving MacCarron had actually jumped into the Tay and swum to safety on that fateful day, but…

The silence weighed heavily. If Ewan said the wrong thing at this crucial moment…

Flexing his fingers, he looked to Shona. The adoration in her eyes gave him courage, but Kendric forestalled him. "'Tis clear," the chief declared solemnly without a trace of a slur, "both clans have sacrificed much for hundreds of years. Nay just at the *Ninth* Inch. And I say Enough!"

There was a murmur of agreement.

Ewan began to wonder if he was just imagining the laird's mispronunciation. No one else reacted at all.

Kendric swallowed hard. "Ye all ken I ne'er wanted to be laird, but when Beathan died…"

He accepted a kerchief from Donald and blew his nose, then gestured to his niece. "Here sits the daughter of yer true laird, a *mon* cruelly murdered."

Tears welled in many a female eye, including Shona's.

Ruadh growled.

"By rights, Beathan's flesh and blood should be yer laird. She'd do a better job of it than me."

This notion made Shona blush and rendered many speechless. Ewan acknowledged she had the will and the ability, but a woman as laird?

"I see ye're nay ready for that yet," Kendric mumbled. "However, today she married a man who has demonstrated beyond a shadow of a doot he can lead."

"Aye," a few agreed.

"He rescued our Shona from her abductors."

Cheers resounded.

"He saved the life of a wee bairn."

Ewan's attempts to give credit to Ruadh were drowned out by tankards banging on tables.

"He rooted out a viper in our midst and kilt it."

The resulting *aye* was deafening. Everyone seemed to be overlooking the fact Mungo had fallen on his own weapon.

Kendric tapped a crutch against the slightly battered cast encasing his leg. "I intend someday to be rid o' this and walk like a man again, but I'll ne'er be as whole as I was. We need a strong leader and powerful allies. I therefore name Ewan Mackinloch as The Camron."

SHONA WISHED MORE cheering had greeted the proclamation, but at least no one voiced an objection.

If only her father had met Ewan. Beathan MacCarron would have recognized his worth. But that was impossible and heart wrenching to even think of.

Her husband remained on his feet, fists clenched, solemnly surveying the people of his new clan. She longed to touch him, but he was The Camron now.

What was he was thinking as he watched folk who were clearly uncertain how to greet the news?

She clutched the edge of the table when Walter strode to the front of the crowd, unsheathed his claymore and pointed it at Ewan. "This day," he declared loudly, "in the presence of all my clan and kinfolk, I pledge loyalty and allegiance to Ewan Mackinloch, Laird of Clan MacCarron."

"As do I," Robbie shouted, provoking chuckles.

Shona startled when her uncle exclaimed, "Nay."

Ewan stared at him, obviously sharing her concern that wine and the *dwale* had rendered him witless. His slip of the tongue in renaming the famous Battle of the North Inch had been the first indication of his rambling. At least no one seemed to have noticed that error.

Kendric shook his head. "He canna be laird until the morrow, when we have proof."

"Proof?" Walter asked indignantly. "Of what? Ye already said…"

"Weel," Kendric mused, "I expect Fynn and David will both be occupied come dawn on the morrow, so 'twill likely be ye, Walter, who'll be hoisting sheets up yon flagpole."

His pronouncement produced the loudest guffaws of the evening.

Walter grinned and slapped Ewan on the back.

Had Shona not been thoroughly embarrassed she might also have laughed out loud.

Jaw clenched, Ewan turned to face Kendric. "Ye're saying I canna be The Camron until I've made Shona my wife in every way?"

Kendric winked.

She squealed with surprise when her husband scooped her up. "That's a *trial by combat* I'll willingly endure," he boasted, eyebrows wiggling, his face split by a naughty grin that sent desire spiraling into her womb.

He carried her out of the hall amid loud whooping and cheering.

"Are ye ready for yer own nine inches?" he whispered hoarsely.

She didn't understand the words, though he'd evidently noticed Kendric's slip of the tongue. However, there was no mistaking the lusty intent in his eyes nor the heat of his nape 'neath her hands.

RAPTURE

As he carried his new wife to her bridal chamber, Ewan cursed his lack of finesse. He *was* a well-endowed Highlander, a true Mackinloch, but mayhap his boast had been a bit of an exaggeration. Then what man didn't brag about the size of his male parts?

It was a relief she clearly hadn't understood his innuendo. He was about to bed an innocent noblewoman who deserved patient tutoring in the love arts, but all he could think of was ramming his needy tarse into her virgin sheath.

Heart racing, he kicked open the door to her chamber, then turned, irritated by the sound of hurried footsteps. If bawdy MacCarron kinsmen had followed them with high jinks in mind…

He calmed when Isobel grasped the door frame with one hand, gulping air. "I came to see to my lady's needs," she panted.

How to explain to a child he intended to take care of all Shona's needs this night, including removing the sumptuous gown, hopefully without ripping it apart in his haste.

Shona came to his rescue. "My lord husband will take care of me, Isobel," she murmured throatily. "Ye can return to the feast."

The maid bobbed a curtsey and scurried off, evidently needing no more encouragement.

Ewan's already swollen tarse bucked. Perhaps his wife did have an inkling of what lay in store and wasn't afraid. Indeed, the slow progress of her tongue across her upper lip as she curled a finger in his hair betrayed a capacity for passion he'd suspected from their first meeting.

He carried her over the threshold and kicked the door shut behind them. Needing a moment to cool his ardor, he rested one knee on the bed and laid her down gently, then stepped back.

He stared hard, willing his memory to forever remember the vision before him. Disheveled golden tresses framed angelic rosy cheeks; wide green eyes studied him with as much intensity as he studied her; naughty nipples threatened to break free of the décolletage; the voluminous red and gold skirts cascaded over the edge of the bed like a shimmering waterfall.

He understood why Odin had ravished Rindr, and if a mighty Norse god hadn't been able to resist the temptation of a beautiful woman, what hope was there for him?

His throbbing cock almost had him convinced there was no point holding back, but then Shona smiled and held out her hands. He suddenly, and astonishingly, wanted more than his own release. He wanted to carry her with him to rapture. "I'm praying yon gown comes off without much fuss," he confessed in a strained voice he barely recognized, "or it will be in tatters soon."

She laughed and tried to sit up, but her struggles only resulted in the skirts forcing her legs up in the air. He gasped at the sight of layer upon layer of frilly white material and long stockinged legs. She righted herself before he could get a glimpse of garters and…

Feeling a little lightheaded, he rushed to the bed to help her rise, discovering that swallowing without saliva was nigh on impossible. He pulled her up against him and put his arms around her waist, so he could nuzzle her ear. "Ye are a temptress, Shona Mackinloch," he whispered, cupping her bottom and pressing his need to her woman's place.

She took a step back. His disappointment fled when she molded her hand to his arousal and looked into his eyes. "I've dreamt of touching ye again," she admitted.

It would take but a second to untie his trews and shove them down to his knees, along with his braies. Then she could fulfill her fantasy. The mere thought of her warm hand on his flesh…

He swallowed again. Even less saliva. The quandary of the gown threatened to drive him witless. Reluctantly, he removed her hand and kissed delicate fingertips, trying to recall how Kathleen's garments unfastened. A waste of time. It was an easy matter to lift a shift over a woman's head. He gritted his teeth and eyed the elegant gown with increased exasperation.

Shona giggled. "Ye look desperate," she quipped. "Here."

She turned her back and lifted the fall of glorious hair to reveal laces. Too many! But he set about unlacing them like a sailor hurriedly reefs the jib before the gale drives his boat aground.

Nearing his goal of having the laces unthreaded from top to bottom, he put a hand on her waist to steady himself—and felt rigid bone. The prospect of more laces was too much. "Dinna tell me ye're wearing a corset too," he groaned.

She glanced over her shoulder, eyes narrowed. "Nay, the bodice has whalebone sewn in. But what do ye ken about ladies' corsets, Ewan Mackinloch?"

He considered a flippant retort but became distracted when the back of the gown parted to reveal creamy skin. His mind filled with the reality that all he had to do was peel the bodice from her body and she'd be naked, at least from the waist up. He opted for that choice, elated when she helped by extracting her arms from the sleeves. He braced his legs, pulled her bottom against his arousal and reached to fill his hands with her breasts, inhaling the scent of lavender that clung to her hair. He brushed his thumbs over rigid nipples, then squeezed.

"Ewan," she breathed, arching her back and stretching her neck to rest her head on his shoulder.

Great as his need was—and his actions had admittedly made matters worse—a peaceful contentment stole into his heart. He'd played many roles in his life. Disobedient son to his stern father; resentful brother and tormentor to the pompous Colin; fiercely loyal clan warrior; loving uncle to his nephew Andrew; occasional bed partner to Kathleen. He'd never cared much about a woman's pleasure, but fulfilling Shona's bodily needs was of the utmost importance. His destiny was to be the harbinger of her happiness.

However, it would be as well to get on with it before he completely lost control like some green lad.

He turned her to face him and sat down on the edge of the mattress, drinking in the perfect curves and rosy brown nipples pouting like little cobnuts nestled in dusky haloes. He didn't have words powerful enough to tell her how magnificent she was, so he put his hands on her bare back, swirled his tongue over a nipple and suckled like a hungry bairn.

She gripped his shoulders and thrust back her head, humming low in her throat. Her hips began to gyrate, causing the skirts to slide with a swish to the floor.

He took a breath, intending to turn his attention to the other nipple, but her waist caught his attention. "Aha!" he exclaimed. "I wondered how they got the skirts to bell out the way they did. It was as if ye were floating on a cloud."

She frowned then smiled when she looked down. "They're called panniers," she explained, smoothing her hands over the basket-like contraptions protruding from her body.

"May I?" he asked before untying the ribbon at her waist.

To his surprise, layers of white petticoats slid to the floor with the panniers.

"It's all one," she murmured.

He could only gape as he beheld a vision, naked except for gartered stockings—and drawers.

He'd dealt with stockings before and looked forward to removing the garters and peeling off the hose—later. He'd only heard talk of the opulent female pantaloons some high-born ladies wore. He stared at the juncture of her thighs, wondering if the rumors were true.

Shona parted her legs, slightly, to reveal darker curls than he'd expected at her mons. "I ken some say they're not healthy," she whispered self-consciously, "but they're slit—for air."

"I see," he managed to reply, though his mind was working on a completely different notion.

A wave of heat threatened to drown him. "I need to get out o' my clothes," he growled, glad of her assistance in shrugging the ceremonial plaid off his shoulder and dragging the cambric shirt over his head.

Like most young Highlanders, he'd spent a goodly part of his life in the training fields. Every Mackinloch knew that a fighting force of fit and robust warriors deterred enemies. If confrontations occurred, men with bodies honed for battle stood a better chance of prevailing, and surviving. He was proud of his body, especially now as Shona raked her gaze over the muscles of his chest and belly.

He sucked in a breath when she grazed his nipples with her thumbs and smiled seductively. "Do ye like that?" she whispered.

He probably replied but his attention was on getting to his feet and ridding himself of his trews and braies.

She gasped when his manhood sprang forth. Afraid he'd frightened her, he took hold of her hand and curled it around his arousal. "Dinna worry, beloved," he rasped. "I'll make ye ready."

Eyes wide, she nodded. "I understand now what ye meant by nine inches."

SHONA HAD SEEN men stripped to the waist before, some with torsos as well muscled as Ewan's. But she'd never been so close that she could see every soft curl that sprang from the chiseled muscles, never felt the pebbled texture of a man's nipples, nor run a fingertip along the line of golden hair that wandered down his tight belly to the impressive male appendage she held.

Right enough, she'd seen mothers bathing their sons at the village pump—wee boys splashing each other and running about with little willies nestled between their legs. She'd suspected from touching Ewan when he was clothed that something bigger lurked there, but was completely unprepared for the thick, swollen lance that sprang forth. The fierce beauty of his male parts sent a feverish wave of heat rushing through every part of her body. A twinge of apprehension only added to the excitement.

In the recesses of her mind a voice whispered there was perhaps another reason for pantaloons to be split, but Ewan was suckling her again, causing cravings—though she wasn't entirely sure what it was she craved.

Then suddenly Ewan dipped his warm fingers in the wetness of her most intimate place, and she knew.

Evidently sensing her trembling legs were about to give way, he pivoted so she was on the bed. He loomed over her, suckling and teasing, slowly then faster. Faster, faster on the very spot she needed him to go faster. She twirled her fingers in his hair and opened her legs wider, whimpering when a finger ventured a little way inside, but quickly withdrew—then in again.

"Come for me," he urged, his voice husky with wanting.

She'd dreamt of the sensations building in her woman's place ever since the first time, but now the touch of his fingers made them hotter, more insistent. Something was coming, something cataclysmic; she had to cry out, give vent to the wildness, but all that emerged as she soared was a guttural moan of pure ecstasy.

She clung to his shoulders, afraid to fall from the heights he'd brought her to, but then she opened her eyes. Ewan knelt between her legs, his hand guiding his maleness to her opening. "This is the one and only time I'll ever hurt ye," he promised with a reassuring smile.

She sensed his restraint as he slowly and patiently filled her, pausing when she flinched. The discomfort passed quickly and the needy cravings began again as he thrust more deeply. She inhaled his pure masculine scent, relished his grunts, sucked on the salty taste of his skin. She felt safer than ever before and knew he would never let her fall no matter how high they flew.

EWAN RODE HIS wife like a man possessed. If he lived to be a hundred, he would never forget the fierce pride that filled his heart when he breached her maidenhead. He couldn't get enough of the heat, the wetness, the tight, tight sheath. He held off his release until he feared he might go mad, but still wanted the thrusting and grunting to go on and on.

He vaguely hoped he wasn't hurting her; she chanted his name over and over, sucked on his shoulder, clenched on his rampant tarse and thrust her hips in rhythm with his own, so it appeared she was enjoying their union as much as he was.

If he had the wherewithal he'd chuckle at the notion it was merely enjoyable.

Hah!

"Fyking rapture," he growled as his seed finally erupted, binding him body and soul to the woman he loved.

It was still dark when Shona drifted awake, but she sensed dawn wasn't far off. She closed her eyes, anxious to return to the realm of dreams.

Had she dreamt the reverence in Ewan's gaze as he'd peeled off her garters and hose during the night before the tallow guttered out?

Had he truly parted her nether lips with his callused thumbs and suckled her juices, all the while whispering how wonderful she tasted.

Her hand wandered down her belly to her female place. She expected to feel tender, but instead found stickiness and heat and…her eyes flew open. She was naked! Ewan must have removed her scandalous pantaloons.

She licked her lips, reminded of the salty taste of his manhood, the exhilaration caused by his groans of pleasure.

She couldn't say how many times he'd pleasured her, but recalled begging him to fill her, again and again.

The feelings, the scents, the growls, the sweating, the laughter, the whispers of love, the physical exhaustion: everything had been so very new, yet there was a peacefulness to it, a sense of completion, of coming home.

"What are ye thinking?" a husky voice asked close to her ear.

She turned her head. The first grey streaks of dawn limned a beloved face—and a naked and aroused male lying next to her. The need already sparking in her womb ignited. She moved onto her side and swirled her tongue over his maleness, then looked into his brown eyes. "I was thinking of this," she admitted, comfortable with her wantonness.

He sucked in a breath and splayed his fingers in her hair to spread it in a drape around him. "My last fantasy fulfilled," he rasped.

"What's that?" she asked.

He eased his hands under her breasts and brushed his thumbs over her nipples. "To awaken wrapped in yer glorious tresses."

She arched her back and thrust out her breasts, anxious for their play to begin again. "I have my own fantasy," she teased, "that ye teach me new ways to please ye every night."

"That's not a fantasy," he growled. "We can start now, if ye like."

COCOON

Ewan narrowed his eyes as the sun's rays caused him to blink them open. He'd never stayed abed so late in his life, but then again he'd never spent an entire night and the early hours of the morning making love. Filling Shona with his seed seemed to have become an addiction. Truth be told, his stamina surprised even him.

She lay atop him now, drooling on his neck, legs splayed and bent so her wet warmth comforted his sated cock curled up at her entry.

A twinge of interest stirred in his balls, but someone tapped at the door, waking Shona.

"Go away," he shouted gruffly, blowing her hair off his face. "We dinna need anything."

"I canna, my laird," Isobel replied meekly. "The lads have buckets o' hot water."

"A bath does sound good," his wife murmured.

That was a fantasy he'd forgotten. Shona in a tub of hot water, naked, Castile soap…

"Come back later," he shouted.

"I canna," Isobel repeated. "My laird Kendric asks that ye be in the hall within the hour for a celebration luncheon. Lady Jeannie and her husband are up and dressed already."

Shona raised her head. "No surprise there," she quipped. "The prospect of another feast would have quickly roused my aunt from her bed. I suppose we'll have to get up."

Getting up was precisely what Ewan had in mind, but, resigned to his fate, he cocooned them both in the linens and gave grudging permission for the maid and her cohorts to enter.

SHONA WASN'T SURE what devilry came over her, but she suddenly had an urge to lick Ewan's nipples under the covers, even though Isobel stood by the *boudoir*, exhorting the scullery lads not to spill a drop of the hot water as they poured it into the tub.

With her head under the linens she couldn't see how many there were, maybe half a dozen judging by the sounds, but in any case she was enjoying making Ewan squirm.

"Minx," he rasped when she burrowed lower and suckled his arousal, savoring the salty taste of his seed and her own juices. She filled her nostrils with the scent she was coming to recognize as uniquely Ewan.

She liked that notion so much she said it out loud when she heard the door close. "Uniquely Ewan."

Suddenly, her husband leapt from the bed and threw off the linens. Cool air caused her to shiver, but it paled in comparison to the apprehensive expectation rippling in her belly, and lower, when she beheld the magnificent aroused male looming over her. "Naughty lasses must be punished," he warned in a teasing voice.

She squealed a protest when he flipped her over and smacked her bottom, but the experience was strangely arousing. He spanked her again then kissed away the sting. "This pleases me," he murmured.

"Me too," she confessed, gasping with delight when he raised her hips and thrust his fingers inside her. In moments she was riding a wave of bliss, as hot and demanding as the other times he'd pleasured her, yet somehow different. As she came back to earth, he carried her into the *boudoir* and eased her into the tub.

She luxuriated in the heat of the water, feeling like a nymph being watched by a golden god, aware of his heated gaze on nipples floating just above the surface. She stretched out a hand but couldn't quite reach his erect manhood. "Come closer," she said seductively.

He smiled the lustful Ewan Mackinloch smile. "Be careful what ye wish for," he replied.

In seconds, he joined her in the tub before she could protest it was too small. His feet pressed against her hips; his knees protruded above the water. She stopped laughing when he took her hand and curled it round his underwater arousal. "Better?" he asked, handing her the soap.

"Much," she conceded, accepting the challenge.

ISOBEL WAS NOWHERE in evidence when the newlyweds emerged from their bath, but she'd laid out fresh clothing.

Ewan eyed the bed on which the maid had spread the garments. "Something tells me she changed the linens," he said.

"I doot she'd think to do that herself," Shona replied, donning her shift. "She's just a child."

He raised an eyebrow as he quickly shrugged the shirt over his head. Watching his wife dress was proving to be as arousing as stripping her naked. "She probably had help."

He pulled back the covers. "Definitely fresh."

She gathered the frock, ready to lift it over her head, but then paused. "This means ye're already The Camron."

Determined to get a last look at the breasts he'd come to know so intimately before she donned the gown, he wasn't really paying attention to what she said.

"The pole," she explained, her voice muffled by the frock.

Without thinking he grasped his hardening manhood.

She shoved her arms in the sleeves and eyed him. "Not that pole, we dinna have time. My uncle is waiting. I mean the sheets…Walter."

He was instantly contrite. Having made love to his wife countless times during the night and early morning, the taking of her maidenhead seemed eons ago. He took her into his embrace. "I'm a typical Highlander," he confessed, "a thoughtless ravisher who cares naught that he deflowered a maiden and hasna even asked if it was painful."

Desire flared when she pressed her mons to his arousal. "The pain was fleeting," she whispered. "The ecstasy went on and on."

"Are ye sure we dinna have time…"

Shaking her head, she pulled away. "Come, Laird Ewan Mackinloch. Yer people await. But best ye put some clothes on first."

UNDER ATTACK

During the luncheon, Shona enjoyed the teasing of her clanfolk as they offered one bawdy toast after another. They seemed genuinely happy for her and Ewan, as well as for Fynn and Jeannie. Their regard glowed in the smiles and winks of everyone from her uncle down to the serving wenches.

When it came to the ceremony confirming Ewan as The Camron, the enthusiasm was more muted.

She couldn't blame them. The clan understood that accepting Ewan as their chief was essential for their survival and prosperity, but he was nevertheless a Mackinloch.

Her uncle was the first to swear loyalty to her husband, followed by the elders; Fynn and David gave their oaths, then Walter led the procession of MacCarron clansmen to the dais.

It was likely she was the only one aware of the slight change in Ewan's demeanor as the lengthy ritual progressed. He accepted every pledge with dignified pride, but an almost imperceptible twitch of his nose betrayed his doubts about the sincerity of certain men. He probably wasn't aware of his reaction, but it confirmed her opinion that he was an excellent judge of character. As she scanned the line of those waiting to offer allegiance, she could almost predict which ones would earn the twitch.

The cheering was louder than before when Kendric draped a new MacCarron plaid over Ewan's shoulder and pinned it with a clan brooch. She wondered if some in the crowd had perhaps also noticed his keen ability to glean the wheat from the chaff. Half-expecting to see his nose twitch again, she was glad when he accepted the gesture with a broad smile.

"Whisky for everyone," Kendric proclaimed.

Amid the resultant din, most failed to notice the arrival of three warriors who hurried into the hall. Wild-eyed and red-faced, they looked like they had ridden hard.

Shona touched Ewan's arm. "Aren't they the men ye sent to bury Mungo?"

Ewan clenched his jaw when he looked where she pointed. He held up his hand to call for quiet. "What news?" he shouted as a hush fell over the hall and heads turned to the entry.

"We're under attack," one replied, striding towards the dais. "We were burying Morley when we espied a war party near Loch Alkayg."

Ewan frowned. "A war party?"

"Aye. Chattan clans. Armed to the teeth. They're nay far behind."

Pandemonium ensued.

A THOUSAND CONFLICTING thoughts swirled in Ewan's brain. His plans for improving the castle's defenses hadn't yet been put in place. He thought he was winning over the MacCarrons, but angry faces and shouts of recrimination made him worry for his wife's safety. Everyone knew the Mackinlochs were the most powerful of the Chattan federation clans.

Suspicion replaced trust on Kendric's face.

Fynn and David frowned in bewilderment.

Babbling servants ran around in panic.

Jeannie's strange eye blinked uncontrollably.

Walter glowered.

Above all, Ewan couldn't for the life of him fathom why his father would want to reignite the feud.

The answer was simple, and it dawned on Shona at almost the very same moment. "Perhaps they've come to wish us well," she suggested with a tentative smile.

He had to trust she was right and bring the mob under control before they rushed off with murder in mind. "Hold!" he bellowed.

To his surprise, most stopped and listened.

"No Mackinloch will attack MacCarron lands while I am The Camron," he declared, hoping he spoke the truth. For all he knew, his father might have died suddenly. Perhaps Colin had decided he wanted Creag for himself and had no intention of honoring the Clunes agreement.

He squelched the doubts. "Be calm. I will ride out with a party of clansmen to greet our visitors."

Fynn kissed his new wife's hand and was first off the dais. David met him at the door.

"Ye'll explain why I canna greet them," Kendric muttered, indicating his cast.

"Aye," Ewan replied before turning to Shona. "It falls to ye to keep order here. If I dinna return," he whispered, squeezing her hands when tears welled, "remember me."

He put a hand on her belly. "And if we've already made a bairn…"

She smiled. "I'll baptize her Margaret."

He didn't know how she knew his dead mother's name, but he loved her for it. He pecked a goodbye kiss on her lips and followed Walter to join Fynn and David.

NE'ER FORGET YE'RE *a laird's daughter.*

Beathan MacCarron's oft-repeated words echoed in Shona's head. Except now she was the *wife* of a laird, a man who faced his first test as The Camron and trusted she was capable of easing the fears of the frightened mob.

Most had calmed, but a few still shouted vitriolic slurs against all Mackinlochs. She pressed both fists into the table, leaned forward and glared. "Ye forget I am a Mackinloch now," she said loudly, "and proud I am to bear my husband's name."

Some cheered her words, others grumbled.

Sometimes men need to be reminded o' their duty.

She inhaled deeply. "Ye all pledged allegiance to The Camron not a half-hour ago. Will ye desert him at the first sign of trouble—real or imagined?"

"Not I," Robbie Gilbertson shouted, lightening the mood.

There's one thing every Scotsman loves above all else.

"Now what's happened to the whisky my uncle Kendric promised?"

There ensued a moment of utter silence, then the servants seemed to recollect what they were about. Trays were retrieved, tumblers distributed amid a murmur of anticipation. It took a few minutes for the liquor to work its magic, but soon nervous apprehension replaced belligerence as the clan waited.

Shona's trembling knees gave way and she collapsed onto her chair.

Jeannie leaned over. "Ye reminded me o' yer father just now," she said with a smile.

KITH AND KIN

THE OSTLER'S LADS soon had their horses saddled. Ewan mounted Liath, glad to be back on his beloved grey despite the uncertainty he faced. Sitting astride an intelligent and reliable steed tended to clear a man's mind. He felt invincible whenever Liath carried him into battle. Colin was sadly mistaken if he thought his little brother would meekly surrender Creag.

They sighted the enemy as soon as they'd galloped past the village. A row of Highlanders, perhaps a hundred strong, waited on the crest of a rise a mile distant, some mounted, most on foot.

Ewan slowed, but didn't call a halt. "We'll approach at a leisurely pace," he told Walter.

"Mackinlochs right enough, I'd say," his friend replied without a trace of apprehension.

Liath snorted and shook his head.

"He knows them," Ewan muttered.

His feelings were mixed. Having convinced himself his father must be dead if Colin had come on the offensive, he was strangely relieved to see the cantankerous old bastard sitting ramrod straight in the saddle of his favorite horse. The three eagle feathers pinned to his bonnet paid no mind to the breeze. But what was he doing here—with a small army? And Colin.

When they came within fifty yards, he called a halt. "I'll go on alone," he said. "If they have war in mind, there's no choice but to surrender. We're ill-prepared."

No one questioned his decision. As he rode slowly towards the rise, his father set his horse in motion until they were side by side. Duncan's stern glower didn't bode well.

Ewan nodded. "The Camron bids The Mackinloch welcome to Creag," he said, extending his ungloved hand.

His father narrowed his eyes but made no effort to accept the handshake. "Ye managed it then?" he asked gruffly.

Ewan should have known better than to expect cordiality from his sire. "Managed what?"

"To wed the lass."

"Aye. Shona is my wife," he replied proudly.

"Sounds like 'twasna the hardship ye expected."

Ewan couldn't resist a smile. "No hardship at all."

His father scratched his beard. "Now, tell me, laddie, do ye greet me on behalf o' The Camron, or are ye The Camron?"

Ewan stiffened his spine. "Ye are addressing The Camron."

Duncan rubbed his nose with the back of a finger, as if he smelled something rotten. "Thought as much when I saw yon MacCarron plaid on yer shoulder." He turned in the saddle and nodded to Colin, who merely returned the nod.

Ewan gritted his teeth, bracing for the terms of surrender. He didn't know what to make of his father's sly smile when he turned back to face him.

"Weel," Duncan declared, "seems we're too late for the nuptials, and we've missed seeing ye be named laird o' this misbegotten clan." Then he winked. "However, since ye offer hospitality, the journey hasna been a complete waste o' time, though I dinna expect Creag Castle to come up to Roigh's standards."

Rendered speechless by his father's wink, Ewan let the insult slide and extended his hand again. "Ye're right, as always, but give us time and ye'll see."

A beefy hand enveloped his in a manic grip. "So long as ye make sure yer new clan pays what they owe—on time."

He might have known the talk would inevitably come round to the coin. Some things never changed. Yet, the firm handshake changed

Ewan's view of the future. It established a bond of mutual respect between two clan chiefs and communicated a father's love for his son.

Ewan's heart was beating so loudly in his ears, he scarce noticed Colin bring his horse alongside until he slapped him on the back. "So my little brother gets to be laird before I do. There's no justice."

Ewan smiled. "Weel, when ye hear of the trials I had to undergo to secure the lairdship..."

Colin guffawed. "Like bedding a comely wench, I suppose."

Duncan frowned. "Ye canna say such things in front o' the lad."

Ewan was puzzled but his spirits soared even higher when Andrew poked his head out from behind Colin. He dismounted immediately and helped his grinning nephew down from his brother's horse. "Ye're a sight for sore eyes, wee *mon*," he exclaimed, hugging the boy.

"I canna wait to meet yer bride," Andrew admitted as Ewan remounted Liath with the bairn in his lap. "Is she bonnie?"

"Indeed, she is," Ewan replied.

"Bonnier than Kathleen?"

Ewan chuckled. "Much more beautiful." Then a thought struck him. "But it might be as well if ye dinna mention Kathleen again."

Andrew beamed an angelic smile over his shoulder. "I understand, Uncle. The lasses can get a mite jealous of each other."

Astonished when even his father smiled at that pearl of wisdom, Ewan turned his beloved grey, and proudly led his blood kin along the trail to Creag Castle.

SHONA AND JEANNIE wandered from table to table in the hall, exchanging pleasantries and trying to act as if nothing was amiss. Moira did her part, mingling with other servants, enjoying their congratulations and wishes for the future.

A few disgruntled clansmen still muttered, but the whisky had quieted many. Shona's jaw ached with the effort of maintaining a permanent smile. She hoped she would still be smiling when the

Mackinlochs entered Creag. For there was little doubt they would come, either as friend or foe, and if they wished to claim her home, there was nothing for it but to surrender.

She briefly wondered if perhaps that had been the plan all along. Had the betrothal been merely a ploy to regain Creag? She was ashamed the suspicion had even entered her thoughts. Ewan had given her no cause to fear such a plot.

She grieved that his tenure as The Camron might be fleeting. The MacCarrons had much to gain from having him as their chief.

She was considering sipping a wee dram herself when Robbie's voice resounded. "They're coming."

All eyes turned to the red-faced boy who'd clambered onto a table.

"I went up to the tower so I could see," he panted.

"And what did ye see?" Kendric shouted.

Shona feared the bairn might topple off the table in his excitement. "Uncle Ewan, er, I mean The Camron, is leading the way."

She breathed again. That was a good sign.

A murmur of relief fluttered through the hall.

"And he's got a lad sitting on his lap."

Curious frowns gave way to soft chuckles as it dawned on everyone that invading clans didn't bring children on campaigns.

Gripping the table to fend off a sudden bout of dizziness, Shona declared, "We are about to host important visitors—my kin-by-marriage. Let's show them our fine MacCarron hospitality and make The Camron proud."

Amid the hubbub that ensued, she espied the harried cook chivvying scullery maids at the entrance to the kitchens. "I hope there's venison left," she shouted.

"Aye, Lady Shona," he replied with a broad grin. "Whisky too."

A loud cheer greeted the news.

WHO IS THIS MAN?

SHONA AND JEANNIE hurried to the courtyard, each helping the other fix a wayward curl here and there. They straightened plaids and smoothed wrinkles from frocks. Kendric hobbled out and perched on his crutches, refusing the chair Donald fetched. A group of clan elders gathered behind them as they watched Ewan ride in. Shona was mightily relieved to see her husband's smile and surmised the boy on his lap was the nephew he'd spoken of so fondly.

The stern-faced greybeard with the eagle-feathered bonnet could only be Duncan, the notoriously bad-tempered Mackinloch laird—her father-by-marriage.

"I'm glad I didna take a sip o' whisky," Shona whispered to her aunt as the new arrivals dismounted. "I get the feeling even Ewan is intimidated by his father."

"Weel, he looks happy to see his kin. I'll wager the lanky fellow beside the old man is his brother."

"Perhaps the smile is because it seems they havna come to usurp Creag."

Moira, Heather and Robbie hurried to greet David and Walter.

Jeannie squeezed Shona's arm when Fynn rode through the gates. "There's my lovely husband," she murmured.

She put an arm around her aunt's shoulder. "Here we are, Auntie, two brides who havna had much chance to share the happiness of being newly wed."

"Right enough, but we will," Jeannie replied.

Shona had an urge to laugh when her aunt attempted a wink, but her amusement fled when she added, "though o' course some things are just between a *mon* and his wife."

Jeannie had misunderstood. Shona certainly had no intention of gossiping about the intimacies she and Ewan had shared. Nor did she wish to hear of what had transpired in her aunt's marriage bed. A retort was on the tip of her tongue, but she felt the heat rise in her face and quickly closed her mouth when she realized her husband and his father were striding towards her.

EWAN LET GO of Andrew's hand for a moment and proceeded to introduce his father to Kendric first as protocol demanded.

"My son told me of yer injuries," Duncan said, shaking the former laird's hand, "but ye seem to be on the mend. My condolences on the death of yer brother. Fine *mon*. We shook hands and shared a wee dram at Clunes. We exchanged swords to seal the contract. I thought ye might like to have yer brother's blade back. As a remembrance. 'Tis in the baggage."

Ewan held his breath. He couldn't recall ever being acknowledged as the man's *son* before and the thoughtful gesture brought a lump to his throat. He knew what it would mean to Shona.

"I thank ye," Kendric replied, looking gobsmacked by the news, "and 'tis thanks to The Camron the perpetrators of the foul deeds that have recently befallen us are dead."

Ewan had only made brief mention of the accident during the short ride, but he was astonished at his father's jovial and considerate manner.

"I brought my eldest son wi' me," Duncan continued, seemingly content to wait for an explanation. He beckoned Colin forward. "He'll be The Mackinloch after me. Few men can boast of two sons who are lairds of great clans."

As Kendric shook Colin's hand, Ewan wondered about the identity of the good-natured fellow claiming to be his cantankerous father.

Duncan put both hands on his grandson's shoulders. "And this young man is my daughter's bairn, Andrew."

Andrew dutifully shook Kendric's hand but quickly looked up at Ewan. "Is that yer bride?" he whispered, nodding to Shona.

Ewan looked at the lass he loved. Her uncharacteristic fidgeting tugged at his heart. She was anxious for his father's approval, something he'd thirsted for many times in his life, but never received. He was confident his wife would win the old man over in short order.

"Ye'll wait yer turn, Andrew," Duncan blustered, reaching for Shona's hand.

"Father, may I present my wife, Lady Shona Mackinloch."

Ewan was aware his sire had attended the court of King Charles on more than one occasion, but was completely unprepared for the courtly kiss Duncan brushed across Shona's knuckles.

If the gesture came as a surprise, she hid it well as she bobbed a curtsey. Folk tended to wilt under The Mackinloch's gaze, but her gesture was polite without being subservient.

Well done, lass.

More incredible was that Duncan didn't seem offended. "My son has chosen well, Lady Shona," he gushed, still holding her hand.

This wasn't the moment to mention the marriage was actually Duncan's doing, and he certainly didn't want his father to know about his efforts to avoid it—at least not until he'd had a few tumblers of whisky.

Andrew tugged at his plaid. "She is bonnie," he whispered. "Can I kiss her hand too?"

"Of course ye can," Shona replied, beaming a broad smile as she extricated her hand from Duncan's grip and offered it to the lad.

Andrew executed a bow worthy of any courtier and kissed Shona's knuckles. "Pleased to meet ye," he said.

"I ken somebody who'll be happy to meet ye," she replied, beckoning Robbie from the curious crowd gathering in the courtyard.

Ewan watched the two boys shake hands and shyly embark on a conversation. If a lad from a MacCarron sept and a Mackinloch could be friends…perhaps therein was the solution to finally laying the feud to rest. He put his arm around Shona's waist as the introductions and pleasantries continued, feeling more confident about the future than he'd ever felt.

"A good beginning," his wife whispered.

"Aye," he agreed.

Historical Footnotes

The enmity between the Mackinlochs and the MacCarrons is based on the three-hundred-year feud between the Mackintoshes and the Camerons. An internet search will provide information about the early 14th century origins of the quarrel that Duncan Mackinloch retells in the opening chapter. It was, of course, a dispute over land and the rightful ownership of Tor Castle (Creag).

It was eventually settled (if feuds ever truly are) by an agreement signed at Clunes in 1665. The Camerons agreed to pay the Mackintoshes compensation for Loch Arkaig and surrounding lands.

The trial by combat at the North Inch did actually take place in September 1396. The temptation to lure Kendric into an inebriated slip of the tongue regarding the name was too great to resist.

The Clan Chief of the Camerons has traditionally been known as The Lochiel, so I bestowed the title The Camron on the Clan Chief of the MacCarrons to provide a hint of the connection.

About Anna

Thank you for reading **Kilty Secrets.** If you'd like to leave a review where you purchased the book, I would appreciate it. Reviews contribute greatly to an author's success.

For a complete list of my books, you can visit my website. I also have a Facebook page, Anna Markland Novels.

Tweet me @annamarkland, and join me on Pinterest. If you want to try another sample of my work, you can download a FREE novella, Defiant Passion.

In my bestselling, page-turning novels passion conquers whatever obstacles a hostile medieval world can throw in its path.

Besides writing, I have two addictions-crosswords and genealogy, probably the reason I love research.

I am a fool for cats.

My husband is an entrepreneur who is fond of boasting he's never had a job.

I live on Canada's scenic west coast now, but I was born and raised in the UK and I love breathing life into history.

Escape with me to where romance began.

I hope you come to know and love my cast of characters as much as I do.

I'd like to acknowledge the assistance of my critique partners, Reggi Allder, Jacquie Biggar, Sylvie Grayson, Alice Valdal and LizAnn Carson.

More Anna Markland

If you prefer to read sagas in chronological order, here's a handy list for the Montbryce family books.

Conquering Passion—Ram and Mabelle, Rhodri and Rhonwen
If Love Dares Enough—Hugh and Devona, Antoine and Sybilla
Defiant Passion—Rhodri and Rhonwen
A Man of Value—Caedmon and Agneta
Dark Irish Knight—Ronan and Rhoni
Haunted Knights—Adam and Rosamunda, Denis and Paulina
Passion in the Blood—Robert and Dorianne, Baudoin and Carys
Dark and Bright—Rhys and Annalise
The Winds of the Heavens—Rhun and Glain, Rhydderch and Isolda
Dance of Love—Izzy and Farah
Carried Away—Blythe and Dieter
Sweet Taste of Love—Aidan and Nolana
Wild Viking Princess—Ragna and Reider
Hearts and Crowns—Gallien and Peridotte
Fatal Truths—Alex and Elayne
Sinful Passions—Bronson and Grace; Rodrick and Swan

Series featuring the stories of the Viking ancestors of my Norman families
The Rover Bold—Bryk and Cathryn
The Rover Defiant—Torstein and Sonja
The Rover Betrayed—Magnus and Judith

Novellas
Maknab's Revenge—Ingram and Ruby
Passion's Fire—Matthew and Brigandine
Banished—Sigmar and Audra (Viking)

Hungry Like De Wolfe—Blaise and Anne
An Unkissable Knight—Dervenn and Victorine

Caledonia Chronicles (Scotland)
Book I Pride of the Clan—Rheade and Margaret
Book II Highland Tides—Braden and Charlotte
Book 2.5 Highland Dawn—Keith and Aurora
Book III Roses Among the Heather—Blair &Susanna, Craig & Timothea

The Von Wolfenberg Dynasty (medieval Europe)
Book 1 Loyal Heart—Sophia and Brandt
Book 2 Courageous Heart—Luther and Francesca
Book 3 Faithful Heart—Kon and Zara

Myth and Mystery
The Taking of Ireland—Sibràn and Aislinn

The Pendray Papers
Highland Betrayal—Morgan and Hannah

If you like stories with medieval breeds of dogs, you'll enjoy **If Love Dares Enough**, **Carried Away**, **Fatal Truths**, the **Taking of Ireland** and **Wild Viking Princess**. If you have a soft spot for cats, read **Passion in the Blood** and **Haunted Knights.**

Looking for historical fiction centered on a certain region?
English History—all books
Norman French History—all books
Crusades—**A Man of Value**
Welsh History—**Conquering Passion, Defiant Passion, Dark and Bright, The Winds of the Heavens**
Scottish History—**Conquering Passion, A Man of Value, Sweet Taste of Love, Caledonia Chronicles, Highland Betrayal.**
European History (Holy Roman Empire)—**Carried Away, Loyal Heart**

Danish History—**Wild Viking Princess**
Spanish History—**Dance of Love**
Ireland—**Dark Irish Knight, The Taking of Ireland**

If you like to read about historical characters:
William the Conqueror—**Conquering Passion, If Love Dares Enough, Defiant Passion**
William Ruadh—**A Man of Value**
Robert Curthose, Duke of Normandy—**Passion in the Blood**
Henry I of England—**Passion in the Blood, Sweet Taste of Love, Haunted Knights, Hearts and Crowns**
Holy Roman Emperors—**Carried Away, Loyal Heart, Courageous Heart**
Vikings—**Wild Viking Princess, The Rover Bold, The Rover Defiant, The Rover Betrayed**,
Kings of Aragon (Spain)—**Dance of Love**
The Anarchy (England) (Stephen vs. Maud)—**Hearts and Crowns, Fatal Truths, Sinful Passions**
Scotland's Stewart Kings—**Caledonia Chronicles**
Jacobites & Mary, Queen of Scots—**Highland Tides**

Made in the USA
Lexington, KY
18 March 2019